# Sarah/
# Sara

# Sarah/ Sara

## Jacob Paul

Brooklyn, New York

An excerpt from this novel first appeared in the publication, *Hunger Mountain*, Fall 2007 issue, #11.


Printed in the United States of America
10 9 8 7 6 5 4 3 2 1

Ig Publishing
178 Clinton Avenue
Brooklyn, NY 11205
www.igpub.com


Library of Congress Cataloging-in-Publication Data

Paul, Jacob.
  Sarah-Sara / Jacob Paul.
    p. cm.
  ISBN 978-1-935439-13-4
  1. Jewish women--Fiction. 2. Sea kayaking--Arctic Ocean. 3. Parents--Death--Fiction. 4. Voyages and travels--Fiction. 5. Jewish fiction. 6. Religious fiction. I. Title.
  PS3616.A943 2010
  813'.6--dc22
                                    2010006743

*For those who walked down the stairs beside me*

## July 16

My father told me he hadn't realized the magnitude of what had happened until he reached Lincoln Center. Traffic was completely stopped everywhere, people fleeing in myriad conflicting directions. But he said it was particularly jammed up where Columbus and Broadway cross in front of the fountain. Three police motorcycles shot out of that mess, sirens blaring, blue lights flashing, heading south; all the emergency vehicles were heading south that day. And then right behind them was this brown Taurus wagon and he had this moment in which he thought, these fucking people have the chutzpah to fly behind the emergency vehicles to get through traffic today. And then as the car passed, he saw taped in its window a sign scrawled in red marker on a torn off piece of brown cardboard: blood. The seats and the back of the station wagon were piled with boxes of blood. Then it hit him, the incomprehensible scale of what had happened. It hit my father, all that blood, racing to get all that blood down there, that much blood.

It was the first time I ever had to call them to make sure everyone was ok. My father could never break his habit of dialing me every time a Reuter's alert scrolled across the bottom of his screen announcing yet another martyrdom operation, yet another bus peeled back, another café disemboweled. He would call whether it was a shop in Tel Aviv, a bus in Jerusalem or a shooting attack in Hebron. Like an allergy sufferer whose compulsive sneezes she wishes were ignored, not blessed, I came to dread those calls and the subtle nagging plea to abandon my aliyah, return to Northport. "A father shouldn't have to fly around the world to see his daughter," he'd say. (My mother didn't pull her punches. She took my aliyah personally, "So you think your father and I are going to hell because we're secular?" No I never thought you were going to gayhenom. I loved you, love you still, and pray that Hashem takes my mitzvoth and applies them to your account, increases your share of heaven).

Then that day came along, and there I was, dialing back home as fast I could, trying to beat the busy signals, find an open line, get through. I'd just come back in from a late lunch and was looking out on Ben Yehudah square from my office window —people had just started shopping again after violence's latest cycle—when Ari ran into my office and turned on Army Radio. It was my turn to call you. Baruch Hashem, you were all right. You'd just gotten through to Eema, and she said you'd called her from what must've been the only working payphone for miles but that you were safe.

Then one thing leads to another thing. You began working on the kayak in earnest; enough so that when the time came, I could not easily dismiss its call. And now Abba, I have also made a journey. Because you had to walk those hundred odd blocks, I have made a journey to take another journey, a trip to take a trip. I set out from far south of downtown Manhattan, far south and far east, and like you, traveled north, north and west. Now, I've been on the coast a full day, in which I only paddled four hours out of what I hope to eventually be a daily eleven.

The sun nods over the mountains behind me. It's always in the same place, sometimes rising, sometimes falling, but hardly at all. In my head, I thought it would be more like a buzzard circling. I thought the midnight sun would resemble that of a spaghetti western, permanently overhead, beating down. It isn't.

I don't even think it's related to its high-noon cousin. Instead, a near dusk spurs all this ancient plant life into a frenzied bloom, a spurt of almost growth, and me too. Me too, I'm also locked into a desperate burst of action, racing in the segue between ice and ice along this pebbled arctic shore. Like these stunted willows' growing season, I have only so much time. Six weeks to safely paddle, paddle and sail really, from my drop-off just east of Deadhorse and Prudhoe to the McKenzie River, to Aklivuk.

I know I'm tired, and I know I need to sleep, but after the mechanical actions of the day are finished, rowing, dragging the kayak up the pebble beach to this night's camp (night, always night and never night), after that, and pitching tent above the highest possibility of tide and spraying everything against mosquitoes and making dinner: Lipton's risotto with dehydrated turkey cooked over a Whisperlite stove, and after sealing every final bit of food in a bear canister, after everything, the sun's still up and I'm still awake. Just me and this journal. Just the kayak my father almost finished building and me and my journal.

I've never kept a journal before. I'm not sure how to begin, what exactly to write in it, to what end I'm keeping it at all. I suppose that the proper protocol would be to log the day's events (for whatever reason):

At around two in the morning (bright daylight), the outfitter, who my Seattle-based trainer, Nancy, had hired, flew me out of Fairbanks in a twin-prop water-plane with my kayak tied to the struts. To not throw the plane off balance, all the gear I would normally stow in the kayak had to be packed into the plane. All of which stretched the limits of the plane's weight capacity. After a beautiful flight over the mountains, and then on across the plains stretching down to the sea, he landed in the cove Nancy had designated, and helped me bring all my supplies to shore. I spent the morning organizing and inventorying my stores, constantly vigilant for bears. Having quite such a bounty out and about unnerved me. Finally, I packed up the boat, ate the first meal of my trip, and set off. There, I guess that's more journal-like. Though I'm not sure that's what I intend.

The trip is really meant for you, Abba, and I guess you too, Eema. I'm finishing your dreams for you. I have to believe you can see that. I cannot believe that this is anything else. But do you need a written account to know that I'm speaking to you? I'm rambling, aimless, using up useful hours whose energy should be, must be, directed, focused, concentrated on getting from here to there while I can, while the Arctic is open and before the grey Brooks Range turns from scenic backdrop, its foothills as lush as the African Savannah, to a massive backboard, concentrating, focusing and directing a barrage of furious weather.

Afterwards, Abba, after that day, you were a lot better about me being in Israel. You said, "It's just as dangerous here, so why come home?" You convinced mother for me, took my side. Not that I would've returned to the states. When you came to visit, yes, she was a little tight-lipped, a little jumpy, but I blamed it on her newfound fear of flying, who would've thought that— Well—This aimless writing isn't necessarily the best thing. Not if I'm to heal myself and go back to Jerusalem; I will go back to Jerusalem. L'shanah ha'bah, b'yerushalaim. Yes, this is my exodus. I've got to get myself to go to sleep. I'm going to go to bed.

## *July 17*

It's easy to keep up with a journal when there's no one around and nothing to do. Something I learned today: Love for my father may have led me to finish the boat, but love's no substitute for skill (or maybe his ability to transform love into craft was better, more desperate, an advanced alchemy. He claimed this boat was his monument, and it lives up to that on the water). But the pontoons I built to balance the sail do not cut, do not break, do not grace the way his hull does. Here's to you, Abba, what you built works wonderfully. This wooden boat blows the fiberglass shells we used on Long Island Sound out of the water, no pun intended (do you think Abba in Shamaim cares about puns, Sarah?). Anyway, this boat belongs to the water. And, I can feel my arms adapting to the current of rowing whole days—if you can call them days without sunrise, without sunset, unde-marcated, obtuse contusions of time I enforce with a waterproof wristwatch I look to as a sole lifeline to civilization.

As if it is civil, as if it is civilization. No. Not again this eve-ning. I don't want to go there tonight. Tonight, I don't want to stop writing only to find myself so full of depressed energy that I end up pacing the pebble beach chucking stones at driftwood and the stray rusted out oil drum in an exhausted stupor until I drift off outside of my tent. Bears do respect structure. They do not respect slight twenty-five-year-olds who've already broken into their whiskey supply and conked out in the open. Not to mention the dangers of musk-oxen and caribou and wolves and whatever else lurks along these shores. Got to be smart.

This place is full of danger. That much is clear already. It's cold enough that I have to put a fleece on as soon as I stop row-ing, way too cold to warm up after a dunk in the water without a real fire. And who's going to make a fire for me if I capsize and can't pull an Eskimo roll and after an emergency exit the kayak drifts from me and I have to swim to shore, the zero degree water ripping away heat faster than a polar bear could tear off my limbs? And if I did make it to shore, my fingers numb, white, frozen, my mind wandering in elliptical fantasies of warmth, would I be able to make a fire, take the necessary steps, assemble wood, kindling, light matches, shelter the first flames, fan them, generate heat, make hot drinks, place warm water bottles in my crotch and arm-pits? (How many other orthodox women think about putting warm water bottles in their crotch?) And that's only one thing to fear. There are bears, Polar bears that can out-swim a kayaker pulling hard, though the Inuit and my father both swear that only the white bears of mythology eat people. And then there is time, also a rabid and uncaring demon, ready to subtract itself without notice, without warning, and hasten the return of ice. And all the little things, a twisted ankle, a bruised wrist, a lost dry bag full of food, a failed stove that can either singly or incrementally damn me to a slow starvation stranded on a shore only briefly forgiven winter's cloak of snow, of darkness. But more than anything I fear the grizzlies. Hungry, angry picked-on bears; these are not the grizzlies of the lower forty-eight, intelligent masters of their ecosystems, appropriately skittish around people. These bears get picked on by their big white cousins and act like cranky children with claws and teeth and a top land speed close to sixty miles an hour. I'm smaller than them and even if I don't smell like my food, my bags sure do.

I see the barren ground grizzlies from the kayak and paddle out further, or tack out if I've got the sail up. They look at me and they're not scared, chasing their berries or ground moles or whatever else they feed on up here. They're also limited to three months or so, a quarter of a year, to throw on enough fat to sleep cozily through winter. And then there's all the wildlife I don't know and don't understand, the grounded molting geese and small shadow animals that flit between tufts of tundra. Tufts, they sound so innocuous. And they are, unless, of course, you don't carefully watch every step as you walk across them and end up with that twisted ankle. Yes, most of all, I'm afraid of what I don't know about this place. And it shocks me that I don't know everything about everything that lives up here.

My father bored us all to tears over umpteen dinners as he planned and replanned and then planned again his retirement trip, this trip. And unlike my mother, I wanted to go. She would chide him, tease him, say, "Henry, by the time they let you out of that job you'll be too old to go out in any boat that doesn't have shuffleboard, blackjack and a swimming pool as standard features." Well, Henry, at least you'll never find yourself courting the West Palm Beach set at swing dancing for seniors on the QE2. I wanted to go with him. His knock's promise of a silent sunrise viewed level with the water was the only thing that ever got me up early during high school. Perhaps Eeema was right, but after I left he swore that when he finished this boat he was done with Morgan Stanley.

That was his way, not rushing the boat to get out of the job, but not dragging it out either. I know that he loved his job, and especially the camaraderie of his coworkers, nearly as much as he loved the water. He filled his office with kayaking photos, many of which featured me. Half the joy he derived from kayaking was earning the respect of his coworkers by doing something truly different. He largely measured his accomplishments by their ability to inspire awe and raise eyebrows at work. But that had all changed; all of his photos and memorabilia were lost with the building. Like me, he believed he could channel everything into building the boat, and that it would then free him on this trip: a memorial equal parts object and action. He would have left within the year, I think. He'd nearly finished the boat.

The tundra amazes me. It's a forest, willow and pine. Just a really, really short forest. I'm walking on plants a thousand years old, walking on them. It reminds me of Jerusalem. There it's all manmade stuff, but equally old. When I go back, I'll walk down streets Solomon's city planners laid out, pray at the temple he built. Here it's nature's antiquity. And that's the beauty of our time, the other use for explosive energy. I can go to these places. They're available. I will go to these places, just as I will wake up after six hours of sleep and will make breakfast and will get in the kayak, set up its pontoons, hoist its sail, and set further off along my unbreakable itinerary.

## July 18

I haven't da'avened since I got here. Perhaps tomorrow, on Shabbat. I can't do anything anyway, can't cook, can't row. Certainly, it's the most important day that I pray. I took Shabbat into account when planning my itinerary. I figured I'd need a rest day each week anyhow. But I should be praying every day. I can't make this trip without Hashem.

Really, I haven't said Shemah, Shemonah Esrai, any of the prayers. I mean I figured I'd immediately give up on tznios; it's not as if anyone here will see whether I'm immodest or not anyway. It's not practical to wear a long skirt and long sleeves while pushing a boat into the waves, while paddling. And there's no issue with shomrei n'giah. I have no one to touch, certainly no man to tempt me into any illicit behavior. I remember going to Rabbi Shem Tov sophomore year of college after a date and blushing when he asked whether kissing a boy made any of my life better. "Sara," he said, "All of us have taivah's, but they only bring us the illusion of pleasure in this life. The beauty of Yiddishkeite is that we're not sacrificing the pleasures of this world for the pleasures of the next. We are discovering the true pleasures of this world that we may have them in the next as well."

I blushed happily, so happily, because it wasn't any fun competing for something I didn't want, a date with some guy, I think his name might have been Jeremy or Rodger, I don't remember, and then playing a cat and mouse game, and marking success in terms of what I was willing to give, what he earned taking. Give and take. The language of compromise, of negotiated treaties only kept out of fear, out of need, should not define love, the relationship between genders.

So why haven't I been da'avening? Why haven't I been praying? It makes no sense to shirk the pleasure of prayer. I'm not sure what's changed, I made a point of at a minimum saying Shemah every day right up until the float plane dropped me off in the surf. There were those who said I'd lose faith after what happened, but clearly, I kept mine. I'll start da'avening again tomorrow. I promise.

As soon as Eema would let him back into the city, Abba began volunteering at the rescue workers' relief station in what had been Liberty Square. He would take the Long Island Railroad into Penn Station where he'd catch the IRT down to Fulton Street. From there, he'd walk up Broadway, forcing him to go past Trinity Church which had become a nexus for the tourists who began steaming downtown almost before building 5, Borders Books, gutted by flame but not collapsed, was torn down. This was well before the fire of a million burning computers had subsided. Large banners signed by well-wishing church groups and third-grade classrooms hung both inside and outside the colonial church. Apparently, they mounted a giant piece of poster board on the metal gates of their small graveyard whose centerpiece declared "God Bless America's Heroes." Abba told me it was a zoo. Middle Americans with aw-shucks sensibilities posed for snapshots with death-weary firemen who were on their way to long sessions of alcoholic self-medication. The Baptists had prayer stations manned by out-of-state cheerleaders dressed in red T-shirts that said "Prayer Helps" and eagerly converted those open to suggestion and the power of larger than life experience.

What I have is more than that.

He called me every day, even the days that I called him, and wailed and railed that first of all, he wasn't any fucking hero; he was as passive as a slaughterhouse cow. The worst part about everything was forced participation in an iconoclastic struggle between faiths he reviled. "And, Sarah, these bastard prayer stations with their cheery-eyed teenage Christ-wannabes. I could knock their blocks off for them. They're like those bastard Mormons posthumously baptizing Holocaust victims, or like those Polish nuns who've set up a monastery at Auschwitz to pray for the Jews who died there. Fuck you and your insulting prayers."

Of course I agreed with him about the Auschwitz nunnery and the Mormon baptismal project for Shoah victims, but at the same time I tried to point out that these were responses to Hashem's chosen people. Prayer does help. And that now, more than ever he should turn back to the faith of his forefathers, as I had. He got nasty. "I forgot that I was talking to my own personal God-Freak, my recidivist daughter who'd like to trade in hundreds of years of progress for medieval customs, a veil, a head covering and second class status." But I did not get angry back. It isn't easy to see the world confront your comfortable, convenient beliefs with airliners full of jet fuel, businessmen exhaled by subexplosions a thousand feet up in the air and a massacre of firemen. He told me about the bodies cascading in clean lines against a back drop of shiny steel rails. He tried not to tell me what happens to a person when they impact on cement. But I know, already, I've seen it. And exploding bodies are simply that, exploding bodies. I'm sorry that Hashem made him confront his life; I'm sorry that it happened the way it did. It isn't nice, it isn't easy, but it is true. (Except when the exploding bodies are yours, Sarah; except then).

Do you remember, Abba, how before all that, long ago, when I asked you about death, about God, when I was just a little girl? Instead of answering, you took me on my first kayaking trip. There's something strange, now, about my days paddling. I mean, yeah, sure, I was on the sound every day for a month before heading up to Washington, and then on Puget Sound every day for three more weeks; and I didn't use the sail. Now, I've got the sail up, and yet every day, all three of them, I'm worried about having the will to make it through. It's all I can do to not turn around and head back. Though here's the thing. There is no back. If I arrived at the float plane drop off, I'd still be nowhere. In a sense, I'm racing home. And I love it—but. Maybe it's the sun, which I'm getting used to now, always there, hovering, doing nothing, maybe it's the absolute solitude. I've been in solitude before, but this is a whole new level. Me, you, Eema, Hashem and the animals, we're all that's here, but I'm the only one who speaks.

## July 20

Shabbat came and went. I observed (no cooking, rowing, writing, burning) but I did not da'aven. I went for a short jog along the shore, figured I might as well give my legs a bit of exercise. And besides, this prolonged a stretch of sand beach is pretty rare. I don't know when I'll get to go on a real run again. But that all digresses from the point that I'm shocked and scared that even yesterday, when there was pretty much nothing else to do, and nothing more important, I didn't pray. But I don't want to think about it too much, either. And I have other things to be worried about.

I forgot to bring the camera bag on the plane. In the long run, doing without binoculars, a guide to North American birds and my Canon won't kill me. But ill-preparedness will, and two things already happened today to make me feel even that inconsequential bag's absence. First, about 10:30 in the morning, right after I'd started off for the day (more about missing half the morning later) I went by a tiny island and all of these round orange birds rose up out of tundra. It would've thrilled you, Abba. You probably would've identified them off the top of your head as some rare species, a once in a lifetime sighting. They weren't large but they were exceedingly round, visibly so even a good hundred feet off. They didn't rise up to fly away but instead created this squawking chaotic mass, the way seagulls do, blanketing the little island. I hadn't intended to stop there anyway, but after that, it was simply out of the question. I don't want to die in some Hitchcockian rerun. But, and this was a welcome change from the anxiety that plagues me, my curiosity about the birds occupied at least as much mental territory as my unease about their angry, unprecedented eruption.

But, no bird book, no binoculars; I worry because I don't think you'd forget something like that, what with your elaborate and redundant checklists. I worry that if I can make little mistakes, I can make big mistakes, that if I'm noticing some things I've forgotten to do in preparation, then there are other, worse things I'm also forgetting, neglecting, overlooking.

Perhaps I'd do better to be concerned about my gradual drift in time. Each day, I've set out slightly later. I mean, I'm still getting my same eight to ten hours in each day; I'm getting to where I'm supposed to be on the topo map before stopping each night, and it's always light out. So what does it matter? I don't know. It strikes me as a gradual erosion of discipline, an acceleration of the time lost traveling west to east, not that time zones are relevant or practical here. I don't know if or when I'll need that time back.

You can jump at your own shadows out here.

I meant to da'aven today. I didn't. I don't know what that means either.

I wished for my binoculars most after lunch. I had the sail up. There was a good wind and the freedom of not paddling, not tacking, made me strangely giddy. I found myself craning in different directions, stir-crazy, half out of the cockpit, looking behind me, shading my eyes. I think I may have shouted out once or twice. That's one of the strangest things about moving swiftly under sail: no sense of wind. You're moving in the wind at the speed of the wind; the water slips past you and you feel like you should feel speed; there is no feeling of speed. I wanted to feel in a way that matched my energy. Dazzling white, breakaway chunks of pack-ice drifted past to the north on my left, occasionally escorting the odd blue iceberg, a lost traveler from the great glacial snouts of western Alaska, or errant wanderers long strayed from Greenland. One stood out, oddly crescent, like the moon of Islam, like a sickle, like the shadow of a hood, pirouetting. I was frantic beneath my spray skirt, feet twitching, knees banging against the wooden hull; I shrieked a series of panting rhythmic whoops and shook my head violently. I was under sail; I grew chilly. I pulled the skirt up after all and felt underneath me for my trusty, fuzzy orange fleece. No dice. It was in the rear bulkhead. You can access the rear bulkhead while under sail as long as the pontoons are out. It's risky though. I decided to lower the sail somewhat, slow pace, and then go for it. I lay my body across the smooth rear deck, its convex crease pressing into my breast bone and carefully, like a precariously perched lookout edging from the forecastle out onto a twisting spar high above the deck, I slid out to the bulkhead. I keep everything tied on one way or another, so I didn't have to worry about balancing the bulkhead cap, just the boat. The fleece was there sure enough, right on top. I grabbed it, and then looked up. And I could see it, sort of, behind me, a swift white floe, about four feet of it above water, moving toward me. It was far away and at first I thought I was seeing a mirage of dry miraculously splayed across the water. It disappeared in a twist of sun and wave. My giddiness departed as if it never had been. My legs no longer dreamed of speed in staccato hull drumming. I gingerly retreated to the cockpit as fast as I could. That's not a paradox; I did it. I got back to the cockpit; and gripping the fleece in my knees, I hoisted the sail and picked up some speed. I looked back and a little closer a crest of white topped a roll in the water and was gone but maybe only to reappear again. I pulled the fleece on and grabbed my paddle, started rowing. But that didn't really add much. The sail's efficient; all I was doing was adding nervous energy to the mix. I decided to head directly with the wind, take it for all it was worth; it took me north. I looked back: nothing. I pulled the spray skirt around the cockpit lip and looked back: something, yes, something but what? The boat lurched uneasily and I realized I'd hit a small wave funny, not a problem, per se, but I was headed towards a chunk of ice. I tacked and then looked back again: yes, something, almost certainly, but something indeterminate, something at roughly my speed, something I could've identified with binoculars.

Uncertain hours last a long, long time. When the waters are with you, when the boat's running as it should, you can simply hang on and watch the ever-changing shore, sloping ridges like long dirt fingers suddenly broken by rifts of rock. The ever-present Brooks Range, defining the southern border of sight, changes as well. For much of this morning its reaches were covered in fog and then the fog dissipated and grey erupted into sun-blessed white peaks. But hours of peeking back, seeing and then not seeing, defining, imagining, dissuading, dwelling, those hours are static, long and damning. But I will not let the lack of a set of binoculars kill me. Even if it was a bear, a polar bear, I doubt if it wanted much with me. I am danger.

But then we are all fear and danger. Once, Eema told me that the terrorists acted out of fear. Abba, you weren't home yet, and so I got her on the phone. "Yeah, they're cowards, Eema."

"Mother or Mom, Sarah, no Eema for me."

"Well then it's Sara, please."

"I bore you, I named you, I'll call you Sarah; you can have your friends call you what they like." I wasn't going to keep arguing with her. "Sarah, the issue isn't cowardice; it's fear."

I let her go on, not understanding, not really caring, waiting for you to get home and take the phone. "The issue is that these men and women, these people, are so terrorized by fear, by anxiety, by uncertainty that they have to share it any way they can. Those men who almost killed your father; they were so crazed with fear that the only thing they could think to do was share

it somehow, perpetrate this horrible terror with planes and fire."
Right, Mom. "That's why your Sharon's policies in the occupied
territories will never stop terrorism. The more fear he creates;
the more fear will seek outlet. People who do not fear, who are
not oppressed, hunted, haunted by occupiers, they strive to avoid
a situation of fear, strive to preserve a status-quo; those kind of
people would never blow up buses or fly planes into buildings." I
asked her if she wanted me to start with her insistence on calling
the land Hashem promised us in the Torah occupied, or would
she rather I addressed the massive success of Jewish passivity during the Shoah, or would she simply rather I dropped the subject?

"F—king hell, Sarah," she whispered—since I became orthodox and stopped cursing, she's taken a special joy in profanity, a
joy I once shared. "The security guard who used to let your father
go in without ID when he had his cast didn't make it out. Your
father's been to his house twice now to visit his wife. He used to
see the man every day, but he only just learned his name, Samba.
Yes, he was North African, Muslim. He was a twelve-dollar-an-
hour employee with a green card who everyone resented because
he wouldn't let them in without their IDs and he stayed until the
whole shithouse caved in and all you can think about is repri-
sals, and right and wrong, and bombing people." Eema wasn't
whispering anymore. "And I have to think about what the hell I
would do if I lost your father and there you are, self-righteously
advocating a genocide of what was a pastoral shepherd folk until
we, yes us, the never-can-do-wrong, always-the-victim Jews
radicalized them. And you use the Holocaust to justify it. My
grandparents died in the Holocaust; don't you ever bring that up
to me as a basis for your twisted manifest destiny. They would
not have wanted others to die because they died; and while I'm at
it, I might as well say that I can't stand the pathetic way you call
it the Shoah. Or call me, Eema! God it makes me angry. Call it

what it is, the Holocaust. Not everything needs a name assigned by some smarmy, bearded self-righteous wisp of a man in a black coat, in a shtetl."

I had to refrain from nervously giggling at her last comment about yeshivah boys naming the Shoah. Nothing I could say would turn the tide at that point, so I delicately set the receiver back down in its cradle on my desk while she continued talking, gaining volume. There just wasn't any point staying on the phone. I was the first one in the office by a matter of hours, gray streaks of cold December light barely beginning to part the buildings ringing Ben Yehudah Square, all so that I'd be early enough that it would be late enough but early enough back there. I couldn't listen; I didn't have to. I would give an awful lot to hear you launch into a righteous tirade, right or wrong, at this moment, Eema. I'd really give an awful lot. I miss you. Despite everything, your misgivings about Eretz Yisroel, about flying, about me, you came to Yerushalaim. Despite all of my belief, despite knowing that everything fits into Hashem's plan, I wish that you hadn't.

But what choice is there but to go on? They seem cliché, the sayings: Changing your life lets them win; the best defense is your daily routine; never bow to terrorism; never again; an eye for an eye; to fear is to lose. But the world rotates on a combination of obstinacy and faith. If you don't believe that you'll die the moment Hashem decides, no sooner, no later, you go insane. You can't survive. There are teenage women in bulky coats dressed up like orthodox women, like me, walking into university cafeterias and devolving into a ground level Fourth-of-July display. Legs and hands and feet and bone and bolts and nails. I shouldn't have told my father what the Rosh Yeshivah where I learned with the women's group in the evening in Kiriat Yoel said about the Jews that died in the Shoah. Of course my father told my mother. Of course she called me outraged. "They deserved it, Sarah? Is that what he told you? That they deserved it? That motherf—r said that my grandparents deserved to be yanked out of their tiny Czech ghetto, out of their shtetl shul, and taken out into the woods where they dug their own graves? Or did the f—t b—d mean that my father deserved to go to the children's labor camp where the commandant used him to teach his son how to strike body blows? Or did he not realize that my father's family was practicing, was orthodox, was devout?" What could I say back to her, to my mother? I answered the way the rabbi answered when the question of the many Orthodox Jews who died was raised, probably not the right answer.

"Eema, it's very hard to accept that we might have deserved it, and it in no way negates any of the Nazis' guilt. They are Amalek, who we were supposed to have killed off in the time of the first temple. But the fact is that all Jews are interconnected and responsible for each other, and if the Jew in Russia (I didn't want to say Czechoslovakia, I didn't want to indict my own great-grandparents, my own grandfather) if the Jew in Russia says Tehillim without kovanah, then there's that much less righteousness in the world, and then the Jew in Germany will break Shabbos, the Jew in France eat pork, the Jew in America intermarry."

That time, she hung up on me, but only after first repeatedly banging the receiver against something hard, the kitchen countertop maybe. I thought I might have heard silverware jangling as it hit. I hung on, listened until she hung up. I thought about my grandfather, how he was lucky that he got to stand all day while a little Nazi solar-plexed him. I was thinking about how it felt putting body weight behind a blow during training with punching bags when I did my tour with the Israeli Defense Forces, the way your shoulder wants to blow out the back of your moving body, and imagining my fourteen-year-old grandfather bearing that impact again and again, glad that his special role as a punching bag made him unique, kept him alive while all other children persished. The least I could do was listen while she slammed the phone and cursed, though the call wasn't cheap. I was in my apartment that time, upstairs from the cafe.

Well the sun isn't going to go down. That's just part of the deal. But there's a lot that I need to do, will do tomorrow. I'll wake up early, and if not totally reverse the lost time, at least begin the reversal. For each of the next four days, I, Sara bat Shmeenah, Sarah Frankel, will wake up half an hour earlier. And that means that I have to go to bed soon, with or without the help of dark.

I don't know if I can go back to that apartment. It's right over the cafe; my windows blew out too. Perhaps I can make this compromise: I'll return to Yerushalaim, but to a new apartment. Ok. That makes me feel better. I can go to bed now. Good-night, Sun, sweet dreams.

## July 21

I see amazing things and I see nothing to talk about. I saw a herd of musk-oxen today. I understand that they're actually a kind of primeval goat. Whales are also a type of goat. Speaking of which, I'm really surprised that I haven't seen whales. I thought I saw blowhole spray in the distance the other day, but it was nothing. In fact, in many ways this trip is tame and it worries me that I am running from Jerusalem. That I do have whole days to meditate, to reflect, that I am not consumed by the trip my father planned is not ideal. The whole idea was to face concrete fears in an environment where I could grapple with them and win. Plus, it leaves too much time for thought.

It makes me lax at times, the seeming casual nature of rowing peaceably through this eerie, unending autumn late-afternoon, because that is what the July here is: an autumn late afternoon, all the time. The light has a red quality to it from passing through so much of the earth's atmosphere and casts long strong warm shadows. The foothills reaching out to the tundra are like high desert, rived by occasional violent water into deeply creased folds of land stretching out like roots or fingers, a combination of dirt and green. On their north, seeming flat absorbs them, and the flat is split by rivers only noticeable at their outlets. Because the flat is deep tundra, it hides the river banks in its expanse, disappearing them the way tall grasses do a meadow stream. To the foothills' south, great grey mountains rise straight up to snow covered tops. And in fact the flat isn't nearly so flat as it seems, but its expanse is so broad and unbroken that my mind averages its rolling nature into a perpetual plane.

I don't want to stay up as late as I did last night. I said that I would wake up half an hour earlier and I only woke up twenty-five minutes earlier, which I would count as close enough except that I was so sluggish that it took me nearly twice as long as usual to break down my tent, cook breakfast, pack everything back into the boat and cast off.

I was in such a rush that I almost set sail without the pontoons. No, Abba, I wasn't so foolish as to almost forget them. Instead, I looked at the wind's constancy, at the water's pacific ease, and almost chose to risk it. I know, no risks when you're going solo. Risk tolerance is zero. But losing time is also a risk, and I'd promised myself to make up what I'd lost. The half hour earlier start was supposed to translate into a half hour earlier arrival. At best I made fift—

—Later—

I feel like I have to write this or I won't be able to sleep. I was writing before and I saw a grizzly on a tuft about forty feet from my camp. I spoke loudly and calmly, but he didn't move. I know, don't run. But pack up your stuff really fast. I got the tent down faster than I ever have. He was huge. He turned his head and looked at me with one eye. And I did the same cause I know that's a sign of non-aggression—but you try believing that when an animal the size of a cow, but with teeth and claws and a bit less ground-clearance paces the distance across Broadway away from you. I couldn't leave stuff behind, but I just shoved it all together into the boat, never taking my eyes off the bear. It took me about five minutes to get my stuff down and in. During that time, he completed a slow semicircle around my campsite. I kept speaking, trying to keep my voice level. Hey, bear. How you doing, bear? Just packing my stuff up here, going to put it in the boat. I don't know why I didn't say Shemah. I think I usually would've said Shemah. It's what you're supposed to say in danger, that or tehillim, but tehillim are really more prophylactic, meant to be said in advance of danger. Often, you say them to protect someone else. If you think you might die, Shemah is the ticket. It's a bit like a Catholic's last confession. I got the stuff in the boat and pushed it down the short embankment. Baruch Hashem the boat was beached fairly close to the water line! When I got close to the water, I was pretty much running, and he began loping towards me, not running, certainly not charging, but nonetheless heading towards me, downhill, his mouth hung open. I was in the water and I swung my feet into the boat and started paddling and then it was all over, a grizzly won't catch a paddler. His water skills don't touch the polar bear's. Why is danger always a he?

It isn't going to be easy to sleep. I keep shouting things out, little warnings, words. I want any bears that might be around to know that I'm here too, that this is my territory, back off. It won't be easy to sleep but I have to. And besides, it'll be safer inside the tent, right.

## *July 22*

I don't think the writing's helping.
    Tonight I will not write about:
Bears, grizzly or polar
My father
My mother
Terrorism
Fear
Loneliness
Hashem
Orthodoxy (why I was ba'al t'shuvah to it, and why I am able
to keep with it despite everything)
September 11
Monotony of kayaking
My campsite, or,
The Midnight Sun

But I don't think I can go to bed just yet either, and I don't
want to break into the whiskey supply, and I don't want to lay in
the tent not asleep, so I think I will write about the mosquitoes.
Yes, in fact, this diary would be incomplete without writing about
the mosquitoes. It doesn't help that the special sun-block I still
have to apply attracts them. The doctors insisted that I spread it
over any exposed skin because otherwise all the tediously sewn
microscopic stitches would become irritated and blossom into a
patchwork of scars. There's nothing quite like mosquito bites on
new skin.

    Abba used to talk about the mosquitoes at dinner. He said
he'd read a book that documented cases of Inuit babies literally
sucked dry of their blood, dying, on account of the mosquitoes.
This is hard to believe. After all, these people apparently survived
multiple millennium, from the time of the Tower of Babel (which

is when I presume they arrived) to the completion of the Alaskan Pipeline, without Off, DDT or any other insecticide spray. So they must have done something good about it, but I don't know what. All the North-Alaskan's I've seen (the few on the way up here) clouded themselves in a mist of the most toxic stuff available. When I was in summer camp, years and years ago, the boys, Jerry Moskowitz in particular, would spray Off on their pants crotches and light them on fire. Blue flames dancing, they would run around the swimming pool separating the boys' and girls' bunks chanting, "Dicks of fire, dicks of fire," over and over. And people say I don't know what I'm missing by rejecting the American dating ritual. The mosquitoes are, in fact, horrendous. Ben's non-toxic spray works, no question about it, but it doesn't last. Yes, I could also measure time in reapplications of bug spray.

In my random wonderings, which I am especially and progressively prone to here, I often wonder why mosquitoes, in season, get worse the further north one is, yet, all major mosquito borne diseases are associated with the tropics. It doesn't make sense to me.

It is fatiguing, no enervating, no debilitating to avoid the questions of one's existence when all alone with nothing but the questions of one's existence. And my questions—shattered glass, dead parents, luck run out, Hashem—And yet my ruminations, my mulling of these issues, has led me into an ever worsening cycle. I come off the water, usually refreshed, and begin with easy questions; soon I've lost sense of where I am. I bounce between ghost-worlds that trump the pacific niceness of my current surroundings, and soon lose grip of myself entirely. (True, last night, the bear wasn't altogether pacific. But out here, so long as you're not moving, you can truly see danger at a hundred paces). I get worked up and can't sleep. I write. I cry. I sing. I shout at my mother and father. I pray. I talk to Hashem. I drink. I assess myself and find that I stick out of the ranks of Orthodox women

I've joined like a chancre; I find myself lacking. I can't sleep. At some point I pass out. I try to make a point of passing out in my tent. Then I wake up late, hung-over, though not so much from booze as from emotional trauma. I row all day instead of sail, though it's slower, though I lose more time still rowing, because it cleans me; it holds my focus hostage until all other contenders for my mental attention fade, recede, are forgotten. But then I arrive and it begins again, the cycle, but worse, because I'm not answering anything. So I think I need to not write about it tonight, not stir it up. Maybe I'm not looking at the problem properly. Perhaps I need to instead ask why I am here.

And I can answer that. I can occupy myself with that. I am here because I want to become something. What will I become? What do I will myself to become? I will become always Sara, not Sarah, for one. I will adopt my Hebrew name entirely, do away with the dual farces of Anglicization and integration. I will be Sara when I return to Yerushalaim.

I will return to Yerushalaim and I will live in a new apartment and I will belong to myself again. I will have meaning. What will my Sara's apartment be like? I will want to be in a religious neighborhood, but not necessarily the old city anymore. No, no more reason to live there. Sara's new apartment will be in Bait viGan, yes, and if it is there it will probably be in a building that predates Israeli independence, which means colonial Palestine, which had a strict building code. Therefore, I will live in a six-story apartment building with a stone façade and a red roof. Sara's salary will, in these recessed (not yet depressed) times allow her to afford a one bedroom with a study (NYC realtors would list it as a prewar two bedroom. Lrge. Snny. EIK. Dng Rm). Sara will find something on a high floor with tall ceilings and expansive views, something on a hill. There will be terraces off the dining room, kitchen and bedroom. I'll fill the study with my father's books and with the framed photographs from our father-daughter paddling trips growing up. Basically, Sarah, you're saying that you'll move your father's study from Northport, from Long Island, to Jerusalem, to Israel. Yes, closer to his bones, and Eema's, where the government buried them while I lay unconscious.

Yes, I will move a lot of the stuff from the house out there. Not everything, there isn't room. And it won't be the only stuff— I want to be able to touch the past, not dwell in it. I'll buy new stuff as well. I'll bring the beautiful old oak dining table and the shaker chairs but leave behind the breakfront, the buffet and the curtains. Instead, I'll buy the rosewood stereo bench Yaakov was selling in the office. No one else will have bought it. And of course I'll hang my own curtains, blue silk from the Sook with rosewood valences. And I'll paint the walls myself; or have them painted myself, in my own colors, a sponged orange. But I won't hire Avram again. Last time he sent some Palestinian subcontractors. And I'm glad I went ahead and changed the locks afterwards because Mrs. Rubin said she saw two strange men, first in the lobby and then on our floor, and there were two men who painted the apartment and they did look strange. I haven't even put anything on the walls yet. Perhaps I'll hang a photo from this trip. Yes, an eleven-by-seventeen of this pebble beach with the mountains in the background would be perfect.

No, Sarah, you idiot, you forgot your camera and won't be taking any pictures. True. Then perhaps I'll find something at Aklivuk at the mouth of the McKenzie when I get there. I'll find something native and dissonant, something that doesn't fit quite right with the rest of Sara's elegant and restrained décor, a shaman's hat made of shells, ivory and fox hide, a carved bowl hewn from driftwood meant for storing seal-fat and whale-blubber, a bear paw talisman, something like that. And people will ask, "Sara, why do you have this thing?" And Sara will smile, will tell them, "Nu, it's just a thing, let it be." But they will persist, "Really,

Sara, what is it? It's beautiful."

And then Sara will tell them, "My father dreamed of paddling the Arctic from Prudhoe to the McKenzie. Instead he came to visit me in Yerushalaim, to see what this t'shuvah was, to see what this aliyah was, to see what had become of me. He and my mother must have been dear to Hashem because Hashem took their neshamot back while they were here, in the pastry shop under my old apartment while we were having morning tea. Which is all a long way of saying that as soon as I was well enough, I finished the boat he was building, and paddled the trip for him." After they overcome their surprise, check to make sure they've heard me right, that I really was in the Heavenly Delight Café and Pastry Shop when it was bombed, after they express their condolences, offer to learn mishnaiot for my parents' neshamot, after they've recovered from their awe that little demur Sara paddled solo through the arctic for six weeks, the gesture's beauty, sacrifice, eulogy will silence them. They will realize that Sara, while most definitely an unpresuming, small, orthodox woman, is also something else, something strong, something resilient.

I will find it in Aklivuk. I will put it in on the wall in Sara's sponge-painted dining room (maybe a flat yellow would be better?), hanging, in all likelihood, over the stereo bench. And that's only the dining room. There's so much more Sara must do to decorate her house. But I must go to sleep now.

I didn't da'aven again today. I still don't understand why.

## July 23

I'm beginning to smell. I'm beginning to smell and I saw other people for the first time today. Oilmen in a Zodiac. I don't know what they were doing. I purposely cast off far enough east of Prudhoe to avoid that kind of thing, but maybe they were on some kind of survey. We were all shocked, myself and the three oilmen, to see each other. They seemed to emerge, fairly far away, from between ice floes, heading back west under full power. Their full power is a lot faster than my kayak to say the least. I waved. They pulled close enough for me to clearly read the Exxon logo stenciled on the boat's inflatable body, about sixty feet off, a respectful distance. Still, I covered my ear with my hand though they were far enough away that I mostly made out what they were saying by gesture: Are you ok? I gave them a thumbs-up and they were off. I would have thought they'd be eager to see a woman up here, would've pulled up alongside and chatted a while, but perhaps not.

Seeing men suddenly after a week is strange and visceral; it reminds me that the stunning landscape is only a backdrop largely lacking human actors, a perfectly composed, scenically set portrait, strangely devoid of the subject for which it was devised. One man sat in the rear of the boat, by the motor. The other two shared a bench though they leaned to opposite sides. All three wore orange life jackets over yellow rain slickers and orange hard-hats. It was the man on the south side of the boat, starboard at the bow, who yelled at me. From what I could tell, he looked almost exactly like Sven, the last goyishe man I dated, not even too much older than Sven would be now. He had curly blonde hair that poked out around his helmet and burnt orange stubble thick enough for me to discern even at my distance. And they were gone like that, off probably to Prudhoe, to the oil-works.

I felt empty with them gone. I'd slipped slowly into an acceptance of solitude. They ruptured it, made me realize the loss of human company, of someone to talk to. But they left, before letting me have any conversation. My father warned, once, that he'd read in Waterman's book that in Canada, the Inuit were incredibly friendly, but the Americans at Prudhoe Bay treated everyone like a trespasser, like an attacking Green Peace boat. If they had pulled up close, it would have been very hard to keep to my shomrei n'giah. I wanted to rub the flat of my palm the wrong way against his orange stubble, anchor my hand with pulling fingertips on the wind-roughed red of his upper cheeks. I wanted to feel flesh.

Afterwards, I found myself rubbing my arms, chicken-wing style, against my sides, tracing the outlines of my eyebrows, my nose, my ears, my lips. I didn't want to touch him sexually. I wanted to feel human contact. I wanted blood-warmth, still want blood-warmth. If we had touched, it probably would have been something more like shaking hands, his hand covering mine while we locked eyes or something silly like that, maybe his left hand on my shoulder, covertly feeling the strength of months training, and a week on the water. I must look so distant from the woman I was in Jerusalem. The past two days I've worn a blue coolmax tank-top and a sports-bra while rowing. My arms are all muscle and brown, my brown hair, chopped short, is undoubtedly matted and bleached by the constant sun and a week without showering. I've lost weight from not eating as much as from exercise. My face must be taught and brown, despite all the sun-block and the special cream. I usually wear a pair of cycling shields while I row to cut the glare off the ocean, though not always. I probably should wear a helmet but I don't. While paddling, I wear red nylon shorts, and sometimes Tevas, if any footwear at all. My legs are almost as pale as my arms and face are brown, staying, as they do, below decks. My sea-skirt mimics the Chasid's cloth belt which divides the mental from the visceral. Of course, only Chasidic men wear the belt to symbolize a separation of their heart and minds from their rutting gear. It's not necessary for the women; we aren't ruled by the need to penetrate, to fornicate.

People often suggest that we orthodox simply don't know what we're missing. They say that we've locked ourselves into a strange cloistered society and simply don't know any better than shadchin, and chaperoned dating. But I am here by choice. What are the chances of happiness through random and competitive sexual interactions? This again goes back to what Rabbi Shem Tov was getting at, Judaism isn't a sacrifice in this world in order to get into the next; it's an embrace of the best way of living in this world which leads to the pleasure of olam habah. I mean, take Sven, AKA The Last Straw.

It was during what I call my dual period. Hillel was already my primary social outlet and I was going to the Chabad House for Friday night services and Shabbat dinner. Yet, outside of those activities, I continued to maintain my secular lifestyle. And so, one Spring Thursday night, I went out to a bar, McNulty's at 105th and Broadway, with my roommate, Marie. We ordered a pitcher of cheap light beer, as flavorless as possible, and sat down at the end of a long table to get to drinking. McNulty's ambience blends the air of a boy's boarding school dining hall with that of an ivy-league college bar. Lot of guys in rugby shirts, no music, just the din of voices. Din of voices! Today I heard the following sounds: the ocean, the crack of sea-ice breaking apart (which startled me), a bevy of grounded molting geese warning me off, the man on the Zodiac's muffled halloo, and of course, mosquitoes buzzing. That's one, two, three, four, five different sounds, not counting my own voice and some tangential noises, like the kayak hull grating against the shell beach I'm pulled up on now, the wisp my lighter makes and the whump of the Whisperlite's priming fuel igniting and then its jet-roar once it reaches cooking temperatures. Even counting all of that, I can still measure all the sounds of my day on two hands. What I'm talking about is the overwhelming din of voices, voices that drown, muffle and coddle with their blanketing fabric of sound.

A couple of guys walked over to our table, mysteriously empty excluding Marie and myself, and asked if they could sit down. Sven leaned over and commented that women drinking a pitcher was ballsass, though we certainly weren't the only two girls with pitchers. Marie rolled her eyes and looked at me with what you would call a meaningful look, Eema, and then told them that balls and ass were a combination that it would take a lot more than a pitcher of beer to induce. Unfazed, Sven offered to buy us glasses of whiskey. Marie suggested they buy the drinks for themselves as it was with each other that a meeting of the pubes seemed most likely.

Nonetheless, Sven proved to be quite a charmer, and I agreed to meet him for dinner two nights later. We went out to an Italian place on Amsterdam Avenue with red checked tablecloths and cheeky waitresses in peasant costumes – again, liberation of sex does not equal liberation of the sexes. I think that might have been the last time, or one of the last times that I actually ate at a non-kosher restaurant. He was outgoing and funny and I let him kiss me in front of my dormitory but I did not give into his suggestions that I follow him to his place up in Washington Heights nor did I invite him past the security guard at my front entrance. We met again, and again I refused the offer to go uptown though I let him feel up my breasts on a couch in the downstairs room at 42O, a terrible bar on Columbus Avenue. On the following date, I had to push his hands away from the waistband of my dress while we listened to an outdoor concert over at Lincoln Center.

But I liked him. He had a penchant for punning that made me smack him adoringly. He was a couple of years older than me, just out of school and working as an editorial assistant at a textbook publishing house. He called me almost every night and after waiting an hour or two, I would call him back. I made it clear that intercourse wasn't in the near future and he seemed ok with that. But after about two weeks of this, he called and said he couldn't continue. "Why?" I asked, hurt, crushed.

"Listen, it's like this," Sven began. He told me he'd picked me up because his therapist wanted him to try picking up different women, one a week for a month, to help him break out of his shell. He'd been following her advice and found that he could talk to girls after all. He said he liked me very much but the future was elsewhere, he'd never really been that into me as a lover, more as a pleasant company thing, and to see how far he could go, now that he had this new personality that he'd purchased at a hundred forty dollars a session. As a side note, I asked how he had all this money for psychotherapy anyway; we'd agreed to pay for alternating dates and his usually involved some free activity. He'd claimed entering the publishing world had impoverished him, which I believed.

"Oh, that," he said. "Well my father is the president of Holt books, that's how I got the job, you know? But I can't have money for just anything, he like gives me cash for specific things." I started yelling at him, cursing—I still cursed then—and he offhandedly mentioned that he owned a gun. I hung up. I didn't really believe the threat—I don't think he wanted to see me at all; he just wanted to get rid of me—I didn't need to hear more. I knew better. I knew where to find genuine people and genuine love and genuine meaning. He wasn't the last boy I dated, or kissed, but it really all ended with him. Ok, yes, I was really scared after the gun comment. I told Marie and she suggested we notify campus security, which we did, and they offered to go to his house, but we felt it was just better that they know about it, we didn't want to stir things further—what if they went there and he didn't have a gun and then he came to find me, angry because I'd snitched? But we didn't sleep well for a few nights, despite the chair we'd taken to wedging under the doorknob.

And it doesn't get better. My father's aunt Maxine started dating again at eighty. The first guy she met, who mind you didn't speak a word of English (we speak the language of love, she'd say, oblivious to the fact that she was quoting Better Off Dead) was about as intolerable as they come; arrogant, snide, self-obsessed. He would pass around topless photos of his deceased first wife at

Sunday brunches in Maxine's Fifth Avenue apartment, approximating, in his pidgin English, a boast about how for him there were only the finest ladies. He'd pinch Maxine's butt while he was doing this, and she'd swear he was a devil in bed. Well apparently, what he didn't communicate in the international language of love or in any other language or linguistic equivalent, was that he was epileptic and had no business behind the wheel of a car. She's lucky she lived through the wreck he got them into on their way out to Montauk. A few years later, she found a new guy, he spoke English all right, only he professed to being a player, and I don't mean bridge. He had the pinky ring, the Italian loafers, the silk sweaters, the iodine-tinted tan and a birth certificate from the roaring twenties. "He's like a mezuzah," Maxine would say, "All the women want to touch him." Need I say more?

No. Giving up dating was not a sacrifice. Losing my parents' respect was. I mean, sure, I gained it back. Or, I gained my father's respect back. But when I was growing up, I was everything to them, and they to me. I never fought with my parents. I wasn't a rebellious child. But this thing began to happen. If I had to pinpoint a start date, it would be when I was on debate team sophomore year of high school. I was up against a pimply kid from Jericho High wearing a yellow button-down shirt with a pink Polo logo and one of those cloth belts with the braided leather ends. I rocked back and forth on my feet behind my podium. I figured: I can take this kid. The announcer called the topic: Organized Religion, irrelevant in today's world. He pointed at me and said, "Yes," at pimple-face and said, "No."

At first, I was a lot happier to be on the side of religion's irrelevance. I possessed an entire rhetoric of that persuasion, inherited from parents, teachers, and daily culture. We each had two minutes to lay out our initial positions. And I felt strong about mine, stronger than the Jericho-preppie. Initial statements were followed by rebuttals and then a short period of personal interchange. I hammered on standardized complaints: war, repression, dissimilation. Up until that point he'd recited a standardized list of religion's perceived benefits: social order, ethical structure, spiritual definition; but then he turned and said, "But you, Sarah, to what degree would you be able to measure and define the meaning and success of your own life without the spiritual constructs of deity and divine order?" I stopped. I mean, I'm sure our debate continued. But for the first time I peeked, however briefly, into the possibilities of life, my life. I saw nothing. I saw years spent waiting, years spent competing for the spoils of living: material wealth, showable mate, enviable career, fashionable lifestyle. I saw a checklist dictated by a society that would never fully accept me, even if through some great effort I managed to tick off every single item on it. A treasure hunt, which if won would win resentment. And it seemed exhausting.

Of course, I was fifteen then. These are my interpretations and extrapolations ten years later. At the time, I didn't even have the intelligence to associate the possibility of meaning with religion. Instead, I simply glimpsed a debilitating life filled with routines I cared nothing for yet felt compelled to pursue. I imagined going to classes every day, doing homework, studying for SATs, enrolling in extracurricular activities I didn't care about, all to get into a good college where I would do more of the same to get into a good job. I imagined going home after the meet, and trying to select the right outfit to outdo everyone else, trying to select the right combination of phone calls and allegiances and friendships and dates, the right car for my father to buy when I turned sixteen, the right TV shows to follow and movies to watch, all to stay ahead, to compete for lousy dates with assholes like Moskowitz who'd stopped lighting his crotch on fire with bug-spray but not really outgrown it; and it all seemed so tiring. The deal with debating is that after the round, you defend opposite positions. One would think that after my soon-to-be acne-scarred competitor so jostled my actual thinking process, I could have easily defended the relevance of religion. Instead, my coach yelled at me afterwards, it was like the will to compete had abandoned me, and instead of my usual passionate, nuanced declamations, I mumbled generic lines that hardly stretched to the edges of my time limits. Jericho had deeply unsettled me. "I thought you wanted to be a lawyer, Frankel," Coach White, our history professor chastised after I tried to explain. "Are you going to sacrifice your clients if a prosecutor convinces you they're guilty?"

But once you begin to look for meaning, there is no turning back. You can't blissfully backslide into not caring about the measure of your life's success, the motivation to continue.

But, Sarah, if you had never found meaning, would your parents have ever come to Israel? Ever stopped downstairs with you to sample rugelach and café au lait?

Abba said that after 9/11 he realized that America was just as dangerous as Israel, maybe more so. He said either you're going to die or you're not. He told me the story of a woman who cheated death three times. She was in an elevator going down in Tower Two. When the plane hit, it must have severed the elevator cables. They plummeted. But somehow, the car jammed in the shaft and came to a halt. They were bruised and in the dark, her, another woman, and three male coworkers. Abba said that they managed to pry the doors open, all the while terrified that doing so would loosen the elevator and they'd fall again. When the doors were open, they realized that they were between floors. The men didn't think they could fit into the tiny space through which they'd have to drop down so they sent the two women first. The first woman dropped through, but when she landed, she twisted her ankle badly. Then the other woman, our protagonist, dropped through, this time guided by the woman who'd gone first. She hurt her wrist and got banged up a bit dropping, but not too bad. Then the elevator did fall. Later, she assumed that the men died in the fall. They certainly died at some point. They were not among her company's survivors. She and the other woman helped each other down the dark waiting area for the elevator bank. At its end was a stairwell. They were on the 14th floor. Inside the stairwell, other evacuees helped them walk down. On the mezzanine level, two firemen led them out to West Street to an ambulance. There, an EMT began doctoring their wounds. All of a sudden, as a rumbling began, he threw open the ambulance doors and yelled, "Run!"

This woman who was the daughter of my father's boss's friend started running through a massive cloud of grey dust as Tower Two began its fateful descent. She clung to her friend's hand, but her friend fell and so she kept running without her. She was barefoot, but hardly noticed. She was training for a marathon and ran her race through a grey cloud of soot, through falling pieces of building of furniture of people. Dark shapes flitted through the anti-light, shadows of ghosts, polygons of longing, vehicles, screaming. She was coated with detritus but felt nothing. She kept running. She broke through the cloud but couldn't tell for sure, her face covered in grey and other things. So she ran on in her serge suit dress, her beige silk sleeveless top, her silk hose long worn through at the feet; she ran. She ran from the death behind her, the viscerally understood but yet unacknowledged demise of her three colleagues in the elevator, the EMT who'd sent them on their way but bizarrely stayed, briefly contemplating the bravery of a sinking ship's captain before debris relieved him of choice, the woman she'd made it so far with, ultimately ripped from her hand either by a blow, her ankle or some other incident, whichever, whatever, dead. And so this woman my age, my generation, a marathon runner ran for seventy blocks, to Hell's Kitchen, straight up West Street.

I never asked my father why she wasn't stopped earlier, and he didn't tell me, so I don't know. But in the fifties, a couple stopped her. Apparently she was covered in other people's blood and dust. They forced her into their west-side apartment. She must have been the same size as the woman, because after sponging her down, after listening, and on that day believing and respecting, her incessant and solitary demand to keep moving, to run—"I have to run." They dressed her not so differently than I dress to paddle, lent her shoes and sent her on her way. She ran to the Queensboro bridge at fifty-ninth street. She ran across it and through Astoria until she reached her aunt's house, some seventeen running miles from where she began. I don't know when she began to speak again. But at the time my father heard the story, three weeks later, over coffee at the Red Cross tent on a shift he shared with his boss, she'd still refused to return to her apartment in the city. Family members had gone and collected her clothing, some essentials. She was staying in Queens.

I'm not like that. I'm resilient. I will return to Yerushalaim.

## *July 24*

I did battle with charging waves of anxiety today; drinking is not my friend.

I cursed the sun last night. I asked it if it wanted to fight. I ripped a small willow tree out of the ground, cutting my hands. Its roots splayed broadly through layers of ancient peat. They were as thick as its branches. I howled and bit its trunk. I screamed. I threw stones at the water. In truth, without resorting to fire, without destroying my own chances of survival, it is fairly difficult to leave a mark of anger on the landscape. The sea absorbs thrown stones effortlessly. The stubby trees are too difficult to pull in any quantity. There's really not much of anything to kick or punch. If there were grounded geese where I was camped, I might have killed one, covered my face in blood and a mixture of molting and new feathers; but there were none. If there were musk-oxen, I might well have been my own undoing. I did manage to get into my tent, knocking over the vestibule on the way in (fortunately, nothing was damaged), and then thrashing against my sleeping bag through the night.

What else did I expect? I spent a night writing to—writing to whomever—my plea against unorthodoxy, somehow wrote the story of a woman who fled from an unstoppable death. I don't even know how to write it convincingly: her near death. This journal was meant to log the arctic for my parents in Shamaim who I must assume watch over me. Instead, I document the touchstones of despair, the neat, clean anecdotes of spiritual collapse, of death, of failure, of misery, in painless bite size chunks, swallowable whole. At a minimum, if I must dwell in the perpetual shadows of all of these stories, I want to capture in writing the pathos I feel. I can't. My parent's death brings personal gravity to everything I hear or imagine, but I can only access my own despair, the truth of my emotions, in the drunken rages that inevitably pursue my written declarations of resilience.

I woke early, head hammering, tent a stinking mess of alcohol-sweat, unwashed body, foul condensation. My mouth was glued shut with dried phlegm as were my eyes. I crawled out from under the flapping vestibule wall whose collapse had eliminated any ventilation in the night, made my hovel into a plastic shopping bag of human moisture. The sun wasn't any higher or lower on the horizon, due south, but it was right in my eyes, just neutral enough through all that atmosphere to tempt me, in my fuddled state, into staring right at it a moment. I coughed and saw thousands of black suns ringed in orange when I shut my eyes. At least I will run out of alcohol soon enough.

I pulled off my orange fleece, already well-funkified even before I'd passed out in the steam bath wearing it. The left arm was matted with something sticky and sweet, soaked in whatever deep enough that my arm hair was similarly matted. I cursed before remembering I didn't curse. I put a cooking-gas-flavored finger in my mouth and rubbed my teeth. When I took it out, where I should have seen a water ring of white plaque, an image of beating out a mad rhythm on the hull of Abba's kayak flashed in my head. I cursed again, and then cursed myself for cursing, and then just decided to give up and ran over to my boat. Sure enough, I'd managed to turn it upside down. Turning it back upright, I discovered how beaten my hands were, are. I have to be smart out here. This is stupid. It's a good way to get myself dead. The other thing I discovered in turning my boat back over was just how much my pits stunk. It was time to wash.

I'm a basically modest person. And I'm an orthodox woman. And I'm shomrei n'giah, which means I have no physical contact with men I'm not immediately related to if I can at all help it (I make reasonable exceptions, especially on business trips, though it's not as much an issue in Israel, where men are accustomed and conditioned to behavior like mine). I carefully looked up and down the beach, though really, I knew no one was there. Everything looked endlessly the same and horribly, terribly beautiful, as it always does: barren, broad, unending. Then I pulled off my tank top and undid my sports bra, which I had to hold at arms length afterwards. I rolled down my red rowing shorts. I couldn't remember, can't remember, the last time I felt a breeze on my bare body, the sun on my breasts. It's cold; goosebumps spread from my pale chest out onto my brown arms. My nipples hardened. I tiptoed over to the tent, shells biting into the soles of my bare feet. Clothing stowed, I ran my hands down my butt, over my thighs, my calves, along ridges and lines, crisscrosses and circles, the contact with goosebumps and new skin sending shivers back up my now spare body, along the sides of my torso, my teeth chattering. I steeled myself, hammering head and freezing body, and walked into the sea.

I'd lost sensation in my feet before my breasts reached the

water. It felt like they'd been slapped with a pincushion. I forced myself to dunk my head, eyes open, and stare at my own bubbles rising the through the green ocean murk. Then I was racing for shore, blue, shivering uncontrollably. I grabbed my orange fleece and used it to squeegee the water off my body in long wet ripples, my hair plastered around my ears, numb in the light breeze coming down from the mountains, rolling out across the water. I felt as if I'd been in a mikvah, a purification bath. I felt cleansed, holy. I covered my nakedness and felt new beneath a set of purple capilene long johns, unworn, still redolent of synthetics and laundry soap. I was inspired. I da'avened for the first time this trip. Everything seemed infinitely better for a while, for about as long as it took to eat breakfast and break down the tent.

I was exhausted by the time I was ready to set off. I hadn't slept much or well. My body ached, and I'd broken out in sweat stinking of old whiskey that quickly mixed with the sea-salt on my body in a sticky brine. With each new action, I caught an instant replay of the previous night, each came with a nauseous wave of embarrassment, of guilty regret. I felt like my head was underwater. I didn't want to row.

But there is no time off from rowing. Yes, I gave myself a week's margin against the weather, the closing of the ocean. But I've only been out here one week out of six. I've already begun to lose time. I cannot give up anymore, waste anymore, bet any of it away on a foolish hangover. I deserve my pain.

For a while, I simply felt a general malaise. The paddle's rhythm eluded me. Then I began to sober with labor. My headache developed into a tense vivid thing. My stomach kept contracting. A breeze kicked up and I began to raise the sail before realizing I didn't have the pontoons out (of course they weren't out. I was rowing and they slow me. And I didn't build them as well as Abba built the hull of the kayak). I turned in to shore, landing on a patch of dirt sheltered in the undercut of a tundra bluff barely taller than myself, forcing me to crouch while attaching everything. Crouching gave me cramps, which gave me—well I had to let go of the boat a minute and squat, and I thought the boat would be ok. It began drifting and I had to go in after it, one hand desperately trying to pull up my pants, which wasn't such a good idea because I hadn't had a chance to wipe. I caught the boat easily, but my pants were wet and cold and my butt itched. I pulled it back to shore and tried to tie it up. There wasn't anything reasonable to anchor it against, and eventually I found myself with one leg on the land, one wrapped around a pontoon rail, trying to wipe.

Eventually, I got the sails up and set off. By now, my hangover, the wet of my pants legs, the chill and immobility were all conspiring against me in earnest. That's when I began to think the hull was sinking ever so slowly. Not really sinking so much as riding lower in the water. Perhaps it's just the sail, I thought, pushing the bow under a bit. I lowered the sail to see, and the hull did seem to rise somewhat. I raised the sail again and the hull seemed to stay level, but then a moment later, it looked like it had sunk somewhat again. A burning coal seam on the shore had forced me out quite a ways onto the sea; I'd rather dodge stray ice chunks than breathe burning coal smoke and the chop wasn't bad. But now I wished I was closer to shore. I wished I was somewhere I could pull over easily. It occurred to me that I was *committed*; I am on a ride I cannot get off.

And at that moment I could not be on the water any longer. I hauled sail and tacked in towards a smoking ridge of gray rock surrounded by black desert. And for the first time this trip, I pulled up my sea-skirt and reached back for my PFD. I slipped it over my head and though I'd been cold a minute ago, the formed life vest set me to sweating. But my hands were freezing. The wind whispered east ever so subtly and I was in the middle of that crazed phantasmagoric smoke, coughing. Coughing, eyes tearing and stinging, blinded. I tacked back out again. Breathe as slowly as you can, Sarah. Try not to breathe at all, but then breathe.

I reassured myself that even if the hull had a leak, even if the whole boat swamped, the float bags would keep the boat going. I tacked away from the smoke. I forced myself out towards the ocean. My heart raced and I thought I would puke. The sea loomed dizzily in front of me, floating ice drifts at the edge of the blue horizon warped and quivered. My heart was going so fast and yet there was no blood in my body. I tacked closer in towards shore, I tacked so that I could see the smoldering ruins of hills where coal had ruptured the surface and now burned interminably. I breathed soot-laden air in great grateful gulps. More than anything, I wanted to be in my parents' Northport home, in my growing up bedroom, on my waterbed, in the dark. I wanted dark.

They should call them uncertainty attacks. Or maybe even more accurately, certainty attacks. Or maybe both. Certainty: my kayak rode lower in the water than the day before. Certainty: I'd drunkenly gone after my own boat the night before, an attack that could have damaged it. Uncertainty: I couldn't visualize ever filling the float bags with air. Uncertainty: I had no confidence in my hull-inspection capabilities this morning.

The fact remained, in my head, I could sink. And if I sank, could I swim? My father would recite the arctic drowning statistics like favorite poems, like onomatopoeic tongue twisters, the tan wrinkles around his eyes contracting with pleasure. Within two minutes the body begins to go completely numb, five minutes and you stop trying to swim, ten minutes and you're gladly gulping water instead of air, if you're bothering to breathe at all. That's if you've got your PFD on. The leading cause of death for Inuit kids is drowning. And they know how to swim. And they know the arctic.

I began to calculate my chances. I figured I was about three hundred yards from shore. I tried to do the math, divide swim times by distance, while accounting for a gradual drain of energy as I spent myself. But all I could think was, I want to get off. I want to get off. I want to get off.

There is no getting off this ride, Sarah. The only way you'll go home is if you row another five weeks east.

You row, every single day.

## *July 25*

I hurled my last full whiskey bottle out into the ocean last night and soon much regretted it. I didn't sleep a wink, my skin crawling with muscle hurt, fear ricocheting off my mind's walls. I left the tent on the hour—about every time I thought I was dozing off—to see if it was bears I heard out on the tundra. All I saw was the flashing tail of what might have been a fox.

I was too tired to make breakfast. Instead, I packed the boat haphazardly and stuffed my shirt pockets with dry granola and pushed off. I fell asleep with the sail up.

I slept nearly twenty minutes, I think. That's terrifying. I easily could have died. I could have sailed through a mystery web of cracked apart ice right to the North Pole that might, as it was several summers ago, actually be open water this year. And what would I do then? Fucking die is what I'd do. I'd die dead. I slept and dreamt. I only woke up because in my dream they were shooting closer and closer to me and there was no where else to turn but consciousness. I'm beginning to wonder if I actually want to make it. I'm beginning to question whether part of me simply wants to die here, curl up in a ball and fade into arctic winter.

This isn't the first time in my life that I've thought I would die out on the water. But all the other times there were specific, adrenaline producing things happening right then and there that made me think I was going to die and fight off death at the same time. This is different. This is watching myself drift further and further from the beginning of what seems a doomed mission, an impossible mission. It's days without end waiting for my own end to catch me like the monster in a nightmare and swallow me whole. It's like living in Jerusalem when the bombs are going off daily in Ben Yehudah Square, and parents are afraid to let their kids play in Har Hertzel and snipers take nightly aim at the streets of Kiriat Moshe. Except here there's no one to buck up in front of, no one to make moribund comments to, no one to share terror with. There's no one. And my nap helped, and when I woke up I was as grateful as I was glad as I was angry because I was alive and I felt slightly if ever so slightly better rested. I was even on course. I felt a tremendous wave of guilt for not da'avening this morning.

Perhaps things will be better without the booze.

I can hardly enjoy the landscape these days, I'm so self-obsessed, so riveted with questions of my own survival, and then questions of whether I care about my own survival and then questions about what that must mean about my faith. I just want a break from my own company, a little time off from myself. There were clouds for the first time today, and I suspect rain will soon be here. A surprising twist, given how dry this climate usually is, precipitation only coming a few times a year, in the winter. Ugh. I once read a book in which the first person narrator stated that the reader should always assume he was smoking a cigarette unless he specifically stated otherwise; assume the same for me about spraying myself down with Uncle Bens. If I run out of this stuff, I'm going to wish it was winter.

At some point I'm going to have to deal with what happened to my parents and my own recovery.

Eventually, I'll have to confront the relief I felt yesterday when I bathed without any mirror to confront me, the way I didn't look down at my own body when I stood up out of the sea.

I can't hide from this text forever.

It's a lot easier to think about my return to Jerusalem now that I've begun planning out this apartment. I pity the real estate agent that helps me find it. I'm not going to be at all open to suggestions. I'll need exactly what I've dreamt up here. But it's happy thinking about my life to come, my life as Sara.

I imagine shopping for the bedroom. Sara will take the bus to Kiriat Yoel to the Lavanah superstore to shop for linens and paints. Of course I picked out the color today, though I don't know what it's called, it's a kind of green, the green of the stunted willows here: pea-green up close but nearly frosted blue when viewed from a distance, cool, soothing, trimmed with dark brown window and door frames and a white ceiling. Even stranger than the apartment is to think of people. Sara will be on the bus and perhaps after a stop or two a soldier will get on and sit next to her, his Galil resting, butt down, between his legs. Maybe Sara will notice something quiet, haunted even, in the way the skin around his eyes sags. He'll catch her looking and smile. A real smile but a sad smile. For a moment, they won't notice the noise of the bus, Army Radio blaring its hourly update of doom, the other passengers jabbering away at each other. For a moment, it will only be the two of them.

Sara will notice that he's not as young as she first thought, just fit and tan. In fact, there's gray sprinkled through his short hair, peeking out from beneath his small, knit yarmulke. And the lines that accentuate his grief also speak of age, place him in his forties even. He'll look away from her eyes, look down at Sara's hands, see her calluses. My hands are getting very calloused from all this rowing, weathered and wrinkled from salt water and sun. Looking at her hands, he'll notice the sleeves that creep below her wrists, threaten her palms. It will occur to him, to Udi—yes, he will be Udi—that this woman is ultra-orthodox, that in the strange caste system that exists amongst religious Israeli Jews, defined for men by yarmulke style, she's really a large black felt yarmulke, possibly even a black hat, not a small knit yarmulke that some aspiring lover, or loving relative, has made by hand and inscribed with the three Hebrew letters that spell his name, ayan, daled, yud. But Sara will speak to him, after all. She'll ask him if it's his forty days. "No," Udi will reply, he's career, a soldier for life. Then Sara will notice the insignia on his collar, realize his rank, colonel. Then why the rifle? Maybe he isn't carrying a rifle. Perhaps he's just in uniform, holding a beret in his hands, his elbows on his knees, leaning forward, that look of loss ringing his face unmistakably.

He will ask Sara why she's so tan. It isn't often one sees an ultra-orthodox woman so tan. "We all have our burdens to bear," she'll point out. And something in the way she'll say "bear," the choice of phrase will make him think she's American, though her face is not American. And after she's said "burden," she will notice the way he swallows his own breath, as if a private tide was rising, one he couldn't afford to let out on a bus.

She'll ask, "Where are you going?"

"You're American."

Sara will nod. He'll squint his eyes shut, his mouth puckering, lips sucked in, a lot of emotion for a colonel. Then he'll blurt it out. "I have to tell a mother her son is dead. It happened this morning. He was in my command. He tried to stop two men in a car. I had trained him not to shoot too quickly."

"And they killed him?"

"No, that never would have happened. Another man, also in my command, a reservist, opened fire. There was a ricochet. His throat. He died this morning. I have to tell his mother."

Sara's own losses will swim around her, and then she'll let her mind drift on a warm red ray of arctic sun. It will calm her, the rhythm of paddling in her shoulders, the trained immobility of legs accustomed to the bind of a kayak's hull. She'll respect-fully avoid staring at the beret Udi slowly twists into a taut felt rope. Then he will look up at her, a look of hope on his face even less colonel-like than his previous show of emotion. He'll seem desperate. He'll ask her to come with him. Not to see the mother, no, but to wait downstairs at a café, and to have a cup of tea after-wards, so he'll know someone's there when he finishes. "I'm not so good with cafes anymore," she'll say, quietly.

"We all have our own burdens to bear. I'm sorry I bothered you. It was inappropriate."

"No, I'll go," Sara will say and laugh (not a carefree laugh, though, more the wistful kind). "I can't stay out of cafes for the rest of my life. Not in this country. Not with my caffeine addic-tion." And he'll laugh too, and sniffle, and she'll realize how close to tears he was.

"Thank you—."

"Sara."

"Thank you, Sara." Udi will say, not even bothering to pretend he doesn't need her, doesn't need someone waiting downstairs for him. And it will occur to her that this is strange. She'll ask him about it later, and eventually, when she learns the truth, that the boy's mother was once Udi's wife, his child's mother, she'll realize his hesitancy, his need in a way she won't have before.

Love is complex but need is simple. Hashem made the yetzer harah to inflict us with taivah. But taivah differs from need. I know that now. It's a complexity I didn't understand for a long time. Needs are forgivable, even by Hashem, even when they lead to sin.

## *July 26*

It is no better and no worse without booze. It is also not the same. The swings are mitigated, the time away from pain reduced, the pain, when felt, reduced as well. I spent a second day hugging as close to shore as I dared. I had to row today. No breeze to speak of. And when there was wind, it blew against me. All things seem to blow against me. You sound awfully melodramatic, Sarah. Yes. But, I'm afraid. I'm afraid of bombs. I'm afraid of planes that crash out of the sky. I'm afraid of abstract and, for here, impossible fears. Every time I try to concentrate on why my heartbeat races and the blood drains from my face, every time I try to capture an image of real danger, of cold, of drowning, of bears, of stampeding caribou, I cry for my parents. I sit in my boat and sob and sob and sob.

It is strange that in this journal writing I don't always disclose everything there is to disclose. I don't talk about the time on the waves mourning. I don't speak about the tears. I never discuss scars. But it's harder to keep those away without the drunkenness, without the booze. With the booze, they came out; but they came out and shortly afterwards I blacked out. And in the morning, it was the sweat of alcohol induced exhaustion that fired my body, that forced what of my brain could focus to focus on the immediate. Now that's gone. I live with the grief, with the fear, all of the time.

The day I let my mother hang up on me, the day I wrote about before, when she banged the phone against the counter, shouting,—perhaps shouting "motherfucker," I'm not sure—it's only been nine days and suddenly I'm comfortable saying motherfucker, fuck—well that day, later on, my father called me. Wait, I want to write about what my father said to me. It's haunted me all day, tear-strokes between the paddle's dip, and such. But I don't want to dismiss my mother, my Eema, so quickly. Who was this woman? That question resonates for me with ever mounting volume.

I have this clear understanding of my father. He was this guy who loved to row, who loved his daughter, who cut deals for the Investment Banking Division at Morgan Stanley. But my mother—often days I scream into the wind, trying to find out who this woman who I interacted with so much during the first twenty-three years of my life really was. And then I fall apart when I realize she can't tell me. Sometimes I worry that the grief will fade, that I'll mourn them less. When that happens, I quickly try and evoke the physiology of overwhelming sorrow. It has four symptoms: your eyes sting and well with tears; your chest tingles, contracts and feels like it's crushing your breath; your stomach knots but feels empty; and some kind of mental chemical release makes you feel awake and as if a gray-orange blanket's dropping over your mental sight at the same time. For me, nothing accesses that reaction quicker than attempting to assemble the fragmented memories I have of my mother here in this journal: fighting with me, slamming the phone receiver down, crying, teasing my father about his plans. Strangely, the woman who raised me—quite caringly, diligently, lovingly— doesn't emerge with clear defining attributes. I realize that the daughter of a Shoah orphan must, necessarily, be an extremely complex woman. I imagine the secrets we might have shared at some point. Her telling me just what did drive her; how she made do, housekeeping, as she did, out on the Island. I desperately want to know how she could be content with that. My mother, who, after all, made my father wait to marry her until she'd completed her doctoral dissertation in philosophy—a story I only know because my father brought it up—how was she so easily sated by that materialistic, nay, perfunctory existence? And it breaks my heart, and I wail, and I know that I still grieve them, that they haven't begun to fade. It comforts me to know that I still hurt readily. But I wish I could know her answer (though I wouldn't believe it, I wouldn't leave the path of righteousness); I wish I could discover what let her tick so easily while committed to little more than her family, defining herself in context of my father, an investment banker who liked to kayak, who while imminently lovable, certainly did not infringe upon the divine.

But I began to write that my father called later on the same day that my mother hung up on me. He was exhausted and I could hear the smoke harshness in his voice, the WTC hack. He wasn't sleeping; he was spending too many days down there by far. "Sara."

He didn't mean to call me by my Hebrew name, but exhaustion and fume induced laryngitis did for me what he wouldn't have thought to do, to flatten the A, roll the R, shift emphasis to the second syllable.

"Sara, I'm haunted by what I've asked to see. These are the pillars of smoke Laban's wife turned into when she looked back at Sodom." I didn't correct him. I didn't tell him that it was Lott not Lavan, and certainly not Laban, and that his wife became a pillar of salt not smoke. "Sara, I should've walked and never stopped walking, never gone back there." I still didn't say anything. I was exhausted. I'd woken up so early, and then had to go to work. My mind wasn't easy at all.

"Sara, for the first time in my life I want to believe in God, and more than ever, I cannot. There's a woman who spends her days sitting outside the fence on Broadway. She brings rotisserie chicken to the national guardsmen and guardswomen who stand sentry at Liberty Street. She sees me walk past each day on my way to the volunteer center and today she grabbed my sleeve. Everyone knows she's waiting to see if they find her husband Before, she split her time between the hospitals and the site. At this point, they want body parts, they want corpses, she's not the only one who stands and waits. She's not the only one. But she grabbed my sleeve and I saw the picture she held, a blown-up photocopy of a portrait. I'd seen her husband before. He also used to get his shoes shined at the place by the gyro shop.

"Sara, I was on the twenty-ninth floor of Tower One. I heard an explosion, my chair nearly tipped over, fire flew past my window. But that was all I really saw that day. Everyone yelled to get out of there, so we went into the stairwell, which was clean, which was light, and we walked down, in an orderly fashion. We were in the bottom lobby when Tower Two was hit, and after making us stay where we were to avoid falling objects, to figure out what was going on, they walked us though the mall level and up the E train platform so that we came out a block north of the complex. About all I saw were two beautiful towers surreally streaming smoke. At the time, I wished I'd had my camera, but if I did—I don't know that I would have made it away before they fell. Only later, first when I saw the makeshift bloodmobile and then when I saw the continuous replay on television, did I begin to link images with what I'd physically felt. Apparently, it wasn't enough. I needed to know more, I needed to hear, to learn to see what all those other people experienced, the ones who saw bodies falling, people falling and becoming bodies, that crazed metamorphosis of flight, the plummet and crash turning flesh into meat. I needed to hear from the people whose escape was visceral. I needed to feel so that I could understand my own survival. And now I'm not sure I can handle all that I've learned. Every once in a while, one of us volunteers at the tent will find a body part, especially us regulars who come in daily and are given tasks that take us closer to the pit. It's like an amateur scoring a hit in the major leagues, our corpse discoveries. I've found the images, the knowledge, the experiences I sought out; I don't know if I can handle them, Sara." He broke into a bad coughing bout, followed by the sound of him spitting into something. Then he cleared his throat and continued.

"Sara, the first time I crossed back into Manhattan afterwards was the following Friday. Somehow word had traveled the country that it was official candlelight memorial night, though that wasn't what I had in mind when I went into the city. I'd found out that we were going to have temporary office space and that I'd be resuming duties the following Monday. That's why I could go back. I had some idea of what would be. I drove down through town, traveling largely backwards along the path I'd taken walking uptown seeing the city. It was an absolutely stunning evening, weather-wise, but you could smell the smoke, see it. It was also the first day they opened below Fourteenth Street to vehicle traffic. At 7pm, or whatever time it was, dusk, people started coming out of doorways holding candles. Standing alone in doorways in the oddest, emptiest places holding candles, looking sheepish and proud and waiting for dark. I couldn't stop. I couldn't look at them. I continued on. Finally I had to pull over, it was dark out and I didn't want to drive any further. I was in the East Village and I walked over to Tompkin's Square Park. There, too, people had set up candles, on the ground, lots of people held candles, were silent, reverent.

"Sara, I was so angry! Not at the terrorists, at the hijackers, at Osama bin Laden or whomever. I was angry at these people holding candles. What right did they have to mourn? I was a survivor. I was in the tower when it was hit. I was in it when it was hit again. My survival was measured in the tens of minutes with which I escaped before they collapsed forever. A few floors separated me from the several thousand who went to work and never came home. Who were these people to hold candles and mourn, Sara? How dare they? Nonetheless, I walked up to the circle. Nonetheless, it was a very spiritual sort of thing, solemn, obviously genuine. Like I said, one wants to believe in some deity right now. One wants there to be a God making sure everything works out in the wash. Someone handed me a candle and I took it.

"Sara, I felt like finally the right person had a candle, finally the right person was mourning; it was me. You want to somehow look more bereaved. You want everyone to notice you. You want them to actually see your greater sainthood or whatever. But no one came to me in specific and said, Harry, yes, you look like you belong here more. No one was interested in doing that. People came and went. They handed candles off to other people and let them have a turn. There were only so many. Parents brought children. There was no disrespect, this was a universal ascension to solemnity, to reverence. Unparalleled, Sara, not a single dissenter. Not a single wise-ass or protesting voice. I guarded my candle jealously.

"Sara, I wish I could hold you. Wish I could wake up Saturday morning and get you out of bed. We'd layer some fleece, grab the boats and hit the Sound. Roll across the water just as the mist was burning off. Yeah, well, eventually, standing there, I began to realize, though I held my candle no less jealously, that we were all survivors, some of us by more, some of us by less, but all of us survivors, the only ones with different rights than us lay buried under burning concrete. And I felt a little better. But I guess I still had to go out and immerse myself in the world of immediate survivors, the world of rescue that's now turned into a world of recovery."

Abba had told me this story before, but I didn't stop him. I liked hearing about the candles set on the hexagonal bricks of Tomkin's Square Park's central walkway, the solemn people lit by candlelight, the Friday night normally devoted to hipster mating rituals subverted and made reverent. It was a religious fable for him, my father. I was too tired to say much anyway. So I stayed on the phone until he was done. And for a second time that day, I lay the receiver back in its cradle after the other end had gone dead.

I really, really, really wish I had something to drink.

Oh shit. I just realized today's Saturday, Shabbat. I'm all fucked up. I wasn't supposed to row today. I wasn't supposed to cook today. And I'm certainly not supposed to be writing this. I can't believe I'm losing track of days like that. It's bad. I need to stop writing.

## *July 27*

This business of rowing close into shore, on the border of the chop, is beginning to wear thin. I ask myself when the hell I'm going to start heading a little further out again. When am I going to head out to the smooth water where I don't have to paddle around every minor contour change the shore makes? I lost time today. And I couldn't use the sail, even though there was more wind, because in the chop, the outriggers I finished don't ride very well and keep pushing me sideways. I can see more of the shore, though, it's very beautiful. After a while, the rippling of green tundra, the seeming endlessness of same, takes on individual shape and structure. The distinct edges of willow leaves, grass blades, of infinite flower stems, come into focus. You can see all of them, sameness becomes unique. And then suddenly, something breaks the spell. Because you're concentrating on edges, you almost don't notice the irregularity. Today, it was a bleached whale skeleton on a shell beach. It must have been at least one winter old because it was past being picked clean; the bones had the dull softness of driftwood. I beached the kayak alongside it and walked over, shells crunching under my bare feet, making me think suddenly of Marie's parents' house in Florida, whose driveway also crunches.

Its ribs came about level with my shoulders. I grabbed two and shook. They were firm, warm; they fit my hands well. I wondered what kind of a paddle they'd make. It was a bit early for lunch, but I went back to my boat anyway, grabbed two power bars and a bag of dried apricots, and returned to the whale. I climbed into its rib cage and sat on a piece of driftwood that had lodged in there during some distant high tide, and carefully leaned back against the spine. I was looking out at the mountains, south towards the sun, which danced along the edge of my vision. The view was like sitting in the very first row at the Met, the stage just above eyelevel, slightly disconcerting. But looking out at that plain of tundra, that field of green and brown broken by tall yellow flowers that waved ever so gently when wind whisked by, suddenly soothed me. For the first time since I'd been out here, I felt a sense of ownership of self. A rightness. I noticed I was smiling. I heard gulls in the air and looked up, blocking the sun with my left hand, and in a cloudless blue sky saw streaks of white dip and dive. I felt free. I exhaled, then inhaled salt and amazingly pure air, totally fresh. The wind whispered by again, and I shivered through my light polypro top. I could feel every millimeter of my skin. Everything was distant but this awesome and empty landscape.

I ate both my power bars, chewing slowly, sipping from my Nalgene in between bites and trying to keep the smile on my face. But for some reason, Marie's voice began to echo out of the wind. She kept asking me over and over whether my move to Israel meant that this was it, that we weren't going to be friends anymore, that I was going to only have Jewish friends from now on. I told her we could stay friends, that my embrace of my culture, of my religion, was not a rejection of anything else. "Not a rejection? Please. Every time I asked if you wanted to go out anywhere during our senior year you gave me that bullshit half-shy look and mumbled some fucking excuse about studying. But I know you were just going to the Hillel House and hanging out with the uber-dorks. Apparently, I was only your friend up until dusk." Marie continued on about how it was only because we'd been friends so long, since summer camp, that she put up with my veto on boys spending nights in our room. She pointed out all of her attempts to save me from the fate I seemed to be choosing. "From having a shitty life living with some stuck-up pretentious Jew who kept you cloaked like a sheik's wife," was what she said exactly. I hung up on her. And though I knew that she wasn't genuinely anti-Semitic, it was convenient to view her that way; and so I broke off contact.

Marie faded from the wind. The vastness before me retained its beauty, and yet, I couldn't hold the ends of my mouth up; I couldn't force a smile, and my eyes twitched with tears. The ocean grew louder at my back. I remembered the phrase: never turn your back on the ocean. I think it refers to wading at the beach. But despite that, my scalp began to tingle with the knowledge of it back there, like being watched, like being stalked. The sea called me. I felt its pull, its inexorable pull, and part of me was tempted to race out across it in the kayak, head straight north, sail up, no outriggers; race away from hope until, inevitably, I capsized, and then not attempt an Eskimo roll, but simply absorb the comfortable numb of frigid, saline water, drown.

But I am too afraid. I keep picturing myself stumbling onto a beach after a capsize, pulling myself out of the water and the constant breeze shocking my system into a quivering parable of painful recovery.

And so, while I sat there, trying to resist the ocean's pull, I thought about Udi's sorrow, the way his eyes welled over tea, thought he didn't confess to Sara right then that it was his son who'd died. I thought about how Sara, for the first time since being ba'al t'shuvah, really wanted to touch someone, not sexually, but kindly. She wanted to reach under the table, and grasp, beneath there, hidden, his rough left hand from his lap. Though she would be taking his hand, feeling the strength in it contrast with his soft, protruding veins, he would capture hers, rub his thumb in circles over her knuckles. Though Sara would not yet know the depths of Udi's sorrow while she fantasized about him soothing her hand, I, of course, already did; and that knowledge triggered the surging sadness lunch had threatened all along. I grabbed the ribs on either side of my log and unleashed my tears' current, my body rigid.

After I had collected myself, blowing snot-rockets onto the shells, rubbing my eyes with my palms, I walked out onto the tundra, careful not twist an ankle, the rough material harsh on my still bare feet, and peed, which made me feel infinitely better somehow. I faced the Arctic Ocean. Blue sky faded across it into a vermillion in the north at the horizon's crest. The sea washed thin teal water and foam over the shells. I stood up and returned to the skeleton. On the ground, near the head, I found a small bone, triangular, white and pitted by the ocean. It squeezed well in my hand. I comforted myself by knowing I would one day give it to Udi, and he would wear it on a strip of leather around his neck next to his dog tags.

I'm tired, I feel the loss of a rest day, and that I totally missed Shabbat like that wears at me. It doesn't surprise me that I feel myself drifting further from people, from civilization, from their constructs out here. But I am disturbed to think I'm drifting further from Hashem. I would have thought that the one thing if anything I would find is my God again, out here. These are meant to be my forty days on the mountain. Instead, I'm finding images and memories, new fears.

I was feeling so devout before I left for Puget Sound. I was learning with Rebitzin Shulman in Midwood twice a week, driving in from Northport to see her. Sure, out on the San Juan Islands I spent a lot more time concentrating on my training than on my Yiddeshkeit, but I da'avened every day. I was a little shook up while there. But that's understandable. I'd just gotten back from the unveiling in Jerusalem. It was the first time I had been back there since I left Israel late last August to finish physical rehab in New York. Marie went with me. She'd heard about my parents, and though I didn't take her phone calls while I was in the hospital in Jerusalem, after I came back, she insisted on taking the LIRR out from the City every weekend and showing up at my porch. I couldn't hold a grudge forever. When I went back for the unveiling, I needed her with me.

Not many people showed up. Funerals are depressing, and there are too many of them in Israel these days, all for people who shouldn't be dead. Yet people usually do attend them, both those with a point to make and those who hope shovelfuls of dirt will cover the new holes blasted into their hearts, their psyches, their security. But few come to the unveilings eleven months later. No one wants to count the funerals they have been to during the mourning period, and so it is usually only family who show up. My grandparents, Abba's parents, wanted to come, but Israel is a long trip. Eema's parents died when I was much younger. I showed up, my chavrusah from the yeshiva, Chana, came, and Ari from the office, and, of course, Marie. Ari was too nice to Marie; he's not religious. Chana distrusted her. I tried not to imagine that I'd brought my parents out here and turned them into a stone over a grave. I tried not to think that if they died on a visit to Jerusalem, I could die on a visit to Jerusalem. (And I thought least of all that they never would have chosen to be buried here so far from the small family plot on the Island).

Marie insisted we go to the café. My subletter in my old apartment upstairs was holding stuff for me that I need to pick up, so I agreed to go over there. They'd reopened. We walked up to the new glass window. Chaim was working. I'd bought an espresso and a roll from him every morning for the three years I'd lived above the store and we made eye contact through the glass. But I quickly looked away. I couldn't go in. I didn't want to be part of the new that represents the resilience of life. I didn't want to surround myself with the shiny metal chairs and new vinyl seats and admire how perfectly they'd restored the old tin ceilings and laugh about how the insurance money had paid for much better appliances than they used to have. I didn't want to catch myself in the large mirrored wall and see there a clean and walking me, with Marie by my side, and a background of happy, loud Israelis babbling at each other and their cell phones, oblivious to the blood-stained rubble this place was just less than a year ago. I did not want to go on. So I turned my head down, and Marie put her arm over my shoulders and glared in at Chaim who was certainly innocent. As we walked away, towards the side entrance, I could see Chaim deflate through a trick of the glass, his eyes sag, an involuntary wringing of his old, heavy hands. I wondered if Lott's wife had only looked back at Sodom because of a trick of the glass, and whether involuntary, unwanted visions could condemn me too. We shouldn't see each other, Chaim and I; it doesn't do anyone any good.

## July 28

I think I need a rest day. I sucked wind today and the tendonitis in my right shoulder flared up pretty bad. I didn't have the energy to cook warm food, so I just ate gorp. I don't know why I'm writing now. It aggravates my shoulder. Missing Shabbat was really very bad. It worries me that I might not have Hashem on my side for this mission now. On the other hand, I can't help asking myself where Hashem was a year ago. But then why shouldn't it be my parents, if someone has to die? If that's what's written in the book of life, then that's what's written. But why couldn't it have been me?

I really want a rest day. I want to sleep in late and laze around looking at the landscape, dream about Sara and Udi. But I feel like I have to continue on. I've missed Shabbat, and there's nothing to do for it but proceed. That's the deal. And since the bear, I'm a bit less comfortable on shore. It seems like a long time since I saw the bear.

Keeping the little piece of bone in my pocket gives rise to a distinct longing to return to Jerusalem, to find Udi and give him this talisman. I know exactly how it will happen. He will come over one evening, a couple of weeks after he's first met Sara. He'll have shown up at her apartment to see if she'd like to go and have tea at a café with him. "You said I should stop by anytime, I'm going to a café, it's the only time you're willing to go to one, and what will become of your caffeine addiction without this?" She'll have offered this, but she won't be ready yet. She'll ask him in. But Halachah forbids me from being in an apartment alone with a man who isn't a relative. This will require that they go through the awkward routine of propping the front door slightly open. A make-believe public thus entering Sara's apartment. While she is changing in the bedroom, whose door will be closed, Udi will pace the apartment in even, deliberate, military strides. Observing and cataloguing decorations and accoutrement, refraining from actually picking each piece up to see it better. He'll ask about the skin in the dining room, and Sara will mention, in an offhand way, that it's from a kayaking tour she took in Alaska, hurrying both of them out the door.

"Alaska! You went kayaking in Alaska?"

"Yes," Sara will reply, pulling the door shut, locking it. "A fun trip, along the Northwest Passage."

Udi, momentarily stunned, will have to hurry up after her as she strides towards the elevator. "Wait," he'll call, "Is it just me, or is the passage a route through the Arctic Ocean?"

"Yes." Sara will say, still flippant. And then, when they get off the elevator, she'll stop cold. He'll nearly run into her. Sara will grab his sleeve, a violation of shomrei n'giah, but not as bad as if she'd touched his bare flesh, not as bad as when she'd found his hand under the table, and she'll make eye contact, pause. Then, Sara will take out the bone and put it into his hand. "Udi, I found this bone, sitting all alone in the belly of a whale on an unimaginably distant shore. I kept it, some backwater superstition, but somehow it comforted me. You take it. Hold on to it."

Udi will take the bone slowly, his hand instinctively acclimating to its smooth heft, the way it fits perfectly in a clenched palm. What if Udi rejects it as avodah zorah? He won't. Just as Sara will know she needs love in a way that lets her grab his arm, he will need love in a way that will let him take the bone. They will have their secret from their god.

## *July 29*

Tired, just way too tired. And I feel the very beginning twinges of tendonitis in my left shoulder. Just the slightest bit of feedback kicks up at the end of each port-side stroke. Not good, not good at all. Hashem didn't create Shabbat for nothing. My flaunting it is making me pay. I have an instant ice pack that I could use on my shoulder, but if I use it I won't have it later, should I need it. I guess I'll just take some ibuprofen and try to get a good night's sleep.

## *July 30*

In certain constructs, it will seem apparent that Udi and Sara are dating. In others, it will seem that they are two unlikely friends brought together by a mutual grief and a mutual perseverance. As in all things, the truth will be between the poles of appearance. Inevitably, Sara will develop some romantic affection for her unconventional new intimate, a mutual affection. But despite Sara's refusal of some of her society's mores, of those admonitions not directly encoded in Halachic law, which dissuade certain associations and friendships—her liaisons with both Marie and Udi are strictly outside standard bounds, and yet valuable and inviolate to her—it would be a grand conceit to assume, therefore, her adoption of Western "enlightened" romantic sensibilities. Sara is an orthodox woman. She does not have a vision of romance; love and enduring matrimony are intertwined and religiously derived for her. And Udi is the same way. He does not have love interests. If, at some point, he decides to remarry, he will pursue that through his community and Rabbi. Which is also not to say that at such time, he might not decide that Sara might make a reasonable partner, and propose such to her—a move that would not be enjoined by a prolonged Western courtship, but, at that point, by a simple decision.

After Udi's impromptu visit to Sara's apartment, they will establish a pattern of late afternoon tea, several days a week. They will meet at Yechil's, a Morrocan-themed café with European pretensions. Its primary appeal will be a triangular, awning-covered seating area, described by the intersection of Rechovs Birchiat and Ben Gurion. When they first go there, Yechil serves them himself, asking only what Sara wants; for Udi, he already has a fresh pot of mint tea, and the appropriate glass tumbler wedged inside of a hammered brass cup.

"You're a regular?"

"Is that a pickup line?" And then, morosely pouring his tea, "We also served together, Yechil and I. When we were kids, after our mandatory tour, we went to India. We were the first generation of Israeli kids to discover their beaches as a getaway."

They won't discuss it, but part of Yechil's Café's appeal is the outdoor seating. In a large open area, they will have a much better chance of seeing a bomber before he detonates. Walls amplify blasts, echoing shockwaves with devastating effect. Yechil's will be a kind of transitional therapy for Sara, a halfway house on the road to full café-recovery. Even the closest bus stop is on the other side of Rechov Ben Gurion and a full half block away. And their meetings will give Udi some structure, a sense of routine, a mandatory, daily perch which will be so important while he wanders Jerusalem's streets, waiting for the expiration of his mourner's leave from the army.

After two weeks of meeting this way, rarely for more than half an hour each time, often hardly speaking at all, Udi will invite her to Shabbat dinner at his friend Noah's house. Noah will also live in Bait viGan, not far from Sara's apartment, making it quite natural for Udi to invite her. After all, he's heading there anyway, and Sara should certainly meet some of the people in her new neighborhood. They will agree to walk to Noah's together from a nearby shul. What will the shul be named? I don't know any of the Synagogues up in Bait viGan. Perhaps it will be Kesser Yisroel. Yes, they will go to services together at Kesser Yisroel, Sara sitting behind the thick curtain partitioning female congregants from male, surrounded by women in the bright-colored cloth of Shabbat finery, silk and wool and linen sleeves and long-cut dresses rustling in warm chandelier light, the smell of fresh shampoo blending with layers of perfume and cologne, rising and sitting and rising and sitting to the rhythm of the prayers, melodic chorus of hundreds of baritones orating Friday night chants.

When they will meet out front, Udi's unfamiliar refinement—a black wool suit and stiffly starched, reflectively white shirt, his hair neatly combed and lightly gelled, a different, crisper yarmulke—will elicit an involuntary tingle down Sara's spine; Udi will look more ambassador than soldier and it will make her straighten up and take notice. They'll walk together, conscious of each other, proud of each other, past throngs of other walkers, equally well dressed, past a mélange of perfumes, scents, and the rustle of wool coat-sleeves against starched cotton.

At Noah's house, they'll be ushered into a living room full

of people about Udi's age. Their easy banter between sexes, the absolute absence of shatels on the women, and the generally westernized dress: shorter hemlines, European business suits, western haircuts, and perhaps most surprisingly of all, a lack of children, clearly define the party as amongst those modern orthodox who treat religiosity as a side note to their mainstream aspirations, not as an all-encompassing cultural dictate. Fortunately, by this point Sara will have grown used to her scars and even in this company, even though dressed far frumpier, more orthodoxly, she will not be cowed. Instead, while Noah grabs Udi's elbow and shuttles him off, she'll sit down on a couch next to a woman at least closer to her own age.

The woman will have dirty blond hair streaked with gray and wear a white shirt with sleeves to just below her elbows tucked into a blue wool suit skirt. Her bold choice of the flag's colors will make her seem dressed for some national pageant. Sara will introduce herself and the woman will shake her hand smartly. "I'm Dalia. You sound American, are you?"

"I'm starving. Do you think we'll eat soon?"

Dalia will laugh, "You clearly don't know any of these people, who did you come with?" Just then, Udi will return to the room, his elbow still in Noah's grasp, nodding his head while Noah talks, gesticulating wildly with his other hand. Udi will catch her eye, smile, and wink before turning back to Noah and, with an obvious gesture of incredulity, launching into some counter-argument. Dalia will lean over conspiratorially, "Udi brought you." Not bothering to wait for Sara to confirm. "He's an interesting one. Too bad about his tragedy though."

Sara will momentarily feel defensive, as if Udi's tragedy is not something anyone else has a right to discuss, has any business involving themselves in. She'll snap, "Are there any of us without a tragedy anymore?" As if Dalia's comment will have been somehow an insinuation about Udi, as if he will have possessed a kind of disfigurement. Dalia will grasp Sara's knee and laugh, then call out to Noah, "Habibi, is there anyone we're waiting for still?"

"I don't remember."

"Well, if they're not here, they're late." Dalia will then whisper to Sara that see, they'd get to eat soon after all. "Shnell, everybody, up for Kiddush."

The ten or so guests will all walk up to the table, Dalia subtly and effortlessly directing them to specific seats. Not surprisingly, she'll separate Sara and Udi, who will shrug at Sara as if everything is out of his control now. Sara, well accustomed to orthodox seating arrangements, won't have expected to sit next to Udi anyway, and would take his implicit apology as mildly patronizing, a response to her American origins, but that she will be so pleased to see him smiling and relaxed, a first since they've met, that she will forgive him anything.

Standing behind her seat while Noah, holding a silver wine goblet aloft at the head of the table, recites Kiddush, Sara will find that Dalia has seated her next to herself. For all the strength and rigidity in Dalia's carriage, her hands will squeeze the high wooden back of her chair to stop from trembling, pushing veins up along the delicate architecture of finger-bones, tensing muscles against the thin, beautymark-spotted skin of her forearms. The group will drink wine, wash their hands and stand silently before saying Kiddush over Challah bread, and then finally sit down to eat. Noah and Dalia will have strategically situated themselves to keep everyone's wine glass full. And Sara will think about how, not counting Purim and Passover, she's only really gone and gotten herself drunk three times since college. The first time was with her father the night he realized that she was going to Israel, no two ways about it. The second time was on September eleventh. Ari took her home from the office and they sat in a little bar in the old city close to her old apartment and split the better part of a bottle of Israeli Orange Vodka. The last time was with

Marie, and that time will still be too painful to bear remembering. Not only does this crowd drink, but it toasts, frequently, and to all sorts of things, serious and otherwise, from the health of the prime-minister to the "saludatorily aromatic effects of our gar-bagemen's most recent affirmation of their right to strike."

Dalia will have a way of seeming to stay engaged in every of the many conversations at once, a sort of second hearing. While serving fish at one end of the table she will interject wittily into a conversation at the far side. While whispering vital stats on some other guest to Sara, she manages to keep track of her husband's description of their vacation in Barcelona, and will correct him on the name of the hotel they stayed at, the peseta exchange rate, and how much the boots she bought there cost. But despite her omni-presence, Dalia won't fully engage in any conversation besides the one she pursues with Sara, which will begin as a cross between outright interrogation and a pseudo-job-interview. While flat-tered by the older woman's interest, and longing for a local girl-friend (Ari's the only person back in Yisroel I've really spoken to since going back to America, which will make Marie, back in the States, Sara's only female friend) Sara will try to change the con-versation. Sara will comment on the beautiful series of prints by Israeli painter Moshe Alon. Except to correct Sara that they are originals, not prints, purchased early in Alon's career, just as the painter migrated from a Degas-like style into his current, color-rich abstracts, Dalia won't be shaken off. What do you do for work? She'll ask. When did you move here? How do you like it? How did you like the old city? Where did you and Udi meet?

The questions will circumscribe a massive event, a two-year hiatus, in Sara's life. Both women will be aware of the looming unsaid. Finally Dalia will break convention, will allude a certain knowledge. Grasping Sara's knee again, she'll say, "Which of us is without our tragedies these days, right?" As if the scars weren't already visible anyway. As if Sara wouldn't have discussed the event she'd like to relegate to just one day out of the tens of thousands she's lived rather than the heart of her entire being. While Sara's head is down, Dalia will continue, "Udi told Noah that you spent time kayaking in the Arctic is that true? Please, tell me about it."

Not sure whether to be flattered that Udi speaks about her to his friends, or annoyed that he's shared secrets, Sara will nonetheless feel relieved to turn to a topic she's comfortable talking about. "Yes, I spent six weeks in the Arctic. I rowed to the McKenzie from just east of Prudhoe Bay."

"I can't even imagine that; you'll have to tell me everything."

"I set off on a wooden sea-kayak after several months of training, dropped off in the most spectacular middle-of-nowhere by a bush pilot, and began rowing along the shore. There's this silence that catches up with you, an absolute absence of humanity like you've never imagined. No people and no impact from people. Just yourself and what you bring with you and myriad animals. I saw every form of wildlife you might imagine: bear, whale, musk-ox, caribou, fox, rabbit and more, more than I can tell. But my most favorite were the grounded geese, great big molting birds no better able to fly than those ornamental members of their species whose wings have been clipped, they ran along the shore, from tuft of tundra to tuft of tundra squawking angrily at each other. It was a fox's paradise. And so many other birds. And seals. But the silence catches you, an aloneness almost beyond imagining. Every voice you've ever heard, the entire of your memory, invades unexpectedly, and fills you with a din of yourself. You can keep this harrowing assault at bay through two mechanisms: sleep and exertion. And so you keep rowing to keep your mind, experiencing an unparalleled beauty of self."

"And what voice were you keeping at bay?"

"My father used to tell me that a musk-ox uses its outer coat of fur to face the winter world. Snow and ice accumulate and freeze onto its long hairs, building a dry barrier around the animal's soft lofty undercoat, which keeps it warm in any weather."

"And your father, he shares your fascination with the Arctic?"

"He said the musk-ox was actually a member of the goat family. So are whales."

"But he didn't come with you, your father?"

"No."

"Is he your tragedy?"

And then Simcha will stand up, wine glass in hand, and loudly toast Udi's dead son. Everyone will stop talking. Udi will stare down at his plate of roast chicken and noodle kugel, fork in one hand, wine glass in the other. Dalia will tell Simcha compassionately to sit down. "What?" he will ask, turning towards Noah. Noah will nod, eyebrows furrowed, and motion with his hand that Simcha should sit. "Ok, I'm sorry," Simcha will say, "But you all know I always loved Elan, he was my protégé, and don't mistake my religiosity, but what is this country that exempts those who engage us in this war, so long as they learn Torah, but a gentle passive boy who makes music with his hands must substitute a trigger for a piano's keys." Noah will half stand but Simcha will already have begun pulling his chair in to sit, an action they will both continue until the sound of exploding glass will startle them. Udi, expressionless, will clutch a broken wine goblet in his hand and then release it, his palm bloody.

"Udi!" Dalia will yell, "Snap out of it."

Udi will shake his head and stand up. "I'm sorry; I need to leave."

"You're not going anywhere, old chap," Noah tells him, standing up as well. "Wrap your napkin around that thing." Udi will do as he's told; the white cloth napkin was already ruined anyway.

A thin woman sitting across from Sara, who Dalia will have

whispered is actually a top intelligence consultant for the Prime Minister, accustomed to selecting militant leaders for assassination, will ask loudly just how long we should be expected to live like this. The woman's husband will immediately shoot back and the table erupt into conversation. Dalia will lean over to Sara again and confide that everyone at the table has lost someone. Sara will ask Dalia if she knew Elan, Udi's son. "Yes, of course I knew Elan. When he was younger, he'd stay with us while his father was away on missions if his mother had to go back to America."

"Elan's mother is American?"

Of course Elan's mother was an American. In her early twenties, she came to work for a year on a kibbutz in the south. Udi, at the time a junior lieutenant, was briefly stationed near her, and on a drive to the Gaza strip stopped in to get fuel for his Jeep. The kibbutz administrator, always eager to recruit "the right kind of orthodox Jew," suggested that Udi stop back in a few days for a social night. He did, met Nurit, and started spending his every Shabbos on the kibbutz. By the end of Nurit's year on the kibbutz, Udi found himself on a flight to the States to meet her parents. A few months after that, they married. Within a year, Elan was born.

"Quite the happy couple."

"Obviously not."

"Why did they split?"

But just then, Udi and Noah will return from the bathroom. Udi, tie off, sleeves rolled up, will display his now neatly dressed hand, turning it side to side for everyone to admire. The table will ooh and ah with consciously exaggerated awe; they will be drunk, after all. Udi will take a little mock bow and then grow serious. Sara will notice the whalebone on a leather strap around his neck.

"You know, I'm not new to any of you. We've known each

other most of our lives. And I've known about this particular monthly gathering for a long time. But I hoped I would never meet the qualifications for entrance. So you'll excuse my lapse. Sara, I didn't warn you. But we are a group bereaved. We meet for Shabbos dinner once a month, not to discuss our grief, but to know we're here. I'm sorry if I brought you against your wishes, without telling you. But I know there is some grief in your life as well. Your loss is obvious. You don't have to share it, just that it exists is enough to get you in with this group."

Will Sara have the strength to gracefully overlook Udi's calling her out?

Will Sara be able to rise from her seat and thank Udi for inviting her, thus putting him at ease, allowing him to sit? Will she then sit herself and quietly acknowledge her own loss? Will Sara be sufficiently healed to say, "Yes, I too have not only lost, but nearly lost myself. My parents and I were in the café beneath my apartment when a bomber detonated. They didn't make it. I, myself, spent months in physical rehabilitation, first here and then later back in the states. None of us are without our loss. Thank you for showing me that I am not alone." I would want her to be able to say this. Why shouldn't she be able to? After all, anyone can see the scars.

Why, when I try to peaceably imagine myself in the future, in a healthy future, where I'm adjusted, why even then do I end up in these situations? I don't feel as if I can simply go back and rewrite the script, change what will happen at that dinner party. To do so would be cheating. No, the future will not be perfect, but I will be able to meet it.

Am I saying then that my imagining of myself, of Sara, upon my/her return to Jerusalem is a true prediction? Yes, sort of. Well come on, Sarah. Ok. Granted, I don't really believe that things will happen exactly like that. How strange it would be to have predicted every conversation of one's life, to know exactly how it will be, to have the opportunity to modify and edit one's responses, utterances, actions, to prepare for hard moments and anticipate those things good in life and to then actually live that carefully constructed, fully described existence.

But it also has a certain magic to it. There's a resonance to what I imagine, a feeling of inevitability. It's as if my imagining of it, my committing it to paper, makes it real. And after all, the very seeming impossibility of such an arrangement would lend a newness and a wonder to that life of impossible déjà vu, making every recurred occurrence new, surprising, wonderful. It makes me believe I will finish this trip, will return to Israel, will move to Bait ViGan, will meet this beautiful sad strong man and his strange group of friends, all of whom have lost; and I will.

I must.

Really, I don't think there's any other way. And that's why I won't try to change the reality that Sara, though healed, will not be fully healed. I won't try to rescript Sara's response and make her even stronger than she is. No, the evening will have already weighed heavily on Sara, the emotions run too high. She will stand up and walk very quickly to the door. She will hear Udi call after her. Somehow, she will be aware of his starting after her, of Noah restraining him. She will hear him say quietly, "I'm sorry. I shouldn't have." She will carefully, quietly pick up her rain coat and put it on, delicately open the door, and gently close it behind her as if she were sneaking out of her husband's bed in the middle of the night to wander the streets without waking him.

Sara will run away for now.

And two days later, on Sunday, Noah's wife will call. Sara won't hang up on her, but will listen to her quiet apology for Udi's behavior, his mistake in bringing her without warning. They will meet at the same café to which Udi usually takes her. Dalia will be there when Sara arrives. Dalia will be dressed in a khaki trench coat with its collar turned up against the building Jerusalem winter. She'll be wearing sunglasses and the silk scarf covering most of her hair will in equal parts suggest the orthodox wife's shatel and Jackie O's fifties chic.

Sara will sit down next to her, feeling suddenly somewhat dowdy, and contritely listen to Dalia's voice gently explaining the realities of grief, of losing a child. They will sit there, the two of them on the same side of their small white metal café table, sipping mint tea and watching the wind blow white clouds through the cold sky over Rechov Ben Gurion. Eventually, Sara will confess that Udi knew about her grief – at least in part. Of course she had a grief. She lost her parents to a terrorist. She should never have lost her parents. Her father had already survived a bombing; he survived 9/11! He was supposed to be exempt.

Their voices won't rise at any point. Their expressions won't betray anything to the world. And slowly, Sara will come around to explaining her trip to the Arctic, her attempts to make amends with her parents' death and her frustration that recovery is an incremental game one never seems to win entirely, and often hardly wins at all.

## *July 31*

I almost didn't row again today. I woke up, my journal, this journal, next to my sleeping bag, the tent walls glowing yellow, and my first thought was to get back to Sara and Dalia. My first thought was to escape. I guess I needed the rest day yesterday. After somehow missing last Shabbat, my body was a mess, my hands chafed, my mind all screwed up; I woke up and couldn't go on. But to take another rest day now would be deadly. And I did feel better than I have in a long time once I got out into the kayak and set off. It's been a nice day, if one can corral a chunk of time and call it a day in a place without any means to measure time. Or at least any natural way to measure time that is. My watch functions accurately enough. It tells me when yesterday has passed and when tomorrow will begin. But we created watches to measure and duplicate a natural function of the world, the cycle of night and day. That cycle doesn't exist here. It's a bit like attaching a speedometer to your couch to measure the speed of the world. At any rate, humans adapt, and my early fascination with the eerie continual light has faded. In ways, my fascination with the arctic itself has diminished.

I wrote outside for a while yesterday, but it got cold, and I felt more protected from bears inside the tent anyway. My nicest day in the arctic so far was spent in a tent imagining not being in the arctic anymore. My return to Jerusalem will be easier than I expected.

But it's not as if my day-to-day existence here isn't fascinating and doesn't change continually. Today was fraught with adventure and with the clean effort of rowing. And I didn't sleep very well last night. I wrote until I was too tired to stay up, but then I found that though my mind was tired, my body itched and twitched and tried to claw its way out of the sleeping bag. Every time I began to actually fall asleep, drift into dream, I would become aware of my own sleep, think: at last! And promptly wake myself up. Short of discovering a cache of booze, I need the exercise to get to bed.

These past few days are also the first time I've gone without a drink before bed this year. During rehab, and then during training, I was good. I wouldn't have more than a glass or two of beer, or just a scotch from Abba's cabinet. I wouldn't get drunk the way I was on the beginning of this trip or the way the people at Noah's Shabbat dinner will. But that bit of drink helped me slip in to sleep. Funny how when tallying Sara's recent instances of inebriation I didn't count my binges here. Now, without alcohol's regular presence in my system, I'm beginning to wake up. Everything feels more vivid. I could feel the echo of the wind on my face while rowing today. Thoughts come and I can hang onto them. But I'm not sure I want to. While I was out on the water, I saw the hump of a rising bowhead. For a moment, I thought I'd seen a submarine. That brought back a memory of my father and I rowing out near a naval base on the Rhode Island shore.

I'm sure it wouldn't be this way now, but at the time, they simply weren't worried about security from small craft in home waters. The idea that a couple of kayakers might be rowing explosive-laden boats never occurred to them. Anyway, on our maps we could see that we were going to go past a base just about as we crossed the border from Connecticut into Rhode Island. And though most guide books recommended against rowing through the waters offshore of naval bases, my father never thought twice about it. As it turned out, the base itself was set into an inlet, and we weren't anywhere close to the docks or boats. Nonetheless, there was storm fencing posted with no trespassing signs that ran out about twenty feet past the low-tide mark—which we blissfully ignored.

We were about halfway across the inlet's mouth, and this was about ten in the morning on a cloudy day in October, so though we had fine visibility, we couldn't really make out what was inside the inlet. But we were trying. In fact, we were trying so hard, and the water was so calm, that we hardly paid any attention to anything else at all until this massive horn blast startled us half out of our shells. I looked around quickly and Abba yelled, "Row forward, now!"

I rowed like mad and then I looked to my right to see what was bearing down on us and about twenty yards diagonally back and out to sea, I saw a submarine's conning tower rising. We kept rowing hard as the boat let out a second blast and continued to rapidly surface. But we turned and watched as well. I had been on a WWII submarine docked next to the aircraft carrier museum on the west side of Manhattan. By comparison, that was a dolphin and this a great blue whale, absolutely massive. And rising softly, sheets of water peeling off its blackish-grey deck – the same color as the bowhead—and foaming around its sides, it thrilled us more powerfully than any recruiting spot possibly could; right then, I would've joined the navy in a heartbeat. I think my father had worried that it would create some sort of vacuum wake effect as it rose, but we were never closer than twenty yards and it never caused more than a ripple. A hatch opened, an officer came out, blinked in the low light, and saluted us. We saluted back. "No pictures, ok?" My father shouted back that we wouldn't take any, and that was it. We watched a nuclear submarine emerge and slowly pull into its base at twenty yards and nobody thought anything of it; that's peace. My father was awestruck. He was a pacifist, me, not so much; but there was no denying the beauty and power of that sea beast rising out of the oily gray Atlantic under the dim quiet of a clouded sky.

But I can't think about my father and water without crying, without thinking that this was supposed to be his trip. At first I thought that this journey would bring me closer to him. Perhaps later I may feel that it has. For now, I try to think of him as little as possible because it's hard enough making myself get up to face my fears each day, get in the boat and row, without also sinking into grief and depression.

It's easier to say that I won't think about my father than to actually not do it. I guess I was about sixteen when we saw the submarine. My father and I had just begun our ideological split. Until then, I was something of a model daughter. I blended into our north shore community's affluent, secular exuberance completely. The curriculum vitae of my high-school life reads like a cliché of lily-white naiveté: honors student, student body representative, small clique of smart friends, track team, Spanish club. My father and I rowed together most every Saturday morning and Sunday's I went with him early to pick up bagels, cream cheese and lox for the family. I followed my parents' beliefs and recited them to my peers as my own. I was a privileged, secular, Diaspora Jew. I didn't particularly excel at anything and was amply proficient at everything expected of me. If there was any point of difference it was my time on the water in kayak. Kayaking's proximity to adventure sport and my exceeding proficiency at it attracted the flirtation of those of my classmates prone to dangerous activity. Northport had its skateboarders and rock-climbers and a backpacker or two. But invariably, my ultimately bourgeois, unrebellious, daddy's-girl nature dissuaded any lasting friendships there. Guerilla-rappelling off the North Shore Savings Bank on weekend nights held no appeal for me. Despite my seeming outdoor credentials, I belonged better with my circle of girls, staging slumber parties in plush carpeted dens, watching rented videos, sneaking bon-bons from the freezer, wearing over-sized college sweatshirts, trading manicures and chatting futures than I did amongst grunge-boys and hippie-chicks. Ultimately, fitting in counted more for me than standing out.

We spent all those nights planning, my girlfriends and I. We would go to Jenny's house and sit in the den comparing cozy clothes, and fuzzy hairbands, and nailpolish tones, fascinations that were the natural evolution of TrapperKeepers, Smurf folders, pencil-boxes, and puffy stickers. We suffered a fatal obsession with accessorizing. And one night, as we sat there discussing colleges, careers, men, families, homes on the Island, as I listed to Dolores redescribe, ad infinitum, her plan for a second house in Montauk, a perfect distance from her folks' second home in West Hampton, my own future appeared as a sort of arc of success that rose until my children reached college-age and then gently waned without poignancy or interruption, like a lullaby muffled by cozy flannel sheets, until I left the world as I'd entered it, naked, incapacitated and alone. And I thought to myself, what is the point of all these giddy collections: of children, of houses, of cars, of jobs, of monies, of renovated redone kitchens and auto-mixing multimode shower heads? I had no answer.

But even then, I sensed that our very lives were the accoutrements of life, not life itself, with no slated change on the itinerary.

It was like a drug, this frenzy of accumulation, of obeisance, of blending. The life planned for me, by me, was an arc that began where it ended, a circle signifying not completeness but zero. And I would write that this ripped through me like a shock-cord, but it didn't. Instead, it was the first in a series of gradual pinpricks of wrongness that I would try to shake from my head, but each shake only clarified my focus, let me see better. I didn't want that life. I wanted something. Equally, I wanted to return to my prior state. Nothing in my experience had prepared me for ambiguous desire, spiritual curiosity. Except, perhaps, rowing.

Subtly—and perhaps Hashem helped—Judaism drew me closer. My parents felt it. They felt an irritated consciousness growing in me that rejected out of hand the comforts in their grasp to provide. My mother clucked and moaned over Israel's responses to the first Intafada and I suggested she go and experience just what it might be like to live surrounded by a hostile populace. My father pursued his romance with German automobiles and I pointedly refused to ride in them (my mother was rather a fan of that). Forty years, I pointed out, isn't very long. But these confrontations weren't the most of it. The most of it was that I began going to the library and checking out books on Judaism. But then I was soon distracted by other possible sources of meaning. I attempted to find a place to fit in by marginalizing myself. I identified as lesbian. A safe choice, as at that point, no one at my school was openly gay, and so I could adopt the persona, the mantle, of an oppressed group without actually involving myself in a homosexual relationship. My parents proved ok with that choice. My father joked that he would be the only boy in my life. But being a marginalized person – which I was not really, no one cared, and so my declaration of lesbianism, without consummation, was as empty as any other childhood threat, and without community, deprived me of the fraternity (sorority) oppression breeds—soon proved to be yet another accoutrement, more a fashion statement than a way of life. Somehow, I failed to see that orthodoxy was pulling me ever closer, and I continued to seek, involving myself next in our school's socialist club.

The socialist thing succeeded in angering my parents. My father was a banker. In the middle of rowing trips he would angrily ask if I wouldn't prefer to go agitate labor unions rather than row around in an expensive boat bought with capitalist funds. (How natural and ironic that my own work revolves around money still). All the while, my emptiness grew. What was socialism but an attempt to spread life's accoutrements more equitably? And while that's certainly a noble goal in its own right, distribution of accoutrements fundamentally engages those very accoutrements that first opened my inner void. I wanted more and drifted away.

There we were, watching a submarine rise out of the morning water, a precursor to today's bowhead whale, and for a moment the tension building between my father and I dissipated in a shared awe. It was awe I was seeking, something that would inspire me to live. Because, when I faced the long path of a zero-sum life in front of me, its most distinguishing facet was the overwhelming effort it would take to end up at nothing and nowhere. It made me want to put on my sweatshirt and comfy tights, grab my fleece blanket and my two overstuffed bears, and crawl between my twin bed's flannel sheets and sleep away the rest of my time on earth. I needed passionate drive and nothing inspires awe more than Hashem.

Later that year, I sought meaning in a man. Maybe at a different age something better could have come of it, but at sixteen pushing seventeen, men offer no solace.

My parents couldn't understand. They mistook my desire for some sense of meaning as a condemnation of their lives' delimiters. It was as if I told my father that devoting himself to his wife and daughter was empty and meaningless. It was as if I was ungrateful for the many advantages he provided me. They were smart, my parents, smarter than me. During all of my flirtations with what I thought were radical identities, they understood that if anything would capture me it would be religion. And they opposed Jewish orthodoxy more than any other possible outcome—understandably. They could refute any other source of meaning that might contradict their own mores except Judaism because Judaism alone can offer spiritual completion.

So why haven't I da'avened in days?

And is it my failure to worship my god that keeps me from solace?

There are all the things the world tells us to do: to stay healthy, to keep a positive outlook intact. Mostly, they attempt to hide the world's true nature which can only be taken in one of two ways: Either life is a cruel and miserable experience, made most so by the tenacity with which we cling to it; or, this is a poetic and starkly just balancing act at the cusp of divinity's embrace. Surprisingly, the advocates of the former view argue for a perpetuation of this miserable existence, they seek to make sure the world perseveres forever. If I held their view, I'd be all for all-out destruction. Push the button and end everything, Baby. Cut the big bombs loose. Those who believe in divine authorship, those like myself, instead long for a hastening of the end. We want the veil of grim reality ripped from the world, a concentrated final tidying of this life's score, and then paradise here today.

I look around me and I see myself surrounded by an unimaginable beauty with an unparalleled ability to kill. All I can see is God's obviousness. No unthoughtful hand could so accidentally fill a world with such beautiful and yet frail life.

So why am I not spending time in prayer?

I know that I should.

I want to go to sleep, but I'm afraid that I'll be giving in to a gradual increase in the hours of each day I spend in my sleeping bag. It can't be good.

## *August 1*

Well I've made it into August. It shouldn't signify anything, but somehow I feel that maybe it does. I have a sense of accomplishment. In fact, the date lightened my spirits sufficiently to balance the added tension of a day along a coast devoid of landing opportunities. Cliffs swept up hundreds of feet from deep seas punctured by massive boulder heaps. Waves echoing off the sheer walls amplified each other and threatened to swamp me, forcing me further out. In fact, I chose to end the day long before I tired because the land formed a sort of peninsula, behind which I was certain to find somewhere to make camp. Unsure of when the next break might be, I pulled in.

Closer now to the cliffs, ever mindful of odd wave patterns, I could see that holes and ledges pocked the rock faces. In them, black and white birds nested. They looked like flying penguins almost, penguins that squawked and hollered at each other. Spying a stream between a break in the cliffs, I rowed in closer still, and the birds angrily kicked pebbles down towards me. Undeterred, I found my way upstream and to this campsite.

Still full of energy, I thought to take a stroll, and then thought better of it, once again wishing that I'd taken along a gun. Everyone suggested that I do so. It's not as if don't know how to use one, or am categorically opposed to weaponry. Like every other young Israeli, I served my time in the military. I am perfectly capable, nay, apt, at wielding a firearm. But somehow as I packed for this trip, as I planned everything out, a gun struck me as an additional bit of weight too heavy for my spirit. Nancy was all too eager to let me stray from military hardware; but then she never really believed in the danger of bears. I simply lied to the bush pilot who outfitted me, and told him I already had one, didn't need him to supply it. With so much violence at home, so much in my life, I couldn't bear to carry a weapon. Now I'm less certain that was a wise decision. In a way, life is violence. And I'm unarmed.

But tomorrow is Shabbat already. I'll be bored, maybe enough so to outweigh any latent anxieties about bears, and twisting an ankle on the tundra. Sure, I'll take a walk then, go exploring, bears don't really want a piece of me anyway, right? My body feels really strong. Resting Wednesday was the right choice even if it makes taking tomorrow off a bit redundant. I can't even imagine what full-blown tendonitis would have meant, and once it truly flares up, quelling it is no easy task. I'll have to monitor my shoulder carefully. Not rowing isn't an option.

### August 3

Maybe things are taking a turn for the better. I am achieving distance. For most of the day, I was glad to be here. I heard the massive cracking of ice to my left and didn't instantly feel my father's hand ripped from mine in the café. Instead, the sound of breaking ice gave me a feeling of triumph. I'm here, after all, I'm doing it.

I woke up and got out of bed eagerly. I was hungry. But before I ate, I washed my hands in the inlet next to where I'd camped, said morning bruchahs, said Shemah. And then ate. Saying those few blessings and prayers brought an involuntary heat to my face, I could feel myself smiling, I felt shy and wondered who I could be feeling shy for. I'll also say Shemah before I go to bed tonight.

I definitely will. And I kept Shabbat yesterday successfully. In fact, I even overcame my anxieties sufficiently to take a nice long Shabbat-afternoon stroll, wandering up along the stream. Purple flowers, lavender maybe, mixed with tall grasses and wild herbs in long stretching fields whose herbaceous aroma enraptured me in each mild gust of wind. My back warm through my fleece in the sun, my body strong, my mind finally freed itself to marvel at the wonder of Hashem's grace, the beauty and intricacy with which he creates this world. I saw the tremendous attention he pays event to the slight details of a small wild flower that emerges from the frozen ground for at most a month or two each year, remote from people. Prayers, psalms, blessings worked their independent ways to my lips and I felt light on my feet. Eventually I came in sight of massed caribou and stopped to watch them for awhile before turning back.

Today, out on the water, I could see the light change ever so slightly, to the long red cast at the end of afternoon, it gave the fields of tundra an amazingly welcoming glow, and I stayed out an extra hour, taking in the view, the combination of colors. I think there will be a moment of darkness soon. Though that denotes the waning of my travel-window, I'm on schedule, and would welcome some physical marker of time's passage.

This campsite has an ideal sitting log, and is littered with old coals. People were here. Not recently, certainly, but at some point in the past several years, maybe even this spring, right after the snow melt. It gives me a feeling of connection. My appetite is up, a healthy sign. For dinner, I made rice and beans with beef sausage, an extra large portion. I finished all of it. I don't feel as restless as I usually do either. This is good. Things are good. I made the right choice to take this trip. My fear is waning. I'm growing stronger. I'll be able to face Jerusalem when the time comes.

## *August 4*

The paradox is this: you can be so afraid of dying that you want to die.

## *August 5*

I was greatly unnerved yesterday.

I spent all night last night sewing my sail. I didn't think it was the kind of thing that could rip; but rip it did. I got off to another really fresh start on the 4th. Woke up, da'avened, ate a nice breakfast, met the sea with anticipation. Chop was strong, in a steady wind, and I quickly decided to hoist the sail. And that seemed like a good decision. I made headway. I easily came up to my fastest speed so far, five to seven knots, a really strong clip. Abba's shell cut through and across the small swells effortlessly, though with each boom shift, my outriggers would crash down on the water. Each time one of them hit, it sent a shudder through the whole boat, and it was loud even over the waves and the wind. At first, hearing that noise every several minutes as I carved back and forth in front of the west wind made me feel like I was fleeing a war-zone. But I managed to catch my mind, harness it. I started cyclical breathing, deep in through the nose, out through the nose. It worked. I calmed myself. The boat could handle it.

I began to enjoy myself. The tension that had been building in my shoulders and lower back drained and I felt that I was finally allowing myself to operate near the limit of my abilities. I pushed myself and it felt good. Better still, I wished Abba was with me and for the first time that was okay. I described the scene to you, Abba. The small wooden hulled craft twisting and turning across blue-grey chop, wind ripping across the sail, the long plains of already-browning grasses dipping and bowing in gusts off to shore. And shore wasn't so close by. I stayed far enough off the coast to avoid maneuvering around every irregular contour in the land. I could just make out a seal sunbathing on a rock spit. Not fifteen minutes later, a flock of birds thick enough to cast a shadow over my boat executed a broad pirouette to my left. Clouds rushed past at dizzying speeds. My arms flawlessly worked the ropes and boom. They felt like—arms, strong, strong, arms; I could feel the muscle fibers in them. I could feel the strength in my hands and fingers. It felt divine.

The seal and the birds, the beautiful shoreline backdropped by stacked rows of mountain are all always there, every day. But yesterday morning they were beautiful instead of threatening.

I'll tell you what felt most divine: wishing my father was here and not having a complete breakdown. Well at least not having a breakdown right away.

After a few hours, squall clouds began blowing past. Every ten minutes or so, drenching rain would whip past me and be gone. Now my supposed policy is to pull into shore in a storm. But I was making great time, even better time than I had. The wind picked up, and I didn't want to turn in because of a bit of rain. Especially not when I was feeling so good.

Then I saw the polar bear.

Reason stands against this being the same bear as I think followed me earlier in the trip, but in my heart I believe it is. I looked back every few minutes to anticipate, and judge the severity of the encroaching storm clouds. On one of these surveys, I caught with my peripheral vision, a flash of white. My instincts immediately screamed, bear. But the day had treated me well so far. I didn't want to slip back into paranoia. I didn't want to retreat into constant anxiety, worry that my hull was sinking or something like that. I decided not to look back right away. Cyclical breathing, Sarah, in through the nose, out through the nose.

Five minutes or so, maybe fewer though they certainly felt like more, and I couldn't take the pressure, the tingling pressure over my cerebrum screaming, they're watching you! I turned back. Storm clouds were immediately apparent. I scanned a full sweep, all clear. I was at the top of my game. Fuck the storm clouds, right? I bent the boat left, tacked with the wind, two wakes V'ing down a sea slope. I tacked right, my starboard out-rigger crashing into the water, shuddering vibration running up my spine, quickly muted by the water's strain. I looked towards shore and there he was, not even remotely hidden, a great white bear between me and the beach, swimming well in the waves. He hovered in view for nearly a minute, keeping pace with me, and then dove.

Everything stopped in me. Keep breathing, Sarah, keep breathing. The bear blocked the shore, apparently by design. I tacked left again, without any thrill this time, and looked back to see building cumulus churning forward, a pincer attack, they planned to trap me between the storm, the bear and the open ocean. I tacked right again, and there was my bear, green haloing his white body as he flew along a foot beneath the surface, a long streak of mint boil behind him. No question about it; his angle would intersect mine within minutes of any shoreward turn.

In trying to imagine evasive tactics, I conjured an image of the great bear hugging the underside of my kayak, four massive white claws tipped in black talon wrapped around the edges of my deck, and then, with a roar, that massive head emerging in front of me, pulling the boat under, bow first, as he climbed the deck towards me. I caught myself holding my breath in expec-tation of imminent immersion and forced myself to expel that reserve of air, replace it with fresh air, expel it and replace it again, and so on. I could see why the grizzlies on shore were so pissy. Like humans, they were born to dominate, and then here are these playful ferocious albino denizens of the arctic, scaring the shit out of us. I felt a spattering of rain. I began to slowly recite a psalm:

*Ashrai haeesh, asher lo halach batzat rishaim*
> Happy is the man who did not walk in the company of evil men

*Oobaderech chataim lo amad*
> And in the path of sinners doesn't stand

*Oobimooshav latzim lo yashav*
> And in a gathering of buffoons doesn't sit

*Kee eembitorah Hashem cheftzoo, oobitorato yehigeh yomam vilailah*
> Because if with the torah of Hashem he explores, and with Hashem's torah he steers himself, day and night

*Vihayah ki'aytz shatool al-palgai mayim*
> And he will be like a tree planted alongside a stream of water

*Ahser peeryo yitane bieeto, vialahoo lo yivol*
> Who will bear fruit in season, and whose children won't be martyred

*Vicol asher-ya'aseh yatzliach*
> And all in that he does he'll succeed.

And that's about how far I got when a gust of wind caught my boat and I yawed on my starboard outrigger, my hull actually twisting backwards, land disappeared, I was in the storm. I aimed for what I thought might be shore, fighting with the boat and sudden six foot swells breaking across my beam and drenching me in frigid water—beyond drenching me, I was passing through literal walls of water. Over and over again I repeated, "With Hashem's torah I steer myself, day and night; I will be like a tree planted alongside water, strong and tall, my children won't be sacrificed." The wind whipped me in fishtailing frigidity. The sea was in me. I longed for warmth, for stop. It was too fast to lower the sail even, and the sail twisted me in circles, in ovals, in trapezoids of definite demise. It seemed that I traveled on the path of sinners. And then the sail snapping free of its bottom mount punctuated the storm's scream. I grabbed my paddle and rowed, adrenalin and frozen sea water mingling somewhere in my middle flesh, the sail flapping loose behind me like the streaming pennant of a doomed army swirling in the furious smoke of it own firing cavalcade. I was sure I was lost. I cried out, Shemah, Yisroel, Adonoi Elohanu, Adonoi echad. Hear, oh Israel, the Lord our God, the Lord is One. But in my heart I cursed Hashem, for not letting me grow like a tree along the water, stronger than the winds of evil men, with longevity enough to bear fruit in season. I cursed, paddled furiously, crested a swell, descended, and crashed into the pebble beach of small island (at least I discovered it was an island later). The ocean tried to suck me back but I harpooned the gravel with the end of my paddle and clung to land.

Suddenly, relative to the wind I was still and seemingly safe, adrenalin draining. Then rain lacerated my face, my head, my now exposed legs, as I yanked the craft above the waves and into a hollow between bluffs. Once the boat was safe from the ocean, I lowered the sail. A second rend ran across its middle. But everything else was ok. I was ok. If frightened, if cold, if totally unsure of my location. After extracting my kit from the front bulkhead, I turned the boat upside down, and lashed it to a couple of boulders. All the while, wind-driven rain invaded every piece of my body. I'd pulled on my shell-jacket earlier, during the first squalls. But I was wearing a bathing suit bottom and tevas and my spray-skirt, which kept catching the wind and throwing me off balance.

Pitching a tent in storm conditions is no easy feat. Everything tries to blow away. I pulled out the tent body and fly, and crawling on top of them, staked down both together. Then I put the poles in between the two, struggling to thread the poles through their sleeves while underneath the fly and buffeted by gale-force gusts. The trick is to thread all of the poles completely before inserting their tip in their rivets and erecting the tent. Three poles went up easily and then the fourth popped out of its far rivet and I had to run around to the other side of the now staked tent, prestrung guy-out lines blown out in the wind and undulating as the unsupported structure bowed dangerously under pressure, yellow plastic tensioners at the ends of the cords describing sines and cosines, dutifully charting the storm's effect on a partially erect tent, sine, sine, cosine, cyclical breathing, undulating fear, urgency, exhaustion and laceration. I gained the far side of the tent and jammed the pole tip into its rivet. The structure stabilized somewhat. I scurried about pounding stakes into wet sandy soil, praying they wouldn't tear, and began fastening the guy-out cords. To anchor the guy-out lines, which stretch down from the dome of the fly, I have to pass them through the ends of the stakes, and attach them back to themselves with plastic tensioners. I fumbled on the first of seven lines, by the fourth and fifth, I discovered that my hands were rapidly morphing into stiff, trembling, wet, blue claws. Twice, the sixth guy-out line ripped free of my hands as I tried to make the cord wrap over the second bend in the tensioner. Each time, it left a red strip across my palm. Finally I got it. The seventh one attached as if in a dream and the tent seemed stable. I'd already shoved the rest of my kit under the fly, and I followed it in. Shelter. Blessed is the Lord our God who created shelter. My face tingled and was numb at the same time. I pulled off my clothes, shivering, blue veins stood out on my chest between ropes of whitened scar and inch-high goose bumps. My breasts had very nearly contracted beneath my rib cage. I toweled off quickly, and layered up: polypro long johns and long sleeve top, wool socks, fleece pants and sweater, fleece hat. I shouldn't have let my hair get so wet. Even though the tent walls are yellow, I could hardly see in there because the storm had so completely blotted out all light in the sky. I put on my headlamp and dug up my candle lantern. I realized I was shivering still. As soon as I noticed that, my teeth started chattering and a strong compulsion to sit and not move came over me.

I made myself inflate the thermarest, a painful process of half breath and lost air as I gasped to breathe, drowning in cold, dimly dying for the shag-carpeted, cozy-warm den of my Long Island youth. Half-inflated seemed good enough. I crawled into my sleeping bag.

I was now laying in bed essentially, on my stomach, but with my head and arms out so that I could dig through my kit which was in the vestibule—the vestibule, which doesn't have a floor, was a bit "palgai mayim"—"a stream of water"—itself. I set up my stove, filled a pot with water from my nalgene, and started heating up the fire. Normally, I'd vent the vestibule to ensure proper exhausting of the carbon monoxide, but in this case that would have meant getting out of my sleeping bag and crawling across the vestibule floor to the door and letting in storm winds. I decided to take my chances with asphyxiation and the rapidly rising need to pee quickly distracted me anyway.

I clearly didn't die of carbon monoxide poisoning though the sonorous whisperlite stove's jet-roar addled by cacophonous rain and wind did ultimately lure my eyelids down; and when I opened them again, the water passing through the vestibule had undercut the stove's legs and the whole thing was about to topple into the tent wall. Fortunately, the water was boiling, and I simply turned the stove off. I wasn't shivering anymore. Hot soup gradually reinvigorated me and I faced the long task of sewing my sail. I thought to wait a day—storms often stay and I'd have nothing to do—but managed to force myself to work. I'm glad I did. This morning, I woke to placid seas, if under a foggy sky. The fog isn't particularly an impediment. Under its weight, the seas seem to calm and the vastness of my surroundings are less imposing. I drift through this quiet soup, blanketed in myself.

Though I was exhausted, almost wishing that the storm continued to pin me down, I began imaging Aklivuk and rowing for it. I imagined walking into a solid, concrete building and sitting down at a table and ordering fresh scrambled eggs (which, believe you me, I'll consider kosher enough at the end of this trip). I imagined checking into a motel, probably built for visiting government officials and mineral workers, and using a hot shower, standing under a stream of steaming water and washing wave after wave of salt and silt from my body. But mostly I focused on that first diner, and running my hands under the faucet in its disheveled bathroom, the artificial smell of pink liquid soap sudsing up in the spray of the sink and the soothing, softening massage of water from a tap as I twist my hands around each other over and over. I knew that Shabbat would come, and with it rest, and resting now means two rest days in a week for the second consecutive week. I can't afford that. And I managed to row. I will make it to the end of this journey and go home to Jerusalem.

## *August 6*

Another long day of rowing, and I'm almost too tired to make food, but I have to. I have to eat; I have to gorge myself, because tomorrow I can't. Tomorrow is the ninth day of the lunar month of Av, on which day both the first and second temples were destroyed after extensive sieges, and so, no eating all day. I'm not sure how I intend to row. Maybe there will be some wind, and I can just sail, which takes considerably less effort. I can't even drink, nothing, no food, no water. But I don't want to sit around on shore either, that would leave me with nothing to do but think about how hungry I am. No, it's better to row, unquestionably better to row

## *August 7*

> Destruction of the First and Second Temples
> First World War and Second World War
> Pogroms and Holocaust
> No Food and No Water
> Fog and Exhaustion
> First Intafada and Second Intafada
> Death of Mother and Death of My Father
> September 11 and The Café Bombing

## *August 8*

It's not easy rowing on an empty stomach. I gorged myself last night after I finally deemed it ok to eat ( which wasn't because it was dark out, I picked a time at random to end the day). At first it felt so good to eat, and then to drink! Water was my best friend. But I quickly bloated, and then fell into a fitful sleep. Nothing brings on nightmares like a good old-fashioned tummy-ache. Bears mixed with bombs mixed with the horrible pain of reconstructive operations. I was attended on by surgeons wearing checkered kaffiyehs who regularly pulled severed limbs from behind their backs. I woke at one point needing to pee but too tired and too scared to get up and get out and do it. And then again at another point I woke convinced I had peed in my sleeping bag, but it was only sweat. After that I fell back asleep and dreamt of the destruction of the Bais haMigdash. In the end, I overslept and woke unrested. I ate heavily again at breakfast and had stomach cramps until well into the day.

Maybe I'm getting my period; I hope not.

There wasn't much to see. Every time the fog begins to break it comes back. It makes the rowing rather dull and there isn't enough wind to sail by. I wish I'd packed Shabbat candles; this will be my fourth Shabbat not lighting them. The candles from my candle-lantern might meet my obligations. However, that means sacrificing two whole candles each Shabbat. I only packed four. It's not as if I have a braided Havdalah candle to light after Shabbat ends either (though I wonder if an actual fire would meet my obligations? Probably). So, I will signify neither the beginning nor end of Shabbat with candles.

*August 9*

I'm not supposed to be writing today. It's Shabbat and I should be da'avening, eating precooked food, resting up, and doing little else. The rabbi at Columbia's Hillel taught us that Shabbat is the holiest day of the year, bar none, including Yom Kippur. And in this fact, I could see, and he helped show me, the egalitarian and granular nature of Judaism. The most important day of the year is not some rarified fete saved up for and passed with breathtaking speed. No, it's a weekly occasion. I remember feeling a great pride that our religion's Sabbath was not a weekly check-in on the way to Easter or part of a month-long fast. But, even as I recount Shabbat's glory, even as I consider that Solomon's Song of Songs, the most beautiful piece of poetry ever written, specifically describes the Shabbat, I break it. I break it to write.

I never had a passion for writing. In the course of my business life I have to prepare papers and so forth. I like to read average much. I'm well educated, I think. But before this trip, I never had the slightest inclination towards letters—or any creative pursuit. But here I am, violating my religious beliefs to scribble away at an imaginary life that I hope to lead, will lead, when I return to Eretz Yisroel.

But how can I make myself move forward each day without a clear sense of where I'm going? I want to get to Jerusalem. I want to meet the people I dream about. It means finishing this trip first, I know. I will finish this trip; I will survive it.

The last time I wrote about my life to be in Jerusalem, Sara and Dalia were sitting at Udi's friend's café, sipping mint tea. Since then, a lot has happened (will happen?). During the following two weeks, Dalia and Sara will meet every several days. During this time, Udi will leave two messages for Sara. The first will be a long apology for his behavior at the Shabbat dinner. Sara won't return his call. Several days later, Udi will call again. He'll ask if Sara got his last message, make another brief apology, ask that she call him at her earliest convenience, and hang up. Sara won't return that call either.

Sara will continue to devote her energies to decorating her new apartment in a bid to make herself a real home in Jerusalem. My last apartment, in the old city, was never fully a home, not in the sense that my high-school friends in Long Island would have meant it. Of course, the new place wouldn't meet their definitions either. It will be an apartment rather than a house for one thing, and in a city not a suburban town, and in a foreign country. But my first apartment, while cute, was a temporary accommodation, a sunny cheery apartment—sparsely furnished and as heaped with clothes and books and things as a high-school girl's bedroom—that I camped out in while waiting for whatever was next. Essentially, it was a marginal outpost of my familial home in Northport. A home is something different. It carries a connotation of arrival, or destination. With my parents gone, there's no longer a place to return to as home; I will have to make one.

In the weeks after the dinner at Noah and Dalia's, Sara will throw herself into that task. Each night on the way home from work, she'll stop at a different furniture store. Though the dining room will be already decorated and figured out, there will still be the bedroom, study and living room. I keep wavering on how much of my parents' furniture I'll actually want to take. I haven't looked into shipping prices to Israel, but I can't imagine it's all that cheap. I assume that I'll have to purchase a portion of a container. At any rate, I don't think it would be economical to bring anything other than the pieces I feel an emotional resonance with. And there's also the issue of wanting to live in a new place, distinctly my own, and not under the shadow of my parents.

So after a night of looking at different shelving solutions to go along with my father's desk and chair in the study, Sara will come home to find her answering machine light blinking. Vaguely worried that Udi's left another message, Sara will delay playing it, fixing herself a light supper of tabouli salad and chicken schnitzel instead. In the middle of benching—the long version of the prayer after eating, necessitated by her consumption of a roll —the phone will ring again. Unable to interrupt her prayer, Sara will try to block out her own recorded voice repeating a greeting in both Hebrew and English. Marie will come on the machine. "Hey, Girl, is this some Jewish holiday I don't know about and you aren't checking your messages? I called you before. Call me."

Marie will hang up just as Sara finishes benching. Contrite, she will decide to listen to Marie's earlier message before calling her back. Sara will notice herself concocting an excuse for not playing them earlier, and realize that she doesn't want to tell Marie about Udi.

Sara takes notes during Marie's detailed message about setting a closing date for the sale of the house in Long Island, and then the truly urgent issue, Marie's grandmother will be back in the hospital with severe clotting in her legs after arthroscopy on her knees. After Marie, Dalia will leave a brief message, "Sara, Dalia here, call me tonight, doesn't matter what time." Sara will find her heart racing. Still, Sara's a sensible person; She'll call Marie back first.

Sarah and Marie will have a long conversation about Marie's grandmother's situation after briefly discussing the house. Sara will briefly think to thank Marie for not being too intimidated by Sara's relatively greater loss to talk about her own fears of losing her grandmother. A multifaceted shame will tingle along her scalp; shame for: viewing her loss as greater than Marie's potential loss, considering that her loss could be considered comparable to Marie's loss, for being so arrogant with her loss to think to thank Marie at all, for wearing her loss as a badge, for failing Hashem in viewing her loss as distinct from, rather than as a part of, a divine master plan. In this scattered charge of emotion, hardly listening to Marie at all, Sara will abruptly interject an offer to fly back to the states and be with her, "I need to figure out everything with the house anyway."

"Dude, I wasn't asking you to fly out here. That's ridiculous. I just wanted to talk for a minute…I'm sorry, Sarah…No, I'm not mad…Don't worry about it. Listen, I got to split. Sorry to whine on and on. It's really late and I need to get to bed."

And with that Sara will find herself setting down the lifeless phone receiver and looking at the clock on what was her father's nightstand, now an end-table in her living room: eleven-thirty— five-thirty in the morning back in New York. Marie will have had to have left her second message past three in the morning, her time. Sara will fight the temptation to call her back immediately, ask if she isn't in worse shape than she lets on, insist on flying out to see her, or flying Marie out to Jerusalem for a visit. Instead she will walk to her kitchen, bare feet padding down the Turkish Kilim Eema bought in Istanbul during her parents' twentieth-anniversary trip there. In the kitchen, she will hang on the open door of her refrigerator, debating a drink, debating calling Dalia at what will now be eleven-forty-five. Ultimately, she will choose to do both, opening a bottle of Macccabee beer while dialing.

Dalia will answer on the first ring, audibly exhaling smoke.

"Dalia, I hope I haven't called too late, your message said-"

"Said not to worry about the hour. It's not a problem. I'm just enjoying a cigarette."

Sara will briefly imagine Dalia sitting at her dining room table, the telephone and an ashtray full of stubs in front of her, waiting in the dim light cast from her kitchen for a phone call like a 1930's private eye drinking scotch, revolver in front of him, awaiting the arrival of a busty, double-crossing assistant.

"Noah's asleep, I shouldn't talk here. Meet me out."

Sara will watch herself agree to leave her house at nearly midnight on a Tuesday, despite her standard eight AM start at work awaiting her Wednesday, and go to a bar she's never heard of several blocks away. Quickly finishing her beer, Sara will throw on a business dress and her overcoat, suddenly aware that she has no casual clothing that won't stand out in a bar.

The bar itself, hardly marked by a sign and hidden between typical British Mandate era stone buildings, will perpetrate Sara's sense of sneaking out past bedtime. Dim track-lighting will cast warm halos on thick carpeting and narrow corridors that stretch off from the main room, all lined with framed reproductions of Jazz-era posters. The bar itself, an undulating rosewood affair, will support the leaning stances of the place's only patrons, several shadowed couples whose murmuring is absorbed and muffled by a light refrain of Sonny Rollins. And of course Dalia will be there, wrapped in her husband's silk smoking jacket, sipping a tumbler of something yellow on rocks and chatting with the bar-tender, himself a seeming set piece, young, tall, possessed of movie-actor aesthetics.

As Sara approaches, Dalia will see her and motion the bar-tender to fix another of what she's having. Sara will gesture that she doesn't really want any of the whiskey that the bartender pours, but her silent miming will be dismissed by a wave from Dalia, and after a brief hug, she'll take her seat next to the older woman, both momentarily silent in the backlit, glass liquor shelving's alpenglow. Sara's drink will come and Dalia slide several shekels across the bar's inlay. Dalia will whisper, "L'chaim," as they softly clink glasses. Sara will sip the whiskey and remember spending a Shabbat in the Arctic wishing for a sip, just a sip, to take away the pain of imagination and to allow her to stop writing.

"You haven't returned Udi's calls."

Sara will shake her head and sip compulsively. Dalia will tap out a cigarette, light it, and exhale a long stream of smoke upwards, sigh. At times, Sara will find herself watching Dalia, and wondering how an orthodox woman absorbed the mannerisms of a Rat-Pack-Era, Hollywood star.

"You would have been perfect for our son."

"Really, would I have?"

"They already knew we would pull out; no one wanted to be the last soldier to die over there. He wasn't the last, but he was pretty close. It makes you so angry—that I had to lose my son after all was lost anyway. You wish that either we had somehow managed to pull out right away, so that Adar could have simply come home, gotten a job, fallen in love, married. Or that his death was a building block in some success, that we were staying there, that our staying there would ultimately mean something. Not that there's much of anything to be gained in Lebanon.

"Stay or go, Adar dead is Adar dead. Death, death, death, our sons, our daughters our parents. Doesn't anyone live a long, naïve, happy life anymore?"

Dalia's rings will scrape against her glass in a strange disharmony with the tumbling ice and the background jazz as she finishes her drinks and orders another.

"You know you ought to call Udi. There's not time to play games."

"The day before my parents died, my father and I were sitting by ourselves downstairs talking. My mother used to get very jetlagged and she was taking a nap. My father looked a lot older, greyer, haggard. I told him so, gently, but told him. The breath left him a bit. Sarah, he said, life's caught up with me. I waited for him to say more, but he just sipped his coffee and watched passersby with this woefulness. It established a dynamic I'd never had with him before; I felt very uncomfortable. Finally, I asked him what he meant by life catching up with him. Oh, nothing, forget it, he said. But at least he turned back to face me."

Dalia will take her new drink and raise it to Sara's, breaking the story. Sara will taste the whiskey burn and remember a morning squatting beneath a tufted bluff along the Arctic shore, shaking with hangover sweats and trying to keep her boat from casting off.

"You were saying?"

"Sorry. Yeah, so my father turns back to me—I don't even know what brought this up—but he starts talking to me about working back downtown. His time as a volunteer was over, deconstruction at the site was completely in the hands of regular crew, the fires were all out, and his company had relocated him to a building just south of the American Stock Exchange on Church Street. He hadn't been downtown in a while, his volunteering had ended months before, and he'd been using temporary space near the UN to reorganize his department and eke some approximation of productivity out of them. He started describing this psychological shift that had happened in him and in the area between his time there supporting the rescue crews and his return. Now, he said, it was as if it was calm, as if the world had forgotten itself, cleaned itself up—it was as if the period for recovery had formally closed and been replaced by an assumption of normalcy.

"But nonetheless, a certain horror persisted. He would walk down the narrow streets, old colonial alleys grown up into canyons of glass and stone powerhouses, and have the awed sense of visiting history. Some places were inherently, obviously so: the Brooks Brothers at One Liberty Plaza for example, whose suited mannequins occupied space used as an emergency morgue for weeks, accented salesmen miming tailors on a floor that had first held displays of corporate-wear, then body-bags, then back to corporate-wear again, as if that was the most natural transition in the world. He felt like a tourist with the rare opportunity to visit a Roman coliseum by himself, and standing at the top of those ruined seats, looking down into the arena, bring to visage warriors, competitions, wild dogs, bloodsport. And in fact the streets were mostly empty. Vast worker populations were gone and the tourists never strayed far from the pit itself. These places of seeming normality, side-streets and office-towers, became similarly evocative; he imagined the new clean sidewalks covered in dismembered viscera, in dust, in running screaming people; he recreated their commutes to work that day, his own commute; the many stories told him by fellow volunteers, rescuers, firefighters, coworkers, vividly populated the geography of his daily minutiae: walk from subway to work, work to lunch, lunch to meetings to work, work to the newsstand, and on and on, always seeing, always mourning, always awestricken.

"A tremendous sense of loss and displacement tormented him, as if he was fundamentally dishonoring the intrinsic nature of these places, as if all of them must permanently live in the full state of that day's horror to exist meaningfully at all. His chest itched with emotions that perversely demanded that the world torment itself so that outside matched inside, so that there might be catharsis. Instead he walked calmly past the hieroglyphia of modernized recovery, subway tunnel collapse notations sprayed in red paint on the sides of deco skyscrapers. He visited a Merrill Lynch office at the World Financial Center, walked onto a floor recently reconstructed, and was riveted by imagined destruction, mourned the lost resonance of scarred girders and burnt body parts.

"I don't really want it to recover, exactly, Sarah, he told me. I want the change to be permanent and lasting. I no longer find resilience uplifting."

Sara will finish her drink and the bartender will already be refilling her glass. She'll look around and briefly struggle to make out the faces of the other patrons, but the lighting will fall such that the few others there are only silhouettes of themselves. All that's visible will be Dalia, the bartender and the liquor.

"I don't know if my father could have kept working or not. He certainly wasn't readjusting. But he had enough money to retire right then and there, go and take his boat ride. I think he was afraid to give up also. And then the next day after we spoke he died."

Dalia will push her cigarettes over towards Sara and raise her eyebrows. Sara will thank her but no, she doesn't smoke.

I wonder if I will die, too, suddenly. Perhaps I'll die out here, in the Arctic, despite having survived a terrorist bombing in Jerusalem. Perhaps my plane will crash on the way back to Israel, rendering this all pointless, this great effort at survival. But then all is Hashem's will.

Dalia will raise her eyebrows at Sara's refusal, and light yet another cigarette for herself, the ashtray, meticulously emptied, never harboring more than a single butt.

"You revel in the past, Sara."

"Look at my face, Dalia. Only through real shituch will someone find me a man who actually wants me, who will be a good husband."

"You're a child, a smart, strong child, but nonetheless – "

"Some ridiculous romanticized notion of self-sacrifice might lead a man to woo me. But then, in time, he'd either become so high on his magnanimity that I couldn't stand him, or he'd realize he wanted someone who he could kiss with the lights on."

"We all have our scars."

"Yes, you keep telling me."

"I'm sorry I called you a child."

"And don't all of you dwell in the past with your dinner club for survivors?"

I'm surprised to see that I will act so childishly when I talk with Dalia in the bar. I was convinced that after this trip, after my return to Jerusalem, I would possess a new sense of calm, an ability to rise above all situations. And I can write myself any way I want to be. I can create anything I want. I'm defining the future that lies in front of me. And yet still, even that seems to be dependant on some order above me. I feel as though I am channeling the actual truth, or a truthful version of what will be. And I absolutely must stay faithful to the truth. My stakes in this projection of my return keeps rising. It is all that holds me together, the thought of returning to Sara's world. I've got to keep it real, take the chaff with the grain.

"I take back my apology; you are a child."

"You called me to come meet you here, late at night. Why?"

"You need to call Udi."

Dalia will finish her drink and hold up a hand to the bartender's gestured offer of a refill. After standing, Dalia will take Sara by her shoulders and look into her eyes.

"Really, please call Udi."

"Ok."

"Promise me."

"Ok."

Dalia will continue searching Sara's face for a few moments, and then let her go.

"How much do I owe you for the drinks?"

"Don't be ridiculous."

Around Dalia, Sara will feel constantly one step less mature, less competent. And yet that very feeling will be an integral part of her draw for Sara. Dalia will bear with her the apparition of a great and secret knowledge. It will be Sara's faith in that supply that will lead her to call Udi, not right when she arrives home, tipsy and late, but the following afternoon, from work. Aside from a mixture of surprise and relief in the way he says her name, Udi will completely ignore his unreturned phone calls, the hiatus in their friendship, accepting Sara's suggestion that they meet at their café as a de rigueur invitation to a standard stomping ground. And so they'll agree to meet that very afternoon.

## *August 10*

What will become of me? Yesterday, I skipped out on Shabbat. I wrote all day, cooked over my stove, didn't da'aven. Basically, the only violation that I could conceivably have done, but didn't, would have been to travel in my kayak. And that's the one thing it might have made some sense to do (though the fog was really too thick to travel; it seems to be fog season here). Today, on the other hand, I da'avened three times, morning, noon and night (the distinctions between which I'm coming to accept as any sense of ongoing wonder at this unmitigated day bores me now). It makes no sense. I don't transgress smartly.

And here is the other thing that doesn't quite jive. Those days on which I da'aven, do follow my structure and order, are my best; and yet I so rarely bother to pray anymore. But really, today was a perfect day. I woke up on time; promptly washed my hands and said the bruchah for that; doused myself in mosquito repellant; said Shemah and Shemonah Esrai; ate, saying bruchahs before and benching afterward; rowed out past the breakers in the fast sea like I am trained; pulled ashore for lunch saying bruchahs before eating, benching afterward, and then saying Shemah and Shemonah Esrai before getting back in the boat.

The afternoon session on the water was equally productive. I felt strong and elected to row rather than sail, blissfully blanking my mind in an exegesis of physical endurance. A small pod of white whales breached intermittently on my left—generally a common sight but anomalous in the dense fog—atomizing a sardine-scented mist that drifted in wisps of otherwise indiscernible wind and precipitated along the lee side of my boat and myself. I really stink now. And then past that interlude, and late in the day, I rounded a rock-corniced jetty, a jumble of leaning shattered gray rock testifying to a lost glacier's ocean border. On its far side, a concavity of black sand beach steeply sheltered the facing side of a frigid trickle rushing through tundra from the hills. I set up camp on a step in the beach's curve well above the high-water mark. Above the beach, all still passes for summer, but the sun will set soon, and once it starts to do that, darkness grows like a bad habit, staying out a little longer each night until it loses itself in a months long binge of black night and effervescent celestial light and death-cold.

I prepared a dinner of rice and beans cooked with butter and rehydrated eggs and ate it wrapped in flour tortillas. Gradually, while I ate, lifting fog uncloaked a broadening landscape. Finished eating, I benched and da'avened for the third time, leery of saying nighttime prayers proscribed for sometime after three stars come out, in what passes for broad daylight here. Finished with the day's obligations, feeling good, swaddled in fleece, top, bottom, head and toes, and able to see the landscape for the first time in a while, I delicately felt my way down the deep rut my hull carved on the way up to what passes for surf here, my down booties finding there slightly less tenuous purchase than on the rest of the steep slick sand.

Near the waterline, the grade relented and I comfortably walked along surf-scum tailings towards a large flat rock I'd noticed on the way in. The rock was about four feet high, and I easily climbed on top of it. Scanning the now-visible horizon, my intention was to lose myself in a meditation on my mother. I perused the ocean in front, beach and jetty to the left, mountains behind, wondering what she might think if confronted with this brutal landscape, empty of people, jagged and raw and colorful. She'd made fun of it for years. I continued my revolving watch. To my right, where the beach abruptly ended in a scrub of brush, I saw the glint of glass. I focused. Yes, the low sun caught something amber and reflective. I thought, well here's evidence of people; trash is everywhere. I thought to go pick it up and pack it out, but figured that with all the corroded oil drums I'd passed and not thought to remove, what difference could this infinitely smaller relic make?

But I have all the time in the world, in a certain sense. There's nothing for me to do, really, once I've rowed for the day. I was under no obligation or discipline to stay on my rock, thinking about my mother, and staring off into space (literally, when the clouds clear, the horizon here ends in space. I'm confident of it). So I sort of slid-slash-jumped off the rock, smashing out twin bootie prints that seeped water like a rotten hull, and picked my way across to the shrub.

I have to say, I've never felt so self-consciously awkward as I did walking over, completely unobserved, to investigate this oddity in the bush. After several weeks of purposeful motion, this luxurious amble made me feel guilty. And how innocent and clear my mind was then. Because this is what I found in the shrub: my whiskey.

Abba and Eema, if you guys are watching over me, please explain what this all means. Am I being tested? Am I meant to hurl the bottle back into the surf whence it reemerged having so successfully followed me here? Am I supposed to carry it out as trash? Or am I being regranted the right to drink having had a recovery of sorts these past several days? Or is the world in fact entirely random as my mother believed? No, I'm way to creeped out to believe that this is entirely accidental.

And have I mentioned how pissed I am that in two week's hard effort rowing   has it been two weeks since I cast off the booze? I should check this journal—I've made no better time than a drifting bottle. Though, in my defense, I have at my best rowed twelve hours in a day while this bottle has plugged ahead twenty-four seven, no rest stops for it. Or has it? Can't it be possible that it too washed ashore from time to time, only to be sucked out by a changing tide, all the while wondering whether it would be better to go backwards or forwards or just stop for once and for all? Could it not have in fact been carried by a playful polar bear great long distances?

Ursus Marinus may well have seen that glinting, highland confection and taking it for a reflective bauble playfully pushed and batted it along the frozen shoreline, carrying it like a dog's toy baby on long northward detours to ice floes past the 85th parallel. Perhaps he showed it to his friends, and in the face of their ridicule—what ferocious white bear, god of the natives, carries a manmade, glass liter bottle around with him—abandoned it back to the waves. Or maybe he had it beside him as he lurked on top of a seal's breathing hole and when making that fateful lunge, slipped, tragically on the smooth, rolling glass, and succeeded in losing at once both libation and dinner. And maybe the seal, inquisitively trailing the stream of bubble accompanying the bottle's temporary plunge, pushed its savior along the bottom of the ice until it reached open sea again, bidding it alas farewell, safe home, good journey. Or maybe the bear stashed the bottle here temporarily. Or maybe it wasn't a bear at all but some people in a boat, or on a beach, who found my whiskey and expecting some special message in that buoyant bottle instead found the best of clan McCallan, aged in oak twelve years. And those people, as they passed this piece of shore, stashed the bottle for safekeeping (unlikely, the bottle hardly seemed stashed, it looked as if it had been entrapped on the backwash of wave, held back in a sieve of stunted willow as the water dropped. No, if in its journey it encountered other humans, they did not willing leave it there. And yet, they may have parted with it as willingly as I, taking that piece of dangerous trash far out into the ocean and dropping it, hopefully to never return.

Or perhaps Hashem, creator the universe, simply ceased the bottle's existence once I cast it from me, and now, for reasons only known to the divine, has recreated it in my path.

I don't know.

I also don't know whether to have a drink or not.

I don't think I'll throw it back just yet.

### August 11

Like a donkey after a carrot, I followed The Whiskey bottle duct-taped to my bow all day. It sits there, glowering, an ever-watchful, never-sleeping bowspirit; baruch Hashem.

### August 12

White-knuckled, not-sleeping, hanging-on-for-dear-life, tehillim-reciting me is still here. And so is It, unopened. Baruch Hashem.

But I passed a long abandoned sod and wood hut today. Something I expected to see far more of than I have. I stopped there for lunch. A track where the last visitors hauled boats out persisted above the waterline. I reached and circled the hut. Behind it, meadows broken by rain-pools stretched back at a gentle but increasing slope into the foothills of the mountains, which are growing ever nearer. In a week or so, I expect to reach their near-confluence with the ocean, which will be the closest I come to the tree line on this journey, one of only two stops in towns, and the Canadian border. The hut's roof was well set into the small rise of land on which, and undoubtedly, from which, it was built. It faced out towards the water. I went inside, an easy feat in the absence of doors. Ancient cigarette filters—lone survivors of butts long pilfered for remnant tobacco—mixed with bits of fur and random decomposition on the floor. The space would have been claustrophobic had the front opening been closed and the sod washed away from the wood walls. In other words, restored, the hut would have been quite unpleasant.

Yet there were conveniences and comforts that made sense for a small outpost on a near empty arctic shore. The center of the floor was carved in lower, the way snow caves are, so that cold air sinks out of the structure. The walls were well shaped to accommodate sitting backs and stacks of fur. A small oil fire in here would be very warm. No longer. This place is like nature now. For decades, passing itinerants, what few there are, have probably used it to get out of the wind, maybe cook a meal. But no one vests an interest in maintaining the hut, or what others like it persist. No one counts on it as a point of return. No, nomadic arctic life is a failing experiment, even amongst those born into it. What am I doing here?

## August 13

But after all, what use would there be in tossing the bottle back into the ocean? If it could find me once, it can find me twice, or thrice, or again and again. I don't even believe that taking the drastic step of emptying the bottle first before discarding it would necessarily put an end to this. Clearly, Hashem sent me the bottle either as a sign or as a test. To discard a sign would be comparable to dismissing Hashem, unthinkable. And a test – it is written that the Lord does not test us beyond our abilities. (And yet I cannot dismiss that this might be in fact a punishment. But if so, it is written that the tzadik is punished for his sins in this life and rewarded for his good deeds in the next; the evildoer rewarded in this life and punished in gayhenom. I must have faith; faith is, must be, enough).

I must have faith. Faith must be enough.

## *August 14*

Why should I care about a bottle of whiskey? I'm making good progress, rowing every day. I'm getting closer. I'm healthy. My faith in Hashem is intact, despite everything, despite my near incapacitating fear, despite being driven from my home, despite the loss of my parents, despite the insomnia, the shakes, the haunting booze bottles, the rifts with friends, the lack of anyone meaningful from my life of orthodoxy at the unveiling of my parents' headstones, despite the fact that though my father survived the single worst terrorist attack in US history, despite my mother's being the child of holocaust survivors, that still they perished horribly in a terrorist attack. Yes, despite everything, my relationship is intact.

Marie asked me. We were post-hangover, sitting in the window of Lucy's Luncheonette on Main Street in Northport, eagerly enjoying the early onset of a fall dusk, Marie sipping an egg cream, myself stuck with coffee in a Styrofoam cup – coffee's kosher but the dishware isn't and I sure would've loved an egg cream if only I could. We sat a while, stupefied mostly by local traffic making left turns to the take-out fish 'n chips place, minivan after SUV after minivan, small mobile oases of loud-mouthed materialistic children and hyper-indulgent parents, in other words, ourselves in earlier incarnations. She shook free from the passing murk.

"Sarah, I wouldn't ask you this if I wasn't fucking hung-over as shit."

I ignored her cursing as best I could. Sipped my coffee: half and half from packets, no sugar. Unless you live amongst Jews, in a Jewish place, the difficulties of keeping faith eventually become overwhelming.

"—but do you ever wonder what would have happened with

your parents if you hadn't become so Jewish?"

"If I hadn't become so Jewish?"

"What the fuck was I thinking? I'm sorry, Sarah. I don't know what the fuck I was thinking."

Right about the time they finished cleaning the pit, some firemen on break ran into my father while he was between meetings, and told him that if he wanted to swing by after work, they'd take him into it. He said he'd thought it would probably be his last opportunity down there before it became whatever it was to become and decided he better go in case he regretted the lost opportunity later. From above, the pit had an antiseptic quality, it seemed cleaned, hosed down, nothing left. Over the months he had reminded me again and again of what it had looked like before the rescue and then recovery operations ended, "No, Sarah, what it really looked like, up close, World Trade Center Four, still standing and smoldering. Giant sections of façade standing like postmodern medieval shields blockading heaps of twisted, burning girders." The perceived smallness of the final pit elicited an insatiable desire to remind everyone of what had been.

But then he descended into it, walked down the long temporary truck ramp they'd erected. "I realized again how massive this structure was, how massive the footprint it had left behind, like a giant leaping from planet to planet, only one foot touching and cratering the earth." Sections of the parking garage by the north tower survived the collapse and were left intact like sundered catacombs. As he descended, he came eye level with first one of these, then another and another. Strings of yellow work lights trailed back from the evenly rusted, twisted facades of fire blasted support girders, casting dim diminishing light, implying untoured depths. Because each level lower survived somewhat better, their darkness was less broken, more eerie as he went. And then he was stepping off the ramp into the floor of the pit, and he realized that for the last hundred feet or so, he'd been kicking up a mud made of pulverized concrete and water seeped from the bathtub walls and his pants cuffs were weighted down with a grey cake they'd never survive. He stepped off onto the bathtub floor itself, the bottom of the pit. The summer sun, though still high at 5pm, was completely blocked from view. He shivered, and looked over at Kevin, the fireman he'd become close with while volunteering at the relief station. I don't know whether my father's account of Kevin sadly smiling and nodding is true, or simply what my father believed he should see. I do trust my father's assertion that they didn't speak the entire time they were down there. Silently, they slowly walked around the floor of the pit, a long slow circle, and then back out again. My father's claim that he noticed his breath's resumption only when he emerged must be fanciful. But I'll always remember that hole in the ground, now slowly filling in, through his eyes, which strangely equated the paradox of apparent smallness and yet true enormity with the telescoping affect of a desert's air, bringing distant objects, mountains, closer, and yet miniaturizing them.

"I love you too much to be mad at you, Marie."

"But you're crying."

"No I'm not."

"My God, Sarah. I'm sorry. I didn't mean—"

"Dude, stop it. I'm not crying."

And then I left and went home by myself and locked myself in my father's workroom and sanded the pontoons and sanded and sanded and sanded.

I still have this fucking bottle of booze that's following me around and it's strapped to my hull—so maybe I'm following it—and I don't know but I worry that placing it so prominently, attaching quite so much significance to it itself might be some form of idol-worship, a certain sin. What am I doing here? Sure, my rowing has improved. I'm moving forward. I'm continuing my father's retirement dream. But each day I become progressively more disconnected from my physical environment. I don't want to be here at all. Yes. I can say that comfortably now. I don't want to be the in arctic. Not now, not later, not ever. But I have no choice. I've got to keep rowing or I'll die. No one can come to rescue me here. No one will.

I just want the sun to set, just for a moment.

(The sun should have set a week or two ago)

I'll hold off on touching that bottle until the sun does set.

(Perhaps the sun sets in my sleep)

At sunset I'll take a drink.

## August 15

I've decided to keep Shabbat this week, and as best as I can tell, it starts in an hour. So, I'll have to keep this short, but I want to document a sudden spike in my psychological fabric. Though I suffered through anxiety attacks, or as I called them, uncertainty attacks, today I experienced something on a totally heightened level, today I graduated to the full-on panic attack.

There's not much to say about its onset. In crossing a river mouth I drifted substantially further to sea than I generally travel, but was still within clear sight of land. I continued on my course from where I was, angling slightly towards shore. And for a little while, that was ok. Then I freaked, ran myself straight to shore without stopping. I made a beeline and rammed a pebble beach—of which there seems an illimitable supply on this trip—helter-skelter, floundering through mild surf and paddling still even after I'd come to a clear halt on land. I flopped out of the cockpit and dragged the boat above waterline, all the while panting, my breath out of reach. Don't go back in the water. But you have to, Sarah. It wasn't even lunchtime yet.

I sat on the beach a while. Part of me grew ever more convinced that the longer I stayed out of the water, the harder it would be to get back into it. Yet I couldn't overcome an equally fixed conviction that any immediate return to rowing would prove fatal because—I don't know why because. I froze. And throughout my physiological contortions—pulse, palms, breath—images of Chaim bobbed. At each approach of calm, he surfaced. I saw him serving his customers, turning the machine on for my espresso as I walked through the glass door in the mornings, my croissant already bagged, the way he looked out the window at me the day of my parents' unveiling. With each buoyant image, rough, frantic waves overtook my psyche. I remembered first going into his shop to wait for the agent who showed me the apartment upstairs. His refusal to take money for the coffee I ordered that day after learning that I was going to be a tenant in the building cemented my decision to take the place. As soon as such images slightly subsided, some new facet of my Chaim memories flashed its piercing beacon. He was a stabilizing force in my Aliyah. He made my little neighborhood feel like home. And today, I felt sick as I thought back to how I threw the vase of flowers he sent to my hospital room against the wall, imagining he'd sent them to every survivor. It felt fucking impersonal, perfunctory. I couldn't help but hate him for having that store, luring me to that building. I don't blame him for not visiting me in person afterwards, how could he? Rocked and riled and nauseous; I was stuck on the beach.

Finally I turned to my last resort, Udi. Just now it struck me that when I get back to civilization, at the McKenzie, he won't be there, of course he won't. Anyway, today, I thought about what will happen when he and Sara meet at Yechil's for the first time after the dinner party. They will show up as prearranged. And despite a precipitous temperature drop, sit outside, lifting upside-down chairs off our usual table. Yechil himself will serve them, weaving through the empty sidewalk seating area, bringing the usual mint tea and Earl Grey as if there had been no break in routine. Despite his obvious cold, Yechil will stand and make small talk, all the while blowing on his raw red hands, until Udi will admonish him for neglecting his other customers inside, behind the warm, fogged window. They will sit across from each other, huddled around their respective hot drinks, amorphous under bundles of clothing, cheeks red.

"You know that I can't do anything for a year."

"Do what, Udi?"

"Do anything formal about you."

"About me?"

"About marrying you. I can't get married for eleven months after my son's death. You know that."

"You thought all American women would want to marry you?"

"I don't think I can wait a year to hold you."

"I don't believe in romantic love."

"What are you talking about?"

But Udi will look at her the way he first did on the bus when they met, with the clear cognizance that she belongs to a sect of orthodoxy far different, far more stringent than his own, in which life conforms to theocratic norms, not the other way around.

"So you were planning on shituch."

"When I'm ready, yes, shituch."

"But what do you need a matchmaker for if you've already found someone you love?"

"I already told you that I don't believe in love."

"Don't believe in love?"

"In romantic love. In the way that you mean love. I don't believe in that desperate, Western construct metastasized only in its ending, measured by the hurt its loss leaves. No thank you. Not for me."

"Who's leaving anybody?"

"Is that what you told Nurit?"

Udi will chuckle, shake his head and roll his cup of tea back and forth between his hands. At Columbia's Chabad House, Rabbi Shem Tov, who'd been picked for his post because of his prior life as classics professor, and I would discuss the western construct of romantic love at length. He believed, rightly, that as an artistic creation, it was subject to definition solely through media portrayal. Due to the nature of dramatic entertainment, love was, necessarily, an emotion measured by the pain of its loss. The key was not so much to develop a relationship via love, but to define oneself in terms of the agony of love. He further tied its roots to early western hedonistic traditions, especially Catulus' excesses in his quest for Lesbos. "Right from the beginning this kind of love was primarily an excuse for self-indulgent breaks with cultural mores." I could easily see what he meant. After all, look at Romeo and Juliet, La Boheme, Casablanca, listen to any pop song: the best kind of love is impossible. Rabbi Shem Tov likened the affects of cultural portrayals of romantic love on America's youth to that of media-induced anorexia. And I agreed, wholeheartedly, which is not to say I was cured.

"Sara, one second you're this very independent mature woman. The next moment you are telling me that you don't experience love, that you don't believe in it. But really, do you deny that there is an empathy, a simpatico between us?"

"Udi, you've just lost your son. You're on forced leave from your job. You have nothing to do. Boredom and restless emotion are strong motivators. I am empathetic to you. But don't extend your empathy towards me past its bounds. Don't feel sorry for me and make some sacrifice just because you need to do something dramatic in your life."

"Sorry for you?"

"Do we have to continue this conversation?"

"I need touch."

At which point, Sara, will carefully reach out and take Udi's hand. She will squeeze it between her palms. His skin will be tough and warm, the veins crossing his finger bones will gently compress against her palms; his nails will scratch along the undersides of her fingers lightly, and shoot tingles through the hackles on the back of her neck. Sara will sniffle and break away from him, stand up. She'll tell him she cares for him but just can't, can't go through what it would mean to be with anyone who hadn't come to grips with her disfigurement objectively, through the cold premeditated calculations of shituch. Sara couldn't bear to cast the image of her love in  plaster of Paris mixed with the blood of her heartbreak after the fact. No, let them be friends. He was welcome to call her.

As Sara walks away, runs almost, scurries, Udi will call after her:

"You're wrong, Sara. Now I understand. You don't realize. You are beautiful. I love you."

A grown orthodox man in Israel will call after her down a midday street, in winter, that he loves me.

With the warmth and contortions of that thought momentarily subduing the jangling buoy that was Chaim-images flashing across my frothing, panicked adrenaline, I thought to set out again, quietly reciting tehillim, rowing in rhythm to:

*Lamnatzayach mizmor lidovid*
*haShamaim Misafrim cavod-ayl, ooma'ahsay yadav magid harakiah.*
*Yom liyom yaviah omer, vi lailah lilailah yachven da'at*
A psalm of praise, a song of David
The heavens speak of God's strength,
And the work of his hand is told by the wind.
Day will say to the day that will come,
and night to night will give this knowledge.

Gradually, singing King David's poetry to myself, I edged

back out onto the water, rolling over chop until I broke free of the surf, first reciting the lines in Hebrew, then translating them to English, I set a cadence for my paddle, and moved further, and further still, along my course. Ok, that's it. I'm going to light Shabbat candles, eat dinner and go to sleep. Tomorrow, I'll da'aven, refrain from writing, cooking, and rowing. I'll generally rest up, refresh myself, and prepare to resume my journey. I'm about halfway there after all. The Brooks Range is racing towards the sea. Any day now, I'll pass the town of Gordon, and then I'll cross the border and be into the Yukon, and from there, the Northwest Territories and finally, Aklivuk on the McKenzie.

## *August 17*

A lot has happened since I wrote in my journal. I saw the sun set Friday night. It had been bobbing within its usual arc of fifteen to twenty degrees over the horizon, behind the mountains when last I'd looked at it. Then, at about eleven-thirty, while I was sitting outside my tent, the clouds over the ocean which as for the past several nights had changed color to a mélange of red and orange hues, transitioned to vermillion and midnight purple streaks and distracted me from my journal (which I was reading over). I turned around, and through an optical trick, the sun, coronating a blackened peak, dazzled and blinded me. But it was almost completely out of sight. Things went on this way for an hour, while in a state of wonder, I watched the sky change color over and over again. The ocean reflected a melee of short-frequencied hues and a flock of geese took flight on new feathers, their molting process complete. My heart raced. I knew I was in for magic. The sky lengthened. I ran to my boat and frantically unwrapped the duct tape from my boomeranging bottle of whic key, desperate both to free it by dark and to not miss any of that most welcome sunset.

I could feel my pupils dilating as darkness descended, and when, after another hour, I could make out the first faint stars I'd seen in nearly a month, I drank long and hard from the burning nipple. Warmth wending wrap-wise around my veins. And then, a freezing hour later, the sun emerged from behind the same mountain it had crowned at sunset. Dawn. I screamed at the top of my lungs, rasping my underused throat: Shemah, Yisroel Adonoi Elohenu, Adonoi Echad. Here, oh Israel, the Lord Your God, the Lord is One. I continued on through the rest of morning prayers, the evening's whiskey still fresh and raw in my mouth, and then went to sleep. Yes, I went to bed without getting drunk, without going crazy, without doing anything stupid.

Today, in Gordon—yes, I made it to Gordon—I learned two things. First, the sun has set for the past several nights; I've just slept through it. Second, Gordon isn't. Gordon must have been at some point, but it sure isn't anymore. If I wanted a town I would've had to stop back in Kaktovic 75 miles, or about eight days, behind me. In what was once the town, or border post, of Gordon, which is now at best a collection of driftwood on a mile wide gravel spit that juts out into the Beaufort Sea, losing itself in a series of atemporal sand bars, I met several Inupiaq men in a metal skiff, who, despite an incessant cycle of cigarettes, noticed, and commented on, my odor. I didn't care. They were people, and better still, English-speaking.

"Kaktovic?"

"Yup."

They laughed, and asked how I'd managed to miss a whole town on the shore. I didn't laugh. I thought about how impossible it would have been for my father to miss something like an entire town while he was rowing. I thought about how impossible it would be for me to miss an entire town. I mean, I'm not even traveling that quickly.

"Kaktovic, how big is it?"

"Your voice sounds like it's been a while since you spoke to somebody."

"Sure."

"Kaktovic's maybe two hundred people. It's just a post office and some stores, a Laundromat, a restaurant. Nothing fancy."

"Yeah. It ain't a whole lot. Some plywood houses, a few buildings. There ain't any real roads or nothing like that."

"I missed a whole town."

"There's been some fog, Lady."

"And Gordon really doesn't exist."

The men laughed again, the eldest of the three turning with his arms wide open to demonstrate the magnificent expanse of this current settlement.

"What kind of maps are you looking at, Lady? Ones from 1952? Gordon wasn't never nothing of a town."

His friends smiled and I was treated to the sweeping gesture a second time. Then the man who hadn't spoken at all started to look concerned.

"Were you expecting to get food here? You got enough to eat or what?"

No, no, I told them, I packed enough food for the entire six weeks. It wasn't easy, but it was necessary, I couldn't expect to find kosher food in the arctic. Well, Eema, you would have gotten a certain joy watching me dig myself out of the hole that revelation excavated beneath me.

"You only eat what kind of food, Lady?"

"Kosher food."

"Is that a special kind of meat?"

"Sort of, but not exactly."

"That's not like being a vegetarian, is it?"

"Sort of, though I do eat meat, just not pork."

"What about Caribou and seal?"

"Caribou, yes; seal, no."

At this, the quiet man generously took a saran wrapped package of oily brown meat from inside his park and attempted to hand it to me.

"Oh no, I can't."

"It's caribou, Lady."

"But I can't eat your food."

"Don't worry about it. We're happy to share."

Meanwhile, a family arrived, seemingly from out of thin air, and two kids started playing with my kayak, which made me very nervous. Well, I didn't want to insult these people, but I also, obviously couldn't eat this non-kosher Caribou meat. I told the man that it wasn't a matter of depriving them of food, but rather that the Caribou wasn't kosher. He pointed out that I'd just said Caribou was kosher, and I had to tell him that Caribou was only kosher if it was killed in a certain way by a rabbi. Do I need to go on? None of my audience, which had grown to eight if you didn't count the two kids playing, crawling in and out of the cockpit of my kayak, had ever heard of a rabbi. Fortunately, by defining rabbis as Jewish priests—always distasteful as we Jews have priests and they're something else, not to mention my reluctance to dialectically imply a liturgical hierarchy in which rabbis rank lowly—I quickly overcame that subordinate linguistic hurdle. However, the idea of priests hunting caribou reduced the conversation ad absurdum. At least they weren't too insulted by my refusal of the meat. They told me, though, that the only way I was going to get a shower was to continue on to Shingle Point, the halfway point for the remainder of my trip, or turn back.

"What are you all doing out here?"

Heading back from Shingle Point themselves, where they had joined several relatives in the Bowhead whale hunt. Yes, they'd killed two whales, and would I like some of the muktuk? Despite whale blubbers' unparalleled attributes as a performance food for artic rowing, and the whale's shared genetic heritage with the common goat—a most assuredly kosher if not down-right biblical animal—in abandoning their cloven hooves to their land-living brethren (and quite possible their multiple stomachs, I'm not sure), whales stepped (or rather swam) out of narrow limits of Kashruth's dictates, and are thus denied me. Fortunately, these first people were as hesitant as I to revisit our long conversation about my dietary constraints and simply smiled, without making any further fuss, when I declined this second offering (no doubt whispering about the bad juju bound to befall me for rejecting this whale's carnal gift. So be it. The kabloona act in strange ways).

We built a nice fire from a blend of McKenzie River driftwood and pieces of what used to be Gordon. They cooked some caribou and ate it spread with cheese whiz; I boiled water in a titanium pot and made myself a meal of resuscitated turkey bits, rice, beans and soup base that I accompanied with a calorie bar meant for the chronically underweight. In the warmth of company and flame, I chastised myself for not making a few fires myself. Of course, I'm writing this without the benefit of one. But then perhaps one fire a day is enough. But really, the weather's turned distinctly colder.

After a friendly warning about wind-blown pack ice intermittently clogging sections of the route between here and Shingle Point, we waved goodbye, and I rowed another seven miles before stopping here for the night.

Given what I learned, several things worry me:

1. My outfitter didn't realize that Gordon was no longer (if it ever was), nor that Kaktovic belonged on my map.

2. I managed to row by the entire town of Kalttovic without noticing it. Granted, there were several days of on again off again fog when I would have been passing it; and the town's

a roadless collection of small buildings. But still, I missed a whole town—and they missed me.

3. My supposedly solitary travels have crisscrossed nomadic natives in boats repeatedly. I am not alone. And this simultaneously makes me vulnerable and more vulnerable. For on the one hand, the fact that I have not seen them, and they have not seen me, though we can't have passed far from each other illustrates the impossibility of rescue. And on the other hand, I am only alone in the sense that there is no one here to look out for me. Should some passing man see me and decide...I'd rather not spell it out, but I'd be at his mercy. So, vulnerable and more vulnerable. That's me now.

4. The subsets of all of the above:
   a. I am ill prepared. I set off on this journey, with, apparently, an ill-conceived conception of where towns were. (Though I've been loathe to inscribe it (inscription carrying a weight of reality I do not wish to face in this instance), I am without topographical maps. What was I to do? There's no turning back on this journey—they were in the same bag as my camera, binoculars and bird book—I forgot it. Yes, I could have gone back with the Inupiaq people I met today. But I—I'll psychoanalyze that some other time. Furthermore, I relied heavily on my trainer Nance to coordinate my trip and prepare me adequately. After we lost sponsorship funding, she tried to save money by using an outfitter who generally took fishing clients to lakes nearer Fairbanks. Apparently, he thought there was a Gordon. Clearly, everyone lacks even a basic familiarity with what I'm encountering. I only hope that Aklivuk is in fact a place I can be picked up. I don't really fancy wintering with the natives. (I'd

have to eat muktuk then. My food simply won't last until next spring. At best, I'm carrying a week's worth of extra food).

b. I am decidedly unaware. As I remarked earlier in this journal, I have grown progressively disconnected from my surroundings, often preferring a day in the tent planning my life in Jerusalem to an active engagement with the environment. The thought's crossed my mind that I might be perfectly happy never going outside again after I get back. Clearly, that disengagement has been less healthy than I thought. Survival in the Arctic depends on active interaction with the natural world. Though meditative and sometimes transcendent, I must remain focused here, if I am to survive. Missing something as obvious as established human habitation—how did I miss a village?—implies that I am also not keyed into tide changes, the subtleties of weather shifts, animal (in particular bear, in particular, particular, polar bear) behaviors. You must tune in, not out, Sarah, you must. No wonder fear dominates my days; somewhere subconscious I realize my stupidity. I've grown complacent, camping between piles of fresh scat, while running in fear from abstractions. A recipe for disaster.

c. Sure, crazy, flaky, tormented, scarred Sarah obliviously rowed past night and village, but the Inupiaq who must have crossed my path? I cannot believe that in a scant generation or two they've grown so out of touch with the nature they depend upon as to not notice such a massive rift in it as my awkward progress, plastic tent, and colorful sail. No, clearly, those who passed me concretely chose not to make contact with me. Either they view me as a trespasser, or, they are attuned to my ill-favored fates, and avoid me for fear of catching some distemper. I will feel always watched now. As if a set of eyes marks my progress and elects not to make contact, not to offer me assistance. I am on my own and yet judged at once.

Conclusively, I'm fucked. Yes, despite hefting the mantle of observance once again, I continue to curse. I'm fucked. And all I can do is preserve faith in Hashem. I am in large part tempted to turn around now and try and catch the people I met at lunch. There's no chance of my puny paddle catching up with their motorized skiffs. Even if I could catch them, I might miss them.

I must reconnect with the origins of this trip. I will start writing this journal to my father and mother—what happened to Abba viEema, Sarah? I thought you were committed to the Hebrew—Ok. I'll keep writing this to Abba viEema. Each evening I write detailed notes of my physical surroundings. I will place my faith in Hashem.

I'm coming home.

## *August 18*

I'm wearing all my clothes and my nose is a bit runny. It's cold. I want to sit outside while I write, but I may not be able to stay away from my sleeping bag. Woke up this morning and realized I haven't had to put Uncle Ben's on in a few days. There aren't any more mosquitoes. I see more ice each day and a brisk chop batters the shore. The seasons really are changing. I've got to keep moving. Nance's six-week estimate is at best uncertain now, in light of yesterday's actions. My body's grown stronger; I'll add five miles to my rowing each day. With that, I might successfully cut a full week off of this journey. Better to wait around in Aklivuk for my ride home than to find myself boxed in by ice, immobile, flipping a coin to guess which'll find me first: a drunken Inuit on a snowmobile or death.

Abba, you expected to find joy on this trip. You envisioned a culmination, a coronation, an apotheosis of every kayaking tour you ever took, in this most rugged and remote and raw of all destinations. The scenery would not have let you down. The undulating northern fork of the continent's spine arched within twenty miles of the Beaufort Sea today. A narrow band of trees separated black rock-ribbed, shining glaciers from arctic tundra. To my left, I could hear pack ice grinding and booming. The geese have feathers again, and fly in ragged formations, Q's and O's and soft-bellied W's, rejiggering and relearning the soaring V formation they'll ride south. We'll leave here together them and me. The scenery is incomparable. I followed in the wake of a baby seal, racing, as was I, between the press of ice and surf. As I grew closer, it raised its whiskered brown snout and then dove, vanishing from my journey. And the tundra: browning wild flowers in jagged patterns of land running out over the giant, gold-tinged pebble-banks of small mountain streams, traversed by the easternmost tailings of the Porcupine Caribou herd, vast numbers of them heading west to their winter grounds. But joy?

The sun runs orange streaks off the glaciers and shines twenty-three or twenty-two hours a day, but I am not invigorated. I imagine slipping into a long dreamy hunger numbed by cold. Exhaustion comforts me. I give in and give up. Eventually, my liver stops heating my sleeping bag and I no longer need to excrete. I surround myself with all the people of my vivid, rich future life. My eyes close and crust over and I wander between silent conversations, Dalia's strange bar and Yechil's café. I'm too tired to struggle through the stages of hypothermia. A last image of a great warm sun swaddling a dark center, like the flaming ring of a solar eclipse, warms me, and then I drift off. Passing barren ground grizzlies in a final prehibernation feeding frenzy scavenge my tent and make short shrift of my desiccated corpse, picking away the soft flesh of my cheeks, my chest, my stomach, my ass. Freed feathers from my claw-ruptured down bag mat my remains into a mottled semblance of an anorexic, Christian angel. Some following spring, my tent's tattered remnants, flapping in an unending sun like Nepalese prayer flags abandoned on an aerie perch, lure an adventurer to shore. She finds me, mummified by time and weather, and this journal. She reads the sad happenstance of my life, my hopes, my parents, my uncertainty, fear and then calm. She notes the vastness of life and death, the rawness of her location and spins, absorbing every visual detail of my surroundings, lit in that twenty-four-hour, red-tinted, late afternoon daylight of arctic summer. She closes her eyes and preserves a starkly curved panorama, a warped image as if she saw my world through a fisheye lens. And then a great compassion swirls her stomach. She kneels beside me, wind in her hair, and lays a hand on my dirty body, revulsion strangely absent, says a prayer whether she prays or not, snaps a photo of my resting place to give to whoever's address she finds in this journal. And then she leaves. Her eyes tingle with both an appreciation and touch of resentment for the unmitigated might of the mountains, the ocean, the weather. Back in her own boat, she questions the reasonableness of her adventurous pursuit. Perhaps she cries for me; I don't know. I would want her to say a prayer.

But I won't give up and die. I want to return to Jerusalem, get a job, find an apartment, marry, bear children, and die an old woman with offspring to sit shivah for a week and then say kaddish for eleven months until my neshamah has definitely ascended from gayhenom to shamaim. I missed my parents' funeral. Not my own fault; tubes and bandages bound me head and foot. As soon as I was able, I went to the yeshiva by my old apartment,

Kolel Am Yisroel, and hired four young men to take turns saying kaddish for my parents. I would have done it myself but a woman can't. They had a whole system set up there for people like me. We're a regular source of income, you know, the grieving women of the unfortunately killed.

I am surprised that this place of so much color and light, bursting with elemental forces and movements, evokes such strong melancholia. I'll have a drink, and carry on.

## *August 19*

Holy sleepless night last night! I had better stop fooling around, imagining bears eating my sadly wasted body and whatnot because they're not waiting around. I'd slept about three hours when I wake up to my tent shaking and a loud grunt. I yelled out, "I'm here!"

A quick snuffling, and I yelled out again, and then I heard the sound of heavy paws on loose talus. It's all very poetic to imagine a bear surviving the winter on my remains after I'm long dead. I don't like it when they try to hasten the process. I'm not dead yet! And if my fear of death is any indicator, I don't want to die any time soon! Well I gave it a minute and then stuck my head out of my tent and saw the slow galloping, wide ass of a big grizzly a hundred yards off. He kept going, so I decided to stay put. Part of me wanted to flee, but logic dictated that he now knew that tents aren't tasty and I'm alive. Of course, the other part of me thought anything but rapid flight asinine and stupid, and that part of me took its revenge by making sure I was awake and at least thinking about fleeing all night long. Ugh! I must be an optimist to have thought I would get any more sleep. I should've gotten back in that boat and started rowing. I think I would've been a lot better rested rowing on no sleep than rowing on no sleep after sweating fear and lying uncomfortably awake for five hours. (Contrary to popular belief, a Thermarest does not fully inoculate one from the jagged torments of a rough talus resting place. Shattered rock hurts the back.)

Things could've gone better in the boat today, if, for example, I had been awake. Yes, I cleared the beach, hoisted the sail, noted a beluga whale on the horizon and dozed off. Second time this has happened. Typically, I dreamt I crashed into pack ice, capsized, desperately pulling myself onto the shattered surface of a floe, frigid, shivering, only to come face to face with Ursus Marinus, the great white bear. The dream ended with me screaming at that goofy, black-lipped, dog grin those bears always have in pictures and waking up to a cockpit swamped in sweat. I was about to create my nightmare. I was heading due north straight into a maze of ice. I couldn't have been asleep more than five minutes, but it was enough to undo the couple of hours of rest I had gotten before the bear attack. I pulled the boat around. And while I was doing that, the disturbing sensation that I might have peed myself in my sleep trickled up the base of my skull like an invading frogman. I managed to wedge a hand between my fleece and my spray skirt and felt my crotch and sniffed my hand. It was damp, all right. However, it's hard to tell apart the smell of sweat-wetted old body and pee. I decided that I'd be really wet if I'd actually urinated, and continued on.

At lunchtime, I rowed up the mouth of a stream until its narrowing banks threatened to clamp around my pontoons. I'd meant to haul my boat ashore and wash in fresh (freezing) water. My plan was flawed. The stream was too deep to get out and stand up in without soaking all of my clothes. Defined by the spring rush of snow runoff, not this late-season comparative low, its banks, steep and undercut, stood several feet above the water, dashed with grinning arcs of permanent ice. I couldn't beach the boat. I couldn't even pull myself out and up the banks onto shore because my pontoons effectively kept me three feet from either side. I backpaddled until the mouth widened sufficiently for me to turn around, after which I continued the rest of the way out to the beach where I beached my boat. I then hiked back upstream, along the tundra. As I noted before, this isn't an easy task. The tundra's uneven and tufted surface perpetually threatens to grab an ankle like a wolf-trap. Plus, I wore my Tevas, which are hardly hiking boots. After a fifteen-minute walk, I reached a spot where the stream seemed clear and fresh, and a minor mudslide had left a cut in the bank that allowed me to easily descend to the water. I stripped and gasped in the wind. Goosebumps immediately formed all over my skin and my breasts contracted in the cold until I had the chest of a man. My stench was far worse than I'd anticipated. When the wind whipped some of it away, I thought my body-funk might have masked the smell of coming snow, not a pleasing thought from any perspective. I got down into the water and I turned blue, my teeth chattered, my eyes bugged. I was submerged up to my navel. I forgot that I hadn't slept; I forgot my name; I was awake and painfully freezing cold. I forced myself to stay in the water and wash myself. Working as quickly as I could with benumbed movements, I squirted biodegradable lavender soap under my arms, in my hair and on my face, quickly lathering up and then dunking myself. A foamy detritus washed away in mild current carrying a tome of stench to an ocean of decoding life.

I scrambled back up the bank as fast as I could go, my soaked Tevas slipping and sliding on the mud. Gasping and clutching myself, wet in the water breeze, fetal, I reached for clothing, a towel, anything. Nothing but dirty clothes. I didn't want to redress in that funk. I'd planned to put on my fresh change of dry clothes and then wash these in the creek. Nothing doing.

Wrapped in my old clothes, but not wearing them, as if that would keep me cleaner, I shivered my running way back down to the beach, ankles twanging on uneven tufts, stands of dying purple lupine whipping against my bared thighs. Mud, spraying from my Teva heels onto my freshly bathed calves like a hail of stones slung by an ant army. Thoroughly chilled, back at my boat, I redressed and took a long medicinal dram of whiskey. The bottle's still close to full. I don't know whether that's a good sign or a bad one.

Too cold to sit around making a fire, I lowered the sail, took in the pontoons, loaded my pockets with energy bars and began rowing. My body's far more familiar with a basic paddle stroke than ordinary conversation now, and despite chilled muscles, blood began pumping again, I found a rhythm, my breath settled, and I continued on through a thick and unsettling fog till I got here and cooked up dinner in an opaque mist.

Shrouded in cold wet, I remember calling my father when I heard about the plane going down over Queens just two months after September Eleventh. In eerie deja vu, Ari ran into my office screaming at me to turn on Army Radio. "It's happening again," he yelled. We listened to the sketchy report of an airliner crashing over Queens, no hard facts. I called my father on his cell phone. He didn't know about the accident yet, but when he heard, he said he was doing his everything not to cut loose and bolt.

"I'm not sure where I'm thinking of running, Sarah. But I can feel my legs swimming in go-juice, my hackles are up. I could easily squat, lighten my load and just go, go, go, get out."

Yes, Abba, much like I feel the need to go, go, go, get out. Except for me that's exactly what I'm supposed to do. I always bucked at his reflexive phone calls each time something happened in Israel, no matter how far or near from where I might be; I took it as a passive-aggressive rebuke for not returning to safe, comfortable Northport. But when I called him—in the process discovering the impetus for all those calls of his, hardly peevishness—I found myself tethered, cell phone to cell phone, to a clinging, floundering man. If he'd been overboard in actual water, I would have had to deck him to get him under enough control to pull to shore. Instead, I reeled in my office chair as he ran, well, walked fast, east along Rector to Broadway. On Broadway, he turned north, heading past Trinity Church, and then up past the Pit, which was still cordoned off and monitored by National Guardsmen. He spoke in long unbroken streams thick with images of fleeing friends, two months prior, on September eleventh. The events that had seemed aesthetic, impossible to believe, when he first told me about them, were now filled with emotional content. He was fleeing with the feelings he retrospectively thought he should have. I tried to catch concrete stories, but names rained around me like falling concrete chunks, actions and events, a coworker's best friend lost while helping her pregnant boss down the stairs, a crying woman touching his arm on White Street and asking if he thought anyone was hurt, a mass of suits ducking for cover behind giant concrete planters, Jeffrey, Dina Chung, Mo, Ben Resnick, his floor's fire warden savaged by glass shrapnel from an imploding window when the second plane hit, Rick, Lisa, Ravi, hordes of photographers, long lenses tilted upwards like the cocked spears of a charging cavalry.

I'm really freezing out here, I'll keep writing this back in the tent.

In the background, Army Radio mumbled a stream of details, the choicest of which Ari relayed staccato. I told my father that the plane had gone down over the Rockaways. Between a description of a cop pushed up against a railing of the E train exit by the herds of evacuees he frantically directed forward (cap askew, hands behind him on the railing, back arched, tiptoes) and a conjecture on that officer's final fate, my father navigated a determined current of wistful Queen's shore nostalgia (a beautiful place to see migratory sea fowl from water level, in the lush salt wetlands, an unpeopled peace punctuated by shaking, climbing jet turbines). His lifetime of athletic training—three days a week in a boat minimum all summer long, alternating days on the erg-master or running in the winter—sustained an unbroken vocalic wind until he reached the Federal Building at Worth Street.

"Shit, Sarah, you caught me on my way to an appointment. I ought to call and tell them why I'm late."

"I'm sorry, Dad."

"I can't tell them I had a PTSD meltdown and fled; that's no way to inspire confidence in a prospect."

"I should've qualified the threat level before calling you. I thought you'd have more information than me."

"Fuck."

"I'm sorry."

"Oh, Honey. Sarah, you know I love you, right? I don't care that you went orthodox on me, that you moved to Israel—all of that, none of that matters—you're all that matters to me."

"Thank you, Abba."

"Harry or Dad, please. I just want to live long enough to get up to the Arctic, Sarah. Even if I can't do all three summers to complete that passage, I want to at least make that first leg from Barrow to the McKenzie."

Well, I'm here, Abba. Even if I didn't start all the way over at Barrow, I'm trying to do this for you, for me, though winter seems somewhat incompliant. I must row harder and faster. I can hear the patter of snow outside.

### *August 20*

Pavlov would've loved this one. First snow of the season and I've got that fresh energetic feeling it always brings. Only, it's nine in the morning and I'm back in the tent cause it isn't just sticking to the ground (an evil harbinger of early winter) but it's sticking to the fifteen-foot-high choss-heap of fractured ice that's grounded itself on the beach. There is no way but no how to proceed. There's no water. And yet I've got a fresh spring in my step. (My step not extending too far lest I lose my way from the tent, tracks in the snow quickly filled by wind drift, a slow death bedded down in the cold.) I made a hearty breakfast outside while big wet flakes slowly swirled around me. My father talked about this happening. He said ice blows ashore, and then in a day or two, it blows back out again. (Until one day it blows to shore and that's just it until spring.) I don't suspect this ice of having formed last night. It wouldn't be so thick if it had. No, tomorrow or the next day, leads will open and I'll proceed. For now I've got a rest day (drink day).

Nothing fights boredom like Macallan 12-year-old, right? (Or takes the pain away quite like it either.)

Self-portrait:

Dirty hair rings my yellow GoreTex shell-jacket's hood like a twenty-first-century parody of Amuudsen's fur-trimmed coat. Torso indistinct: I'm sporting a down coat and a fleece sweater beneath the shell. Legs are similarly immobilized, mummified in fleece, nylon and waterproof bibs: think yellow, fisherman's coveralls. Feet are in neoprene booties. I'm sitting on a log that must've floated a good five hundred miles to get here; it's covered in snow. A pervasive mist sways in irrational gusts like milk pooling in oil. I can see about ten feet in front of me, where what looks like collapsed seracs beneath a glacier is theoretically ocean. Footprints, obviously my own, extend ten feet out/up the snow-covered ice, then abruptly turn back where I had a pleasant little uncertainty attack. (Certainty: ice impassably covers the water and parts of the beach. Uncertainty: perhaps the ice is shifting just a bit, perhaps I'm standing on a thin crust of mostly frozen slush, and with the placement of a second foot, I'll sink through, plunge into thirty degree sea water, too cold to bother to drown.) I hold this journal open on my lap with a double gloved hand, layer of fleece, layer of shell. With my other, equally clad hand, I write with my father's Parker pen. Between sentences, thoughts, paragraphs, or at a particularly poignant gust of wind, I look up and scan an obscured horizon; a suspension of billions of aqueous lenses lightly veils my tent and boat just yards away. I stuffed my pockets with goodies—peanuts, granola, raisins—and also break to put down my pen and nibble. I could be twenty feet from a polar bear and have no idea of it. Large flakes hit my journal pages, leaving furtive, moist footprints before I brush them off. Oh yes, and my good friend Mr. Scotland sits between my feet (which I mentioned earlier as an activity, but it belongs in my aesthetic rendering of self as well). A slug here and there lends this white, white world a log-cabin coziness. Ah, August.

I let my mind and eyes drift, aimlessly chewing my snacks, and a second of sun, far past my position, glints off a formerly obscured ice dome and I see the mosque at the temple mount. I last saw it when my father and I went to visit the Wailing Wall while my mother researched the Holocaust name register for remnants of her father's family. So much happened during the four days we spent together in Jerusalem. If that trip's denouement hadn't eclipsed everything else—if they hadn't died, been killed, been horribly murdered by soulless terrorists in an act against humanity—those four days would have been a positive reference point in all three of our lives. Tourists mixed with Chasidim saying Friday afternoon prayers at the wall. And despite a ban on Palestinians under age thirty-five attending the mosque, the chance of violence by exiting worshippers manifested in omnipresent, hair-trigger security.

Throughout their visit, my father's new demeanor struck me. It wasn't that he necessarily looked older, or that he was more fragile, but rather he seemed oblivious to life's white noise by virtue of a sad and otherworldly empathetic tenderness that bordered on infirmity. His shoulders bowed slightly; he didn't lift his feet quite as high; when he met people, he cradled both their extended hands in both of his; he made eye contact with everyone, but not to assert his existence; instead, he futilely beamed an incessant pardon, a desperate compassion for a complex humanity, a plea for mutual understanding. At the wall, though he towered over the army sergeant who checked his identification, he managed to meet the man's eyes from below, and search his face for some indication that this soldier would think twice before firing his Galil, no matter how urgent the provocation. It infuriated me to see this new, unstated, holier-than-thou saintliness in my father, and it broke my heart. He walked around Jerusalem stuffing American dollars into the pockets of everyone and anyone remotely begging. Each time he did it, my mother looked at me as if my father's transformation was a direct and unfavorable product of some conspiracy between Arik Sharon and myself.

I followed my father through groups concentrated like breaking whitecaps to the grass-chinked stone blocks of the wall itself. My father gently ran his hand over its surface, stopping when his fingers contacted small rolled papers shoved into a crack between blocks. He began to pull out a weatherworn message. I told him to stop, that they were other people's prayers.

"I know, Sarah. I want to see what they ask."

"You can't do that."

He stopped; he sighed; he looked at me with a world-weariness that made me ashamed and angry; he gently pushed the note back into the wall. We stood there, not speaking, the drone of young men da'avening a few feet away filling our minds. My father put his hand on my shoulder. Years of kayaking together had taught me that this was a signal to silently follow his stream of sight. Neither egret nor fox nor narwhal came into view, but the young man to our left. His black hat stopped within millimeters of the wall each time he rocked forward, foot together, emulating the angels' single leg, eyes bunched shut, hands clenched in supplication and shaking in rhythm with his murmured, fervent prayers. While we watched, he tilted his head skyward, still rocking back and forth, eyes open now, and shook his extended hands towards heaven. For a moment, this ritual that I too practice thrice daily alienated itself completely, like I was spying on undiscovered, rare wildlife. Then the man bowed, and took the three steps backwards followed by the bows to each side that signal the end of the Shemona Esrai, and represent the exit from an audience with a king, Hashem. We looked away.

"Do you pray like that, Sarah?"

"Do you mean do I pray at the wall?"

"I mean, do you believe the way he does?"

"I believe."

My father took my head in his hands and kissed my forehead the way he used to before I went to bed when I was a little girl. Tears moistened his crow's feet. He smiled and took out his handkerchief, blew his nose.

"I'm jealous, Sarah. I really am."

"You don't have to feel jealous, Dad. You can go to synagogue, too. No one's stopping you from observing."

"They've left one small section of wall at the World Trade Center, thirty feet long by fifteen feet high. It's on the north side of the site, and I think it must have been part of building six, but I could be wrong. The façade's stripped away, it's just raw cinderblocks and cement punctuated by rusted steel rods. If you look at it while you walk from the east, you can see the chipped-away remains of a staircase climbing its backside. The steps are full width, but adjoin nothing on their south side, and each is chiseled round and smooth. I think they intend to keep it. Use it somehow in the new structure. Maybe it will connect a walkway from seven, which they've already begun rebuilding."

"But that wall isn't holy."

"Our every conceit is destroyed, and yet some remnant perseveres, and whatever it is, we end up worshiping it more and longer that we ever did the original."

Well, I stopped bothering to argue with him then. I rather felt the way my mother did about this sudden world-weariness and sensitivity. So his office tower was destroyed by terrorists. I didn't know anyone in Israel who didn't know someone who'd died when some fanatic decided to blow himself up. Get used to it, get tough, fight back. Unasked-for tragedy hardly entitles one to airs of unearthly, conceited wisdom. Terror holds no special truth—I wish the wind would come back and blow this ice out to sea, cause otherwise I'm going to end up walking to Aklivuk.

The glint of sunshine was a ruse. Grey mist engulfs me. I'm glad I filtered water last night. I'd have to tie a line from the tent to my waist to find my way back from the stream (if I could find the stream). But not being able to see comforts me. I understand the blinders horses wear. On clear horizons, my peripheral vision picks out source after source of anxiety, indelibly identifying every potential cause of danger. I am afraid—without direct object, and of every direct object imaginable. And I'm much happier not to know, not to see. Sure there could be six grizzlies closing in around me like invading armies marching towards a besieged city's central square, guided by scent alone to my food-filled dry bags, but I can't see them; they don't exist. Nor can I see distant tundra shape-shifting in low-angle light every time I turn my back. It's a relief not to face the myriad objective hazards posed by currents, cold water and wind. I'm happy here with my journal and my bottle and my snacks. In a little while I'll build a small fire to warm myself and cook a nice meal. I'll row tomorrow. I'm looking forward to getting home.

The outfitter picking me up in Aklivuk will fly me back to Fairbanks, and from there, I'll take an Alaska Airline jet to Seattle where I'll spend two days with my trainer evaluating the trip. From there, I'll fly to New York City and spend some time with Marie before heading back to Jerusalem. Ari's set up a two-month sublet for me, just somewhere to crash while searching for my new dream apartment. I'll land at Ben Gurion with my allotted three bags, read my new, temporary address to the cabdriver, and then probably go straight to bed. It's a long flight and I'll be tired. Some days my future life just doesn't arouse me as much. I think about Sara sitting there at Yechil's, Udi telling her he loves her, and it all seems so distant and impossible.

No man will ever love me.

Scars cover most of my face. I don't have eyebrows. I'm missing half of an ear.

The plastic surgeons did what they could, carefully, and at great expense, erasing the savage craters left by two-cent screws, scrap bolts and exploding glass. But eyebrows can't be replaced, and no matter how minimized or fine their lines, a web of scars makes looking at me like looking in a shattered mirror. Makeup helps. It's not as if I have to hide in public. I'm not hideous in a horror-movie-monster sort of way. But no one could ever find me sexually attractive. A little girl at Gordon tried to touch my face, embarrassing her parents who declined to punish her (though they did prevent her from actually tracing the tissue ridges). So what am I doing fantasizing about Udi? I don't believe in that kind of love anyway. It never worked for me before. It's not condoned by Jewish law. I don't want it now either.

And yet, there is something inevitable about that encounter at the café, about the way Udi will laugh and hold my hand. (I know that when I last wrote about this, Udi was to have yelled after me as I scurried out of the café. I've since realized that isn't quite what happens). Yes, I will stand up to leave, but he'll grab my hand and pull me back to the table. I will tell him that I am shomrei negiah.

"So don't run away and I won't touch you."

"Are you threatening me, Udi?"

"Do you want to leave?"

I won't answer, but I won't get up either. Though I don't trust any man to love me, given the way I look, I am also not embarrassed or ashamed. I am a survivor. I don't need to run away. Udi will lean back in his chair, mocking levity vanished, and sip his mint tea. He'll look away and down the street at a row of three-story houses with sharply raked roofs in stepped heights. On top of each, rows of solar panels will bask in grey light, glinting nothing. His eyes will tighten into a trembling squint, seemingly focused far past the rooftops, and I will wonder if this isn't a long practiced, well-affected look, the faraway stare in advance of relating matters of great import.

"Sara," he will begin in a tone that furthers my suspicions. "Sara, I don't know how far you intend to take this shomrei negiah thing. I long ago concluded that—" He will turn back to me, eyes wide, focused on mine, and grin goofily. "Oh, my, oh, Sara."

"What?"

"You're too hard on the world. Yes, I believe. I can't not believe. Who would want to think that the world just continues, from day to day, impractically spinning its way through space while we concoct the strangest absurd superstitions, driving ourselves to great advancements only to use them to ravage each other just in case. How can there be a world that includes the word sacrifice but not God? I don't think it can be. I don't want to believe it anyway. But just the same, I also think that any way people can mitigate life, they ought to do it, and not withhold comfort because some antique rabbi claims the Torah implies its prohibition."

"Either you have faith in Hashem, in which case you should observe his laws, or you don't at all. And if you don't believe in Judaism, Udi, then you're fooling nobody but yourself by wearing that yarmulke."

"Your modesty smacks of a certain self loathing. And I should add it isn't justified at all."

"Now why the fuck would I be self-loathing, Udi?"

"Fuck? So the yeshiva girl isn't so prim after all."

"Good enough, Udi. I think maybe it's time I left. Don't hold me back this time."

"Come on, Sara. I don't want to play this game where you threaten to leave and I beg you to stay."

"I think you're trying to tell me you want to fuck me."

"That's a crude thing to say."

"Not interested."

"You're an idiot. I love you and you've got brains and you're determined and I admire you. But you're also a fucking idiot."

"You've got five minutes to convince me that I should ever talk to you again."

"What the fuck is that?"

"Starting now."

"I grew up orthodox. I grew up Israeli. Religion was another fact of life like school was then, or army service. I liked religious classes as much as anybody. I mean, learning about all those old guys, the prophets, the kings, history really, that was interesting stuff. But what I never got into was the law, the halachah, the Talmud. All that debate about the finer points of which days of the week you could get married because how would it interfere with slaughtering animals on Shabbat. Or when a man can divorce a woman without paying, or she, he, without a Get because of disfigureme—"

"Because of what?"

"I'm sorry. That was an incidental example of something else entirely. I was saying I didn't care about that stuff."

"Because of his or her disfigurement."

"This is my five minutes to speak."

Udi will reach into his coat and pull out a pack of Time cigarettes and a brass Zippo lighter.

"Since when did you smoke?"

"Only when I'm nervous."

I will sigh in exasperation, loudly, and lift my bag into my lap. Smoke will drift towards me as Udi exhales a thick double funnel of grey down at his mint tea. Disgusting.

"This conversation is going in circles."

"Well what do you want me to do? Get on the floor on my knees? I'm being honest with you. I try to tell you a story about myself and you take offense during the preamble."

"So tell me this story about yourself."

I will cross both my arms and my legs, aware that I'm taking on the mannerisms of a western woman modeling after a romance movie, and yet powerless to stop.

"I don't know. I don't have a story. All I was going to do was to tell you that when we were growing up, despite all of the religiosity, the orthodoxy, whatever—we pursued our hearts. None of us believed for a moment that there was anything wrong with finding a beautiful Jewish woman, falling in love with her, relying on her, marrying her. I don't need some two-cent, old-world, Ukrainian Shadchin with six hairy moles on her upper lip and body-odor that could wake the dead sitting around in her dirty black clothing and mumbling to herself in Yiddish about what the right woman for me should be. No. Definitely not. I don't want some formulaic determination that because of this and this, and that and that about me, I'm only worth x or y. Fuck that. Yes I'm a soldier, yes, I'm divorced. No, I will never be a talmud chacham the pride of some yeshiva, an anemic scholar with a limpfish handshake. But I can go after what I want."

"Would you listen to yourself, Udi? Everything you said, you put in context of aesthetics, and how you can get a better woman than what you're worth. Well I'm not that woman. A man could marry me and divorce me without a Get because I'm ugly. I'm interested in that anemic scholar who will love me because I can help him reach heaven."

"You're not interested in an anemic scholar, Sara."

"Why not?"

"Because you won't be able to take him kayaking, for one thing. And he won't let you go either, for another."

"I don't care if I never see sea-water from a cockpit again."

"And he won't understand you if you spend a little time angry at God."

"I'm not angry at Hashem."

"You will be."

"Udi, your five minutes have almost completely elapsed."

Udi will reach across the table and take my upper arm in his left hand. With his right hand, he will hold his cigarette behind his chair.

"Sara, we came together because we understood one another. You felt a certain kind of grief, had an appreciation for it. I had just lost my son. By sitting with me in a café over tea, you provided a haven, and I began to fall in love with you. I cannot change your face or undo your fate—but I can love you, and accept you, and with Hashem's blessing, eventually let you see that your disfigurement is nothing to hide, that you are very attractive. I don't want to lose or wait for that. Please, if you need to go home and think, go home and think. But don't cut me out of your life."

"You are much older than me."

"I'm forty-two, you're twenty-six. It's not a lifetime."

"Let me go home, Udi. I'll call you."

"Ok."

I will walk across the street to the bus station we determined was just far enough away to not threaten the cafe. After such a long uphill battle to regain a sense of self and strength, after completing a grueling traverse of the first leg of the Northwest Passage, uncertainty, conflict, struggle will seem indecent, an inescapable farce. Riding the bus back to Bait viGan, Sara will wonder at her strength's defeat, at her uncertainty.

This is a major blow. I thought for sure that when I returned home to Israel, it would be as a cured woman. And I mean cured in the sense of self-sufficient, at-peace, certain. Like some New Agey guru's apprentice, more than anything I yearn for that sense of quiet, aloof assuredness so popular in movie sheriffs and Chasidic rabbis. When I first got back to Jerusalem, and took the new apartment, and started going by Sara, I had that certainty in my life. I faced everything solidly. I called on a huge character reserve. There I was with my apartment half furnished from my parents' home, half furnished with new, living in an orthodox neighborhood in a nice modern apartment, working and living and functioning, *without fear*. In fact, I can only imagine that my confident compassion attracted Udi in the first place, and without that, he will find nothing desirable in me.

Why continue on with this trip if I won't emerge strong and capable?

How can I be expected to continue living when every day is a trauma of what might happen, each moment told in a lexicon of indecision, every decision point a pinnacle of exhaustion?

I can't. I need some respite. Yes, the weather now provides a pause. There are no decisions to be made. I simply have to sit here, either outside in the blowing mist, snow drifts like miniature sand dunes against my log, or in my tent's nylon-filtered, yellow glow. I need make no decisions. I will encounter nothing. I love this immobility; but, I can't sustain it. To live, I'll have to continue. The idea of new movement, of parted sea ice and possible forward progress explodes into anxious nausea and a trilling pulse.

It wasn't always so. I was not indecisive. When I told my parents that my future lay in making aliyah to Israel, they called into question every premise of my faith; but I went. I packed my bags, quit my job, said goodbye to my friends and boarded an El Al jet out of JFK without wavering at all. Now, I flinch at every rounded shape in the water, baby seals scare me, the threat of cold water brings me to the edge of hysteria; and a life-threatening impasse of ice, the one thing that genuinely deserves to strike fear into my soul, comes as a welcome excuse to avoid forward progress.

I'm such a whiny jerk, sitting out here sniveling into my diary. If I was Sir Scott, and weather had impeded travel on my fated attempt to return from the South Pole, I would have written something along the lines of: *Snow falls today and we make no progress. I cannot help but commend the spirit of my men. Though food stocks are low, and Johnson shows signs of severe frostbite on his left foot, none has given into imprecation or despair. We are spirited unto the last. As for myself, I am glad to have carried on this far, and hardly feel worthy of my companions. I have lost all feeling in both feet and one hand, and find it hard to progress. Rough corn snow hampers our attempts to pull the sled. If we can make the next cabin, with its fuel and food cache, we should survive this endeavor.*

And Scott really was dying. I seem ok, no physical ailments, gear intact, several weeks' food. In short, nothing to worry about. So why can't I shake this anxious fatigue?

Drinking helps, actually.

My father whispered to me in the morning while making eggs in my poor excuse for a kitchen that it wasn't just my mother who'd developed a newfound fear of flying. "I used to fly fifty flights a year, easy, you know that. I never thought about it. Now I feel like I've been in the air so much that something's bound to happen. I've used up my allotment of safe planes." My mother wasn't secretive about her own airborne neuroses, nor was she pleased about them. I didn't, don't, suffer from that, or at least no more than I do from any other anxiety. But I understand now what my father meant when he said that it was as if he'd become aware of his surroundings for the very first time, that he now actually heard distinct engine notes, the changes in pitch, the screaming sounds of tremendous forces at play. I understand how he hinged his fate on every change and whine, his desperate yearning that the plane acquire a single sound, a single altitude, and stick with it, even if that meant gradually running out of fuel at 30,000 feet and then silently, slowly, with the lights out, accelerating towards the ground. "Sarah," he said. "Every plane is actually a missile." Yes, Abba, every airplane is a nascent projectile. Such is the true nature of planes. I understand, Abba, around every bend, in every face, in every act of nature or tool of man I vividly realize the potential, nay, likelihood of great destruction. That woman in the baggy black overcoat's vengeance was to thrust open my eyes to a world of what could happen, make me into a soothsayer of the potential doom in daily habit.

Yes, every ice floe conceals a camouflaged polar bear; every man boarding a bus intends to explode; behind every tussock lurks a grizzly ready to spring; in every cockpit sits a pilot despairingly deciding on spectacular suicide by the outcome of rock-paper-scissors solitaire; each wave yearns to surge into tremendous swells; each new spit of land hides unnavigable currents; the earth revolts against life, and we in it are all ready to kill each other. Like a deer in the high-beams, I am ever so aware that the very fact of impossible, inexplicable light bearing down on me is proof positive of flight's futility, and so my instincts scream to stand still and face fate's steamroller head on, row due north.

The day stays a constant muddy white, but the hand on my watch moves forward. The treats in my pockets are all gone. I haven't made a fire for food, though I'd planned to hours earlier. At each minor weather shift, I pray for strong southern winds. But apparently, watched ice doesn't blow away.

I flip back through this book and wonder just what a diary should do, anyway. I mean, are these abstractions, rants, wrung hands appropriate to this document? I intended to write to my parents, meditate on what I was seeing, and thus take the trip for them, for my father. But I hardly think of them, or write to them at all anymore. Sufficient presence of mind comes at the sacrifice of retrospection. I either have the freedom to think any thoughts that come, i.e., mourn for my parents, consider the divine chicanery of their demise and wallow here uncontrollably, or, I must enforce a rigid mental discipline in which only a narrow range of those thoughts located in the present and future earn mental real estate. It's not really a healthy tradeoff, but otherwise I die, I suppose. Drinking lets me leap those carefully constructed barriers a bit better. And yet I don't know where the reflective, enabling drink becomes the disabling, tree-biting binge. The first explorers' diaries were a hybrid scientific journal and ship's log. Objectivity and observation were the order of the day. But I am not discovering anything undiscovered here (though clearly what was once discovered is hardly publicized as my mess of planning proves). The only things new are in my mind. When else have humans, entirely sheltered from fear or ideology suddenly found themselves besieged by terror? This is uncharted ground.

## *August 21*

Ice, snow, grey skies, hangover, negative outlook, can't sleep, won't write.

## *August 22*

I'm as grey as the ice and the snow, empty as the clear glass of the top half of my bottle, flat as the backlit fog. At least I won't have to worry about keeping Shabbat this week; the ice will enforce a day of rest (another day of rest). My muscles are starting to cramp from inactivity. I'm chilly. The cold's here. This is the third day of nearly identical weather. Wind pushes fog swirls like curling stage smoke, muting daylight aryhthmically, a world of frequent and irregular almost night and almost day inside a universe of near-night, near-day. I wonder where I am. Just how far is it from here to Aklivuk? Imagine if it was so close that I could simply pack up a bag and walk there in a day. Imagine. (But then I'm forgetting Shingle Point, which may or may not lie ahead of me, may or may not be a full-scale town, and may or may not have slipped behind me when I wasn't looking). If only I could vaguely see my way through the fog I might stretch my legs, exercise this body that already feels atrophied, stale.

At least I'm not as hung-over as I was yesterday. I couldn't even summon the focus to write. I walked outside, inside, muscles aching, skin itching, no position comfortable. Starving, of course, yet repulsed by food, unable to eat, I tried to read back over my exploits thus far, but the writing was static on the page, letters randomly shifting in and out of focus, disconnected from sense and context. Eventually, I abandoned that pastime as well. I strove to stay awake until nightfall. But I fell asleep, an uneasy sleep, bothered by a restless stomach and dreaming of a cornucopia of dehydrated peas, carrots and turkey, rice and noodles

You reach a certain point, level, continuance, of discomfort, and it seems impossible to ever recover from it. I'm there now. It seems like I'll feel this way forever. But then, soon, I'll continue forward on my trip, and then I'll reach the end. There will be showers, hot food, congratulatory toasts, maybe a write-up in the local paper; headline: Jerusalem Terror Survivor Solos Stretch of Arctic. Everything will seem simpler. The trip's bad days will compress and vanish, spectacular moments multiply in retelling. But right now, it seems endless.

Those aspects of daily existence that make life worth living lie on one side of a scale and those that make it unbearable on the other; and I pin so many of my hopes on the presumption that with time, the balance will swing in favor of life. Which, when considered, means that I am living solely for the future. And what does the future hold?

After leaving Udi, Sara will ride back to Bait viGan. As always, her mental calculus of doom will come somewhat into play—she'll consider which stops will most likely be targeted, imagine the faces of other passengers reprinted in black news type. In fact, Sara will have grown so accustomed to the physiological arc of fear as to not pay it much mind at all. She understands that her fears are statistically irrational. She forces herself to ride buses everywhere, never taking cabs, thus empirically establishing her safety. But those intellectual truths, looping through her mind on permanent auto-playback, aren't working. Perhaps her sense of defeat after meeting with Udi will contribute to her general lack of mental discipline. Whatever it is, the group of Chasidic high-school girls crowded against her since she transferred buses at Beit Elan will make her feel like the bull's-eye in a prime target. Sara will inhale deeply through her nose, close her eyes, and attempt to marvel at the great and real danger she overcame in the Arctic. Instead, the smell of fried chicken schnitzel emanating from one of the girl's clothing will make her think of Shabbat dinner. That in turn, inevitably, calls to mind Dalia's group of survivors, though Dalia would never serve anything as pedestrian—and old Eastern Europe—as schnitzel. Yes, odds will stand strongly, starkly against anything wrong happening on the number seventeen bus. But it happened to every one of them there at dinner. And to Sara. And to her parents, twice. You can't really rely on stochastic modeling. There's always a hundred percent chance of survival or of death. You only know which after the fact. But that unknowing is the most unbearable of all the burdens weighting the scale in favor of death.

Sara's eyes will open against her will at each stop until she squeezes into a seat and finds herself waist level with the bevy of long black skirts. It's easier to keep her eyes closed sitting, easier to concentrate on cyclic breathing. As always, she debates saying tehillim. On the one hand, doing so wards off danger, on the other hand, resorting to them acknowledges her expectation of calamity. She won't say tehillim. Instead, she'll gently murmur to herself, "You've always made it, always made it." But even then, her hands will involuntarily slip up around the scar that was her ear, and rub the rough tissue there (a habit I have now, but have not chosen to record). At the Braishit shopping center, many more people will push onto the bus. Unable to force her eyes closed, Sara will scan and assess the threat potential of each new passenger. Her pulse will race when a young woman with nervous, almond eyes and layers of clothing covering an oddly shaped body pushes towards the center of the bus. But then the woman will turn and talk to a friend who laughs; suicide bombers don't board buses in pairs; Sara will exhale.

The line will stop as the driver stands up. All sound will fade into the blood pounding through Sara's skull like frantic war drums. There must be some problem, an alert, something. She will find a view between two of the yeshiva girls' cloaked shoulders. The driver will demand that an Arab man (Israeli or Palestinian, she can't tell) step down from the bus and open his large backpack. Collective murmuring ripples back and forth through the bus as those still waiting to board will step away from where the man stands opening his bag.

Obediently, he will take out a bag lunch and display an orange, a chunk of black bread, a Tupperware container of hummus. What looks like several university text books will follow and finally a large box covered in wrapping paper with a homemade card taped to it. The man will gesture with a broad hand motion that this is all he has, see, there's no problem, let's everybody get back on the bus. But the bus driver will point at the wrapped box, and indistinctly, Sara will overhear or understand, she won't quite know which, him order the man open that too. And the man's hand will fly up in protest. He will begin to shout. Sara will distinctly hear him say, "I'm an Israeli citizen. This is an anniversary gift for my wife." Everyone on the bus will gasp as the man reaches into his back pocket, and sigh as he pulls out nothing more dangerous than an Israeli passport.

Still the bus driver will insist that the man open the package. To Sara's left someone will whisper that this is a perfect example of the kind of humiliation he had been talking about that would lead to a third front. The girls in front of her will mutter that no Arabs belong in the land anyway; it serves the man right to open the package. Apparently, the man's box will not explode; Sara will lean forward to catch a glimpse at what he takes out. But inside the box there will be another box, also gift wrapped. The man will pause but the when the bus driver motions, he will continue unwrapping this box. And inside of it will be another yet smaller gift-wrapped box. This time, the man won't even ask, but simply unwrap it. In all, he will unwrap five successive boxes before revealing a small wooden jewelry case. No longer hesitating, the man will open the case and take out its single content, a silver locket on a thin chain. Of course, Sara will not be able to see the picture in it, which the man will show to the driver. But she will be able to distinctly hear him say over the now hushed crowd, "It's our only son."

The bus driver will wave, he's sorry, and shrug to show, what can you do these days, and offer to shake. But the man, shoving everything back into his bag, crumpling his wrapping paper an boxes in the process, will refuse the hand. Sara will relax further when the bus driver doesn't insist on shaking, but simply boards everyone else rapidly and quietly. As the man passes, Sara will think that he could die as easily as anyone if the bus blows up. But looking at his face, the way he clutches the largest of his once proudly packed boxes which wouldn't fit back in his pack, she will wonder to what degree death matters for him, or for that matter, for herself. Perhaps there is some kinship between them. And then the man will have squeezed past and gone towards the very back of the bus and the remainder of the passengers will have successfully struggled to insinuate themselves into the already overfilled vehicle. Turning back around, Sara will find herself inches from another man's waist. She will look up and see a lumpy military coat, whose sleeves are too long, buttoned all the way to his collar. He will be in his early twenties, black swirls of hair covering the backs of his hands. On the crest of an adrenaline-wave, Sara will see the truth in the trough below: this is the man, the bus driver searched the wrong guy, this is the one. Free fall rush of blood.

She will clutch at the insight she's just gained from the poor humbled man behind her. But hope will elude her. She will think, this is how it happens—and—this is the last thing I'll ever see. The bus will grind away from the curb before Sara can act, get off. And it will not blow up right away. Sara will remain staring at the waist of this man as the swaying of the accordion connected back section bounces her around. No, the man won't detonate right away. He'll begin fiddling with what must be a watch under his left sleeve, taking his arm partway down from the hanging metal strap to reach and twist something in between bus jerks that force him to grab on or fall over. Screaming panic will yo-yo in Sara's esophagus, bile searing her vocal cords. The watch, or wristband, or whatever, must be the detonator. But he will fiddle with it several more times and no explosion. Instead, she will realize that he knows she's staring; she won't be able to stop. Perhaps he's supposed to detonate at a specific time, and that's why he keeps looking at his watch.

No one has ever blown up on a bus that Sara's ridden. This man will not blow up either. But it will become increasingly difficult to believe that anything else could happen. And given their proximity, if he does blow, Sara will not survive. She will find herself guiltily wishing one, or several, of the yeshiva girls would work their way between herself and the man. She will want to get up and reseat herself elsewhere, but will be incapable of doing so, certain that the man will realize her suspicions, and be deeply embarrassed if not confrontational and outraged—presuming he's not a bomber (of course he's not a bomber). Even if other passengers came between them wouldn't their exploded bodies penetrate Sara? She will collect a whole new array, a second coat, of shrapnel scars, her body torn by bodies, bone punctured by bone. (I have often wondered if some part of the woman who killed my family still resides in me, if the part of my heart that has a harder time with faith can be directly and proportionally attributed to the biological taint of that fiend).

Sara will will herself to calm down, close her eyes; clearly the man will not blow up! If he was going to kill everybody he would have done so already. Bombers don't take quick tours of the city before completing their missions. And still she will not be able to slow her heart rate, nor to fight her nausea. At any moment, she will scream. The bus will shake under the impact of brakes, startling Sara (if one could be any further startled, any more keyed up). It's just the brakes, she will reassure herself. The man will move as if to get off. Fixated, Sara will not move at all. It will occur to her that perhaps she's already dead, the man's already exploded and all this an imagined continuation of life instantly dreamt between impact and death.

The doors will close with a pneumatic exhalation, reminding her that people breathe, both in and out. And yet impossibly she will have continued to hold her breath. The man will not get off. He will pull on his watch again, shift from foot to foot. Now, even more disturbingly, he will begin to cradle and shift the odd shapes beneath his jacket pockets. It must be a bomb belt under there. It has to be. For whatever reason he will not have detonated it yet, but he will, surely he will, surely he must. Sara will be aghast that she elected to remain on the bus even another stop. The next stop is further, on the side of a highway that wraps around a hill. Why did she ever take the express bus when there are so few opportunities to escape?

Her body will momentarily relent. Adrenaline production will decelerate, hormones will course back to their uptakes. She breathes in and out. The man doesn't even really look Palestinian, really. So he's got some stuff in his pockets. Whatever. Life moves on. Certainly, she will not be able to afford to live with this level of mania. She will not survive if every man in a bulky jacket frightens her. Breathe in; breathe out. What's this? The man is sweating. He will wipe his face with his sleeve and then continue to nervously feel out the strange, hard edged shapes beneath his jacket with his forearms. He will twist the band of his watch back and forth on his wrist, never exposing enough for Sara to discern wiring in his sleeve's shadows. There will be no question in Sara's mind, the man's a bomber. That he won't have exploded yet will only prove that his device is somewhat faulty. (It's bound to happen, a faulty device, from time to time). Or perhaps fear will stall him, some lingering doubt temporarily staying his immolation (that's also bound to happen, but likely won't last). He will reach into his pocket and Sara will know that his hands are feeling out the connections, preparing to manually trigger his mass-immolation. Just then the bus will come to its highway-side stop. Sara will desperately push her way out to save her life. As soon as her feet will land on pavement – in the middle of nowhere basically, the wall separating Arab East Jerusalem from the highway backs the stop she's gotten off at; a steep, undeveloped hillside rises across several lanes of traffic —she will feel her breath return to normal, her vision clear. She will become aware of her sweat-wet pits and clammy palms. The bus will pull away with a grudging grind of gears and a diesel fart.

Not a hundred yards away it will explode spectacularly, first throwing Sara backwards and then sucking her into the resulting vacuum, a rain of hot fragments lightly precipitating on her trembling, prostrate body. A piece of metal will clatter out of the sky in the distance, ringing a ragged death toll.

No it won't. The bus will pull away safely, and vanish down the highway, leaving Sara stranded. Another bus will come in half an hour. Unhappily, she will face the necessity of boarding it. She will realize that she's just let a bus that did not explode slip out of her grasp, and now must take the same chances all over with another one. In fact, her actions will have increased her chance of riding with a bomber because she will now take two buses instead of one. She will refuse to let herself cry. At least, standing outside waiting for the new bus will be more pleasant than sitting cramped between all those girls. But clearly, that man was never a bomber. He probably was a Jew, for God's sake.

Fuck, I just realized that I got my, hmm. Just write it, Sarah: I got my period. You're so prude. It's a period, everyone gets them. (Though they probably don't write about them in their journals, not in real time, not at twenty-five).

—Later—

Despite double-bagging everything and putting it in the bear canister for trash, I worry that I still smell like blood. Yes, it's an irrational fear. I've been pretty irregular to begin with and wondered if taking this trip, the exercise, mild calorie deficiency, wouldn't have stopped my cycle. It came close. The flow is awfully light (though not realizing that it had begun made a bit of a mess). But bears have an amazingly keen sense of smell. I've heard recommendations against campers having sex in their tents in the lower forty-eight (which never concerned me). And I've read accounts of bears sniffing out wrapped snickers bars in tents. All this invokes the fear that some bear will pick up the faint trace of my blood and come after it. I really thought my period would stop altogether on this trip, apparently not.

My trainer suggested going on the pill to suppress everything altogether. She said it would be more convenient; I figured she thought I would have sex with someone. I wish I had gone on the pill; I don't want this here, now. Even if I wasn't susceptible to the fearful suggestion that my body has secretly sought to contact predatory bears, I would not want to deal with double-bagged used pads, cleanup, hygiene. Either way, the obscuring fog that smothered my fears in a bliss of unknowing, now threatens me. I imagine those animals, long competent at olfactory navigation, even now establishing a siege just yards from my tent site. And I can't know. You can never know anything, it turns out. Faith. Faith, faith, faith, faith faith.

But what good is faith when its primary purpose is to force one to accept the unintelligible, undecipherable twists of worldly activity as belonging to some plot beyond comprehension? What good is a faith that says everything happens for a reason when what happens is so damning? Am I to believe that my parents deserved to die while visiting their daughter in the midst of her attempt to be more religious? How can a faith like that prevent a bear from tracking down the infinitesimal scent of blood I leave behind and mauling me? This faith only tells me that I deserve it. (And if I keep on like this, I will deserve it). But, I want a faith that reassures me that evil will not happen. I want to face fear and say, "Sarah, nothing bad will happen because your God is watching out for you." Of course Hashem spoke to Adam and Eve, displayed his presence beyond all questioning—without evil, without crushed hope, without the bodies of loved ones to bury, without fear of death, why would one need to assume a god? But we are cast out of paradise. This is no paradise. And I must believe in God to stomach this rancid, fear-wracked, prolonged suffering. (It's bad enough that faith doesn't prevent evil; to think that evil happened outside a divine plan is unbearable). I want a bear to leap out of the woods and crush my head, once and for all; I pray that it doesn't happen.

There's nothing to do but go back to my future which pulls me forward. But even there, what happens?

Sure, the bus will come in half an hour, maybe a little later, a bit off schedule, to pick up Sara alongside the highway. Its bright headlights will remind her of dusk's quick passing, of the possibility of sniper fire over the wall she stands against, homemade mortars even. She'll walk up to the bus and look up at the driver, take out her ten ride pass for him to punch. But then with her left foot on the fist step, she will apologize, turn back. "But this is the only bus line that stops here, lady." No, it's the wrong bus. "Suit yourself." And he will close the door, the kneeling bus rising. Through the door panes, Sara will see the bus driver looking into traffic, and turning, hand over hand, the big flat wheel in front of him with the steady constancy of a fisherman resignedly rowing his dinghy out before dawn. Like a lantern light fading, the bus will slip away into darkness. There will be no point in hoping to board the next bus, in another half hour (or hour, depending on the schedule's vagaries). Turning defeat over defeat, with great difficulty, Sara will punch Udi's number into her cell phone.

"Can you come for me?"

"Of course. Where are you?"

"A bus stop on the highway"

"Which line? I'll just ride over to you."

"Come for me in a car."

Udi, thrilled at the invitation, its implicit pardon of his prior indiscretion, will not question her request. He will listen carefully to her directions, and promise to be there in less than twenty minutes.

Sure enough, twenty minutes later to the dot, Udi will arrive in Noah's Fiat. Sara will open the passenger door and see a bouquet of lavender, bluebells and irises in the seat.

"Going to visit someone after you drop me off?"

"What gave it away?"

"You've got these flowers on the seat. Shall I put them in the back or hold them in my lap?"

"If you don't mind holding them—"

"Then it's the least I can do since you came out here to pick me up."

"Well thank you. Do you think she'll like them?"

"They're very nice."

"Smell them."

"I can smell the lavender already."

"Does it remind you of the artic?"

"Being afraid reminds me of the artic."

"You're afraid to ride the bus."

Is that, then, where it all ends up? I struggle through my fears out here—assuming I do survive being icebound in the fog while bleeding like near-carrion—only to go home to Jerusalem and find myself too PTSD to ride a city bus? Look at me. I stink. I'm cold. I'm stuck in the middle of nowhere, at the top of the world, in a pea soup fog, afraid to go more than five meters from my tent for fear of getting lost.

I want my parents.

I'm in over my head,

I can, will, do this.

Do what? There will be no rowing today, nor tomorrow, nor likely the day after that. My father's kayak, which has brought me so far, no longer can help me. I'm stranded. I need Udi to get me now, not later in some future life. But I must break free, because there is a future life, because I must have that peace.

Sara will get into his car and they will drive to her apartment. Once in Bait viGan, Udi will circle the block until he finds an overnight parking spot. Sara won't stop him. They will get out of the car together and Udi will drape her in his heavy coat, brushing his arm across the back of her shoulders. Sara won't stop that either. When she neglects to take the flowers, Udi will hand them to her and without discussion, they will walk between the long planters lining her building's open air lobby to its elevator bank, ride up, walk down Sara's hallway, and into her apartment. This will not be the first time Udi's come up to Sara's place. But unlike last time, they will close the door, despite the religious, legal connotations.

At the dining room table, a Long Island relic, Udi will retrieve his coat from her back like a matador snapping his cape, and fold it over the back of the chair at the head of the table before seating himself in it. Sara will sit next to him, her clasped hands on the table in front of her.

"I messed up, Udi."

"Good days and bad days, Sara. That's the end of it."

"Why don't you exploit this opportunity to say how much we're alike and how you were right at the café and everything else."

"Would you want that?"

"As much as I imagine myself here, I imagine myself as a suicide bomber wandering from bus to bus, searching for myself before exploding."

Udi will look at Sara, at me, his handsome soldier's features ill-equipped to express what he will feel: confusion, repulsion.

"You *imagine* yourself?"

"I imagine myself as a Palestinian double of me. An uncertain woman bundled in layers—clothing, bomb, clothing—wandering between buses, unsure of when to explode, unsure of why, but knowing that she must, knowing it will be a relief. And what I know about this person, who is me, and who I imagine, but that she does not know about herself, is that she's waiting to find me on one of those buses. One day, as she wanders aimlessly from potentially caustic moment to moment, she'll see a young woman with facial scarification dressed in long clothing who looks like herself. Mimicking me, she'll trace the edge of her left ear, discovering for the first time that it is tattered like mine. I won't ask how she came to such an identical injury and she won't speak to me either. Maybe we'll try and flee from each other. I don't know. What is sure is that when that moment comes she will detonate, and the two of us will both be gone. In the morgue, they will accidentally mix our bodies and so the final death count will only tally half of me, and will accidentally tally half of a suicide bomber whose death Israel would not officially chose to acknowledge. Our burials will be similarly mixed—an arm of hers attached to remnants of my torso. Perhaps my head will end up wherever they put the bombers' bodies—"

"They cremate the bodies."

"How do you know?"

"It's common knowledge. They hope that denying proper burial will act as a deterrent."

"It doesn't seem to be working."

"No, not particularly."

"I imagine her unable to think properly, vaguely afraid, some asinine phrase circling through her head—a song lyric, or maybe an instruction. She forgets things and then remembers them, panics that she's forgotten them. All the while, wondering when the right moment will be, hating her hesitation, trying to focus. She's a grenade with its arm wedged against the side of a munitions box and its pin pulled out, all in the back of a pickup truck with a shot suspension, racing down a pocked dirt road, waiting for the right bump to set the whole thing off. And then she remembers, in a hot flash, someone telling her, she's not sure who, that if she focuses on killing a particular person, makes herself into a bullet against that one individual, then it will be easy."

"And that's when you see each other?"

"That's when we see each other."

Udi will studiously remove Sara's left hand from her right, gently prying the fingers lose, as if he was untangling a knot or defusing a bomb. The hand free, and Sara looking away, Udi will rub her palm gently with his fingertips, then slowly work his way up, massaging her wrist with his thumbs. Sara will fidget with her free arm, look away from Udi, threaten to break away from him altogether, from this clear violation of shomrei negiah. The silence of her apartment, the cold emptiness of all her things will weigh on her. She will turn to him, her mouth full of silent words, a gasping fish mouth, a screaming beached whale. Now tracing gentle circles along her forearms, Udi will cock his head from side to side, falsely inquisitive, miming the mute to speech. Her free hand will slap down on the table like a hull breaching a wave, a fat thwack stinging her fingertips, her wrist. And mean-while, the soporific fondling of her arm will continue, repulsive and welcome, a dream-drug whose incumbent inoculation she fights.

"What, Sara?"

"I don't know. I don't know. I don't know."

"Tell me."

"Just stop it."

She will pull her arm away from him, ghost tingles mesmer-izing its flesh, betraying her will. His hangdog face and submis-sive, sympathetic willingness will drive her to a near internal fury and a strong desire to grab his shadowed cheeks in both hands and kiss him, hard, her nails biting into his skin, leaving marks, her teeth driving against his lips, mashing them, making them swell purple, like a plum's skin. She will want to hit him.

"I'm afraid, Udi. I'm afraid."

"I know, Sara."

"I'm afraid because there's this girl in the Arctic and the ice has closed in around her and she's trapped in her tent and she can't move and winter is coming. I'm afraid that the weather won't change again and she'll be stranded, slowly running out of food, unable to move, nowhere to go. I'm afraid that she will die there by herself in the cold. I'm afraid that none of this will happen."

"It's all right, Sara. You've made it. You got out of the Arctic. You're here."

"You don't understand, Udi. I'm afraid that the ice will trap me, that I won't escape, that I'll die there."

"Be here, Sara."

"I want to be."

"Be with me."

"I'm trying to live so that I can be with you."

"You are with me so live."

"You can't understand."

"Try me."

"You can't because it would be impossible for you to understand that all this life only exists as long as I experience it. That if I die, you die with me, that my doppelganger is the destroyer of all I would live for, not just my life itself, because my life creates all of it. You can't possibly see that I am icebound and fogbound for the third day in a row, only mostly recovered from a massive hangover begotten by a bottle of near-mythic whiskey that's still half-full, fully potent. Udi, I can drink the rest of that bottle and walk out onto the ice in my underwear and in an hour it'll all be over—but I want to be with you. I want to live for you. I want to survive and believe that you can really love me."

"Sara, I do love you."

"But I'm trapped by the ice."

"You don't have to be."

Udi will recapture her hands, both of them this time. Panic will share space on his face with patronizing sympathy, his lustful overcaring.

"You don't understand, Udi. I am in a tent, in the Canadian Arctic, and I don't know that I'll make it."

"Of course you will. You told me once about being trapped

by ice on your trip. And look at you now, you're here. You broke free."

"Really? What happened?"

"Let me try to remember."

Udi will guide Sara by her two hands, up from her seat and across to his lap. Willingly, slowly, like a forgiven child, she will sit side-saddle across his legs, demurely.

"Tell me, Udi."

He will nuzzle her good ear, inhale her hair, slowly, casually encircle her waist.

"The ice broke free."

"How?"

"The wind came, blew the fog out, and sent the ice to sea. The sun returned and conditions improved. You got back in your boat and you rowed. Favorable conditions allowed you to make up for lost time. You were fine."

"Tell me again."

After furtively glancing at the hands Sara's placed on his shoulders, Udi will resume.

"Strong winds came from the south in the night and blew the ice out to sea. In the morning, the sun burnt through what was left of the—"

Sara will stop nibbling on Udi's earlobe and murmur, "Keep telling me."

"The sun burnt off what was left of the fog and you quickly broke down your camp. You repacked your kayak and launched it into light, following seas. You easily breached the surf and made good time heading eastward. The weather held and soon you were out of danger."

Sara will have brought her left hand down Udi's side, feeling his hard chest muscles, ribs, ease into the soft side of his stomach. Her right hand will have strayed down his back, her mouth now on his neck, biting and kissing, tasting almond aftershave and sweat. Udi will move his head to kiss her, briefly his lips meet hers. She will want to press into him, to cry, to shove her tongue into his mouth, to bite, to wail. Instead, she will take her hand out of his lap, grab his chin and turn his head away from her.

"Tell me again how the ice broke, how I lived."

"One night, after several days spent pacing your campsite, your tent whipped in the wind. Startled from sleep, still in a dream-daze, you imagined you heard the fire-roar of wind in trees, the creaking of winter-bare branches in a storm. You braced yourself for danger but slipped back out of consciousness."

Sara will lick the underside of Udi's chin, his nascent stubble abrading her tongue; his jaw will press her jaw down as he whispers. Her hand will find his shirt buttons and expertly, singly undo them. He will move a hand onto her thighs, ok. But when he will reactivate it, begin to search her out, she will slap him; he must not be distracted, will not be.

"You woke early, the tent calm now, sunlight glowing against its yellow walls. Occasional gusts still whipped by, rippling the fabric in waves like a string of prayer flags on a mountain. Still inside your sleeping bag, you pulled on the mid-layer of insulation that you slept with at your feet: fleece coveralls, wool socks, hat, fleece sweater. God that feels good, Sara."

"Don't interrupt."

"You pulled on your neoprene booties and stepped out of the tent shivering, immediately blinking in a strong sun barely five degrees over the mountains. Eyes shaded, half-crouching, you turned towards the ocean."

His shirt completely open, Sara will kiss across Udi's now-exposed chest, her fingers tangling in the gray and black hair on his stomach, her right hand will claw at the nape of his neck. Her tongue will find one of his nipples inside an eddy of black hair; she'll pull it into her mouth, suck, then bite hard, making him yelp.

"The ocean was clear, pancakes of ice still littered the shore above the high tide line, but the water was open as far out as you could see. You hurried back to your campsite and cooked a quick breakfast of oatmeal and tea over your whisperlite stove, then hurriedly stashed your gear back in your boat, downing a meat-stick while you dismantled your tent."

Sara will turn, straddling Udi, and push his shirt off of his shoulders, feeling down his arms' curves. Her tongue will dally in the cleft of his neck, run rings along the seam of his chest. With the backs of her nails, she'll scrape his skin in long, needy strokes.

"With the tent fastened, you dragged your craft out into the surf, half-running. After days of inactivity, you elected not to use your sail, but row instead. You wanted to feel strength in your arms, muscle ache, blood pumping. You waited as a receding wave sucked the water from under your boat, pulled it slightly further out, got in, and braced yourself. A swell broke over your bow, pouring off the sides before reaching you and the cockpit. Suddenly buoyant, you began to row hard, the wave pulled you north. And then you'd broken free of the surf, were safely out over deep water. Leaning right, you pulled the boat around east, and set off."

Scared and eager, Sara will look down at the tab of Udi's belt she's just pulled out of one half of its buckle. He will suck his gut in as she pulls the belt backwards to lift out the buckle's tongue. And then it will be free, flow easily apart. She will notice a fresh crease in the black leather across the hole she's unfastened and older, deeper creases further towards the tip. Next she will open the button of his trousers, only to find that an internal clasp keeps them closed as well.

"Beneath you, the water was brown with silt runoff, but further out, it turned an oily sunset blue. Exuberant, you rowed hard, warmth and pain mixing across your back and along the tops of your shoulders. For the first time in weeks, you reveled in your surroundings. White mountains sparkled in a wall of barren, articulated mass to your left, rising behind a landscape covered with snow. Over them, a blinding orange sun hung like an over-sized set piece, disproportionately present. In front of you, ocean bent away towards the thin line of island shores far distant. You wondered if the silt washing around you wasn't actually McKenzie runoff and not a local phenomenon of the melting snow at all. Cold air cycled through your lungs, and you leaned further into your task, sure, certain, and free."

His pants undone, Sara will slowly slip her hands around Udi's waist. She will draw them over the sides of his butt, feel his firm, warm haunches inside her palms, his boxers silky, worn cotton secreting the backs of her fingers, palms, wrists. As she draws her hands up over his thighs, in towards his crotch, she will feel his breath shorten, his legs tense, and his hands jerk, desperate to move, confined by her will.

"Despite your urge to rush forward, your training overtook you, forced you to adopt a steady, sustainable rhythm, a commitment to the long haul ahead. Though you hungered for the end of your journey, wished to row frantically for days on end without food, without sleep, fully exploiting your twenty-two hours of light, and perhaps the hours of dark as well, you slowed, realized your goal was at hand, controlled yourself. Midday, you took a break; stopped rowing, and ate granola bars while drifting, slowing, holding your position with your rudder."

Sara will slip a hand behind the small of Udi's back and pull herself forward, hiking her skirt up in the process. Pressing her body against his, her breasts into his chest, her pelvic bone into the top of his crotch, she will moan into his neck, grind down. He will start to stop; then he will resume in a broken, fast paced whisper as she brushes the bottom lip of her open mouth along the ridge of jaw below his ear, her eyes slitted.

"You finished your lunch. You started rowing again. The ocean was calmer than it had been for most of your trip. Everything worked well. You'd found your groove at last. The cold air and the sun conspired to keep your body temperature perfect. For the first time you realized you'd miss the arctic after you left."

I can't do this. Not yet. It's too early. It's not me.

"Why? Is something wrong?"

It would never happen; I can't pretend that it would ever happen.

"Sara, are you ok?"

Sara will pull herself off of Udi, pushing her skirt down with her hands, and then jam her hands into her hair. Her damp panties cooling around her crotch will smack her, make her shiver. She will look over at Udi's disarray—open shirt, open pants, erection fading beneath his boxers, which are damp, damp with her—and she will want to scream or vomit or hurt herself. Udi will quickly stand up and turn away from her as he buttons himself up and tucks himself in.

"I'm sorry, Udi, this isn't right; it isn't me."

"Don't play with me, Sara."

"I shouldn't have gotten you all worked up."

"This is cruel. You didn't have to do any of this. I would have been happy to just hold you."

"I'm orthodox. I want to believe. I want to observe. I want to be rescued by Hashem."

"This isn't right, Sara, to treat someone this way."

For one thing, I have my period. If I keep on, I'll attract bears.

"Why didn't you say it was your period?"

Udi will turn back towards her, smoothing the front of his shirt. Facing him, Sara will notice they've adopted identical poses, hands flat against their waists, heads tilted forward, legs slightly more than shoulder width apart—ready stances, action stances, the soldier and the adventurer preparing to grapple with—

"I wouldn't have even if it wasn't."

"What bears?" Udi will gesture broadly with one hand, indicate the whole of the apartment. "What bears are you afraid of, Sara?"

"You can't understand Udi. You have to stop being rational, stop questioning, and just trust me. Trust me."

"Trust you that there are bears?"

"There are bears behind the fog, still hungry, still searching for food—urgently searching for food, fattening up before hibernating." Udi will blink, and in his face's softened expression, Sara will see an entirely new wariness, the very caution she's feared to find in him since the very beginning: pussyfooted tenderness towards damaged goods. "Don't look around this apartment like I'm crazy. It's a mirage. All of it is a projection of my fantasy, Udi. But the real truth is that I'm lying in a tent, writing in my diary, hoping that the storm breaks so I can proceed. And I have my period. And I'm afraid that if—and with my period—and—well—that everything united the smell—blood—will draw bears."

He will sit back down in the same chair, sigh, lift his hands and then drop them, sigh. "You know, Sara—"

"What, Udi?"

"Well it's just that—"

"What, Udi? Just that what?"

"Fucking hell. If you're fantasizing everything. Then why can't you fantasize that we have sex? Why do you have a fantasy all twisted up and convoluted? If this is a fantasy, then why do I have free will?"

Sara will sit down as well, somewhat cowed.

"I don't know."

"You don't know what?"

"Any of it. I don't know the answers to any of it." She'll reach across to him, gingerly make for his hand, but he'll move it out of reach, into his lap.

"I'm sorry, Udi." He'll begin to crack; she'll see it in the softening of his lips, the droop of his shoulders. "Udi, I do love you."

"Maybe I should go home, Sara."

"Only if you want to."

"Do you want me to stay?"

"I don't know."

Udi will stand up, pull on his coat, and walk over to Sara's chair. He'll quickly cup her chin and kiss her forehead. "Udi—" But he will continue on to the door, and she won't stop him.

And so there I am, alone. Even in my future, I end up by myself, sitting in my apartment, lonely, afraid. But there is a future beyond that moment, Sarah. It may well happen that Udi will return, that time will elapse and he and Sara will marry. In time, Jerusalem will cease to be a battlefield. Your fear will fade.

Maybe. But, now it seems likely that I will die here, in my tent, terrified of the deepened gloom outside.

*Elohim yechananu viyivrachanu, yaayr panav eetanu, selah.*
> God will favor us, and bless us, he will turn his face to us, Selah
> He will make the path clear to the world, every people will cry unto him.
> He will be known to the nations, our God, known to every nation.
> He will be rejoiced and feared in all other countries because he will cause them to judge honestly towards the path.

This is what I remember from a letter my father sent me:

> Patchwork cement plugs fill in for trees razed to make way for rescue trucks; orange checks cover the backdoors

of buildings, dated by search completion; the Deutsche Bank building wears pinstriped black over its broken face, and only in these tragic alleys can I capture and live in my fear. Paddling out into the Atlantic, mild water waving off into rounded blue, sine, cosine, sine, sine, cosine, sine—infinity, for me, means no deity, but a mathematical summation of emptiness; I scrambled for shore, heartbeat racing, scared, terrified. I'm only all right where I can cry, where I can see damage, scars, rent fabric and ashes.

## August 24

Much has happened; my doom is sealed.

Two nights ago, just as Udi predicted, wind blew from the south, I woke to my tent fabric rippling then snapping at gusts, like a sagging sail drifting into the trade-winds' tailings. Sunlight lit the walls cheery yellow; between the wind, I could hear surf; I knew the water would be open. I sat up in my sleeping bag and inhaled crisp ocean air. Hastily pulling on a fleece and booties, I scrambled out of the tent. For the first time in days, I could see where I was. My tracks were melting in the sun, and the snow covering my boat had formed an icy glaze. And there it was, an arc of wave-eroded snow, followed by sand and then open ocean, green murky sea. I stretched my arms out under the sun and whooped. My stomach flip-flopped with anxiety and anticipation—and then I remembered: it was Shabbat. I couldn't row.

Glumly, I looked out over the water, and then walked back through icy slush to my log, found my butt's indentation on its snow-covering, and sat down. Clear water; no travel. Fuck. I reasoned with myself that if Hashem had opened the sea for my passage, then surely I would not be penalized for observing his most important sacrament, the Sabbath. I thought back to Rabbi Shem Tov telling us how the Moshiach, the Messiah, could be forced into coming if just once, every Jew in the world observed Shabbat. That's all it would take: one Saturday of every Jew not turning on or off lights, not working, not cooking, not killing, not traveling. One Shabbat of no one TRAVELING and the messiah would arrive on his white donkey blowing the other horn from the ram Abraham sacrificed in Isaac's stead up on Mount Moriah. At the time, it seemed so frustrating that the Jews hadn't done that already, hadn't forced the point, brought God to earth, ended this madness of living, of terror, of grief.

But there I was yesterday, sitting on the log, staring out at the first clear water in days, *days*. And it was hard to have faith. All the while that I sat there trying to muster Shabbat prayers to my lips, a mad drummer thumped out, go, go, go. Now is the time, now is the time, now is the time, now.

And so I began preparing to embark from my then-well-settled camp. I moved slowly at first, like a nervous escapee, timidly, delicately, creeping through tall grass barely past the prison walls before reaching the tree-line and breaking into a sprint. What I would give to be within the tree-line now. Boat packed, excitement tingling along my scalp, I pushed off into light breaking seas and easily cleared the surf. My body eagerly rushed back into activity, arms pulling long broad strokes of clean water past my bow. I hit my stride, my groove, my pace, perfect paddling freedom like I've rarely experienced on this trip. Gale remnants whipped by chasing rippled streaks of freshly freed water and lifting my tangled hair from my shoulders. I wanted to shout with glee; I did shout out; I caught myself shouting: Shemah, Yisroel, Adonai Elohenu, Adonoi Echad—and instantly felt guilty. I couldn't declare God's unity, sovereignty, while breaking Shabbat. Yet I kept rowing.

And what if yesterday was the day, the one day that every Jew but me observed Shabbat? What if my not rowing would have brought the moshiach posthaste? Then I wouldn't have had to row ever again. But it's hard to believe that every Jew observed Shabbat, or that even half did, or ever will. Yet if they all went through this mental exercise just once, and we all chose opposite of the way I chose yesterday, then that would be enough, but they won't ever do that. And if never, then will the moshiach never come? Will the pain of this world never be ended? I'd rather not dwell on these questions. One must will herself to faith.

The day was so beautiful that my spirits couldn't stay down. Sure, the temperature hardly rose above forty degrees Fahrenheit at any point, but the sun, low-angled as it was, warmed me, as did exercise. The cool air refreshed my lungs with each inhale. Snowmelt returned to the sea in dark rivulets splicing angled sections of gravel beach into a continuous line of safe landings, if necessary. I rationalized that Hashem meant me to row, Shabbat or no. And likewise, since this all seemed to follow Udi's predictions, I imagined that the broad easy beaches were in fact prelude to the McKenzie's mouth, that I'd already passed Shingle Point somehow. From there it would only be a short distance further to Aklivuk and home.

Now I believe nothing but Hashem. I realize that yesterday was a tease and a test, a test that I failed. I paddled through the day, singing zmirot to myself, the cheerful Shabbat songs seeming appropriate to a day so obviously a divine gift. The rhythm of the waves, my oscillating paddle strokes, and the wind all conspired to drive me forward. In the late afternoon (which differed little from either morning or noon), formation upon formation of small orange breasted birds fanned out across the water, heading west. They broke across the point of my kayak, granting me a berth only several feet wide, so that as they passed, roughly eye level, the world was made of colorful wings. And the water beneath them danced with long shadows of their aggressive flight, exaggerated black forms flitting across a metallic green surface against a blue-orange sky. My heart fled to my mouth and I thought: this is creation.

Immediately I remembered my father, and I tried as hard as I could to enjoy the sight on his behalf rather than dwell on my loss, his death. But melancholy wound through my elation. Even when the sun started to sink behind the mountains, and the long snowy contours of land turned gold with its refraction, I couldn't help but cry—both because my father never lived to see this and because I don't enjoy it enough for him. Life is very hard. Each gift comes at great expense and I can only hope that the difficulty of the test is a measure of the ultimate reward. I'm so tired of living sometimes.

And even if my father is in Shamaim, and he and my mother were looking down at me, they can't have been happy. No, I cannot entertain an idyllic daydream in which he nods to my mother and points out the sun-sparkled water tipping off my paddle blades and says, "See? That's why I wanted to go there." No, I cannot imagine that yesterday my father took pride and comfort in that the kayak hull he crafted so deftly with his banker's hands was ferrying his daughter onward with such great efficacy. No, if my parents are in Shamaim, then they knew the truth about yesterday. They knew that every stroke further forward took me one step more outside Hashem's grace. They knew that I wasn't just traveling on Shabbat, but that my travel literally carried me away from salvation.

Because here is the awful truth: after my longest day yet in the boat, after a record day, I pulled in to shore, ate a cold dinner as to not cook on the Shabbat, erected my tent (a violation) and went soundly, peacefully to sleep. And when I awoke in the morning, this morning, mere hours ago, my tent walls bowed in the wind like a galleon in a gale. Eyes squinted against stinging, sideways snow, I pulled my sore, stiff limbs out of the tent and made my hunched over way towards a foreordained spectacle. Great, grinding slabs of ice stretched from shore out past visibility (itself not far, in the storm). They hadn't yet welded to each other and so crashed and boomed like warring barges in some surreal bumper derby. My doom was sealed, is sealed. Where was my faith in Hashem? How could I have not trusted that if he cleared the waters one day, surely he would keep them clear if I kept his Sabbath? Shabbat is the most sacred thing of all! Solomon called it God's bride! And I rode away from his grace, his watchful eye. There is no hope.

At best I can spend my time now doing penance, hoping for forgiveness enough that when cold and winter and hunger finish overtaking me I will ascend into the company of my Lord and no longer be alone. For now, clearly, he has turned his back on me just as I turned away from his sacrament.

I am going to die.

I don't know which would be worse: the current storm destroying my tent, in which case I'll quickly die of exposure, or, surviving only to remain here, trapped, only to die slowly once my rations run out. And if the latter, I wonder whether I'll exhaust my supply of food or fuel first. It would be easier to run out of food, and slowly starve, my body shutting down, piece by piece, unable to keep itself warm. Running out of fuel carries a particular horror. One moment, I will be in full health, and then the next, I will find myself unable to convert snow into water. Starvation may be a fine way to die, but surely dehydration is not. As the gaping maw in my stomach grows, I will attempt to fill it with dry food, eventually turning to my dehydrated stores even, anything. I'll melt handfuls of snow in my mouth to loosen the dry leather of my tongue, my cheeks. You can't get enough water eating snow, it's mostly empty air. And even what you do manage to eke out from its crystalline mass deprives your body of more calories in lost heat than you gain in hydration.

I'm very scared.

I'm scared of a painful death that follows a long wait with little to do but anticipate and imagine that death. I'm scared because in the hinter-light of the storm, out on the thrashing ice floes, I saw demons. They rode on frozen plates as they smashed into each other, dancing, laughing, howling. From floe to floe they leapt across the seas, teasing and taunting each other, fueling the chaos of ice, wind and snow. I can't have seen what I saw. Tricks of light, fear, guilt, horror combine and collide and emerge as fantastical agents of my demise. Yet what if they are Hashem's minions sent to turn weather meant for my passage into a crushing jail? I can't think about it.

But, looking back at these pages, I cannot refute a simple fact. I am afraid of dying just as much as I don't want to live. Given everything, I wonder why I don't simply leave the tent, walk out onto that pitching deck of the ice outside, and keep on until either I fall beneath it or sit down depleted and give up; all this struggle, all this pain, would be over by tomorrow night at the latest. It's not as if I'm sitting around hoping for a brighter day. The facts are clear. I'm not going to make it. For whatever reason, I've missed the window of safe travel. So why don't I just end it quickly, proactively, with strength and dignity? I'd like to say I don't because Hashem forbids suicide. I'd like to say that like Sir Scott, I believe attitude is everything, and find it more important to die hoping impossible hope than to despair (though one of his men, who knew he was holding the party back, walked off into the snow to save them the decision to leave him). Yes, like good old Robert Scott, I'll end my days in a tent not far from my goal. But I only persevere because I'm afraid of dying. I'm only sticking this out because it's easier to struggle though several painful miserable weeks until death than to get it over with quickly by my own hand. I'm pathetic.

I just remembered that I have my whiskey; all is not lost.

## *August 25*

What's the point? I'm surrounded by ice, hemmed in by wind.

Udi, if you are out there somewhere, I want you to know that I love you.

## *August 26*

I got a little drunk Sunday, and really drunk Monday, and now am out of whiskey. So that's the end of that. Drinking, not drinking, chucking the bottle into the sea, recovering it from the ocean, taping it to my bow like a masthead maiden, and finally finishing it. Whiskey all gone. Sarah mostly gone, too. Drunk as I was I didn't slip into the violent, animated rage that marked my first artic romance with the bottle. It's too cold outside and I'm too tired to run around screaming and breaking things. I drank the way my father and I used to play game after game of cribbage on a travel-sized board during our trip through Puget Sound when rain confined us to our tent every evening, just passing the time. Take a sip, wait for sleep, sip some more, wish for sleep. Then at least, we'd look forward to sleep, because when we woke up, it would be light out, and we'd row even in the rain. Rowing in the rain along that verdant coast added a wildness to the temporal rainforest stretching down from the Olympic Range, whose summits lay behind waves of mist and rain and fog. Here it's always wild, obviously, and there's no point in sleeping, because it just means waking up with renewed energy and no way to expend it. It's not like I'm anticipating a brighter day and sleeping away the wait; this is all I've got. I might as well be awake for it. I can't row through solid ice. Besides, when I force myself outside to empty my pee bottle or squat, I can hardly stay erect the wind is so strong. Three days of wind and the tent remains standing.

On the first several nights of the Puget Sound trip, my father desperately forced conversation. Despite our close relationship, largely fostered by rowing, he seemed to believe that at nearly seventeen I must be leading some secret existence. He was determined to do his paternal duty and ferret out the nature of my love life, limn the parameters of my drug experimentation, determine the nature of my nascent independence. Of course there wasn't much to say; his interrogation made me squirm with embarrassment and answer in half sentences describing the rumored activities of several lesser friends.

All those friends are gone; I don't talk to anyone from high school anymore. My father's brother and sister held a small memorial service in Northport after I returned there for rehab. Some of my mother's friends showed up, as did my father's coworkers, and of course his two siblings. Then there were journalists from local papers, including the *New York Times*, writing follow-up stories on the man who survived 9/11 only to die in Israel while visiting his daughter. Over my time in Northport, more than a few reporters asked to interview me. And when it became clear that I wouldn't speak to the press about either my parents' death or my planned trip, I lost my sponsorship deal with Cold Summit Equipment and had to outfit this trip on my own. (In and of itself, no big deal. What else would I use my inheritance towards?) And of course Marie was there. But the only person from my high school, the only remnant of my slumber-party toe-nail painting youth there, was a young man taking pictures for *The North Shore Daily* who asked if we hadn't gone to school together.

He looked at my long dark clothing, my covered neck and wrists. He saw the brace protruding below my skirt along my left leg, and the cane I used on that side still, the fresh red scars on my face. At least the hat I'd begun wearing covered my damaged ear. I remembered that he too was Jewish, though not religious, and as he looked at me, I saw repulsion mix with and overcome his journalist's inquisitiveness. I knew that he thought I'd chosen an awful and wrong life and now what stood before him was a willing victim of the worst of many worlds, someone who'd foregone the American dream, traded the ideas of progress and liberation for fundamentalism and something just short of an Islamic woman's garb. He saw someone who in his mind had willingly gone to the heartland of the century's greatest scourge, terrorism, and brought otherwise innocent parents there, paid for it. And now he saw a leper, a difficult sight, a possible opportunity to advance his career by documenting the Other in breathtaking terms.

"Yes," I told him. "I think we were in high school together."

Marie materialized at my side like an ever-present security guard and the photographer turned his eyes towards her even as he offered me his hand.

"She can't shake," said Marie. "It's her religion."

He lifted both his hands, and tilted his head, indicating all was well, and turned his full attention towards her, assessing, I'm sure, her rather lovely aesthetic qualities.

"Do you mind if I take a picture of the two of you together for the paper?"

I told him I'd rather he didn't. Marie emphasized, don't, and he walked away. But I still saw, and see, that picture the way he conceived it. I imagine him titling it "Old Friends," shooting it in black and white, reveling in the contrast between the dark, scarred survivor and her effervescent, pristine, nubile friend, a slightly out-of-focus cemetery and funeral party in the background. I see him daydreaming about national wires picking up his chance-of-a-lifetime shot and beautiful women, long out of touch, calling him to express their admiration of his artistic vision, his bold choice to eliminate color from that stark scene. He probably tells his buddies about that lost photo over beers at local pubs still, descrying the one that got away, trying to seem sympathetic to my plight while denigrating my base character and ultimate life choices. I never saw anything of my high school class again after that. Though, the woman serving me coffee at Starbucks and the junior partner at the law firm handling my parents' estate might well both have been alumni of my class. Who knows?

My mother had a far better sense of my day to day inner development. She didn't worry that I was smoking pot, or snorting lines in the atrium ceilinged foyers of my classmates' absentee-parent mini-mansions. She knew very well that I was neither invited to those sexualized forays nor wanted to attend. This worried her more than anything, for she read my apathetic approach towards north shore living for what it was, a spiritual-seeker's dismissal of an empty life. She recognized the potential for my t'shuvah to Hashem and it worried her. Perhaps she discussed it with my father and in all likelihood he dismissed it as a phase, or maybe he even recognized it as something desirable. Certainly, throughout my warring with my mother, his primary complaints were that I lived too far away and that I fought with my mother, not that I'd adopted the faith of my forefathers.

My mother's anger at the Holocaust, that it happened, translated into a bizarre distaste for Judaism tinged with paranoia. Though she hadn't gone so far as to intermarry, I think she secretly hoped that I would, and that she would have grandchildren who'd made it to the other side, escaped Judaism and its many burdens. And I guess I can understand that. Our people seem to suffer disproportionately. The secular Sunday school classes my parents sent me to were history classes that essentially listed all the hells my people have toured: In the past century alone there were the pogroms of Russia and Poland, the fable of the Elders of Zion and its resultant pogroms, the restriction on job and housing opportunities in the United States which persevered well into the 1950s. Then, of course, there was the Holocaust, but that hardly ended things. Following the Shoah, the Allied forces found they had no immediate place to repatriate the survivors and temporarily reinterred many of them back in former camps. Britain certainly wasn't letting them into Palestine, though many made it there despite that failing empire's enmity. After Israel won her independence, the Arab nations massacred and/or expelled their long persecuted Jewish populations. In all, about 800,000 Jews were uprooted by Muslim nations ranging from Morocco to Iran between 1948 and 1968. Even China forced its 20,000 Jews out. And those Jews that survived the Shoah only to find themselves stuck in Stalinist Russia were subjected to horrible persecution and frequent murder. Now, at the dawn of the twenty-first century, suicide bombers besiege the gathering places of Israel's young and old, the Arab nations are once again disseminating the Protocols of the Elders of Zion as gospel; Europe has made a pastime of burning synagogues and renewed a time-honored fashion of hating Jews and siding against Israel. Even in the United States, the mindless popular opinion of college youth believes that Israel is evil, Jews are self-serving and disproportionately influential, while somehow, bizarrely, the perpetrators of the greatest loss of civilian life on American soil in a single attack EVER are defended, for fuck's sakes DEFENDED as only levying what America, as an imperial power, was long due.

Even I am persecuted, out here, by ice-riding demons and a trip I can not complete. Why?

I've got a hangover. I'm bored. I keep fiddling with the whale bone I'd meant to give to Udi. It's a strange thing to wait for death. I'm not really so much annoyed as impatient for something to happen. There's not much to do in the tent but write in this journal and sit around trying to stay warm. I look forward to melting snow, to cooking, to eating. All are activities that require preparation, decision making, deliberate steps. But I'm also reluctant to melt too much snow. Now that I no longer direct my energies towards survival, I find myself making choices that will influence the kind of death I'll have. I really don't want to die because I've run out of water after burning all my fuel. That would definitely be the most painful option. In fact, if I do run out of fuel, I may well take a drastic step like walking out onto the sea ice. Anything's better than lying here and drying out. I much prefer the soporific succumbing that follows hydrated starvation. (There's a religious prohibition against placing oneself in the way of certain danger, a prohibition that led to a ban on new people smoking (existing smokers were grandfathered). I wonder if I have violated that prohibition by being here, if my choice to take this trip was itself tantamount to suicide. And if so, I wonder whether actual suicide might not be a sin in my case, or rather, might only be a sin I've already committed, and so not wrong. But then I'm too afraid to take that step anyway, right?)

I thought to write more about my adventures with Udi and Dalia, but now that future life will never come to pass. Much as I want to, I cannot instill faith in the events I imagined would transpire. They are dying with me.

I think to recite psalms, but all that comes to me is the book of Job. I'm no longer asking for deliverance from danger. I'm convinced my fate is sealed.

## August 27

Blah, blah, blah, blah, blah, blah, blah, blah, blah, blah, blah, blah, blah, blah, blah, blah, blah, blah, blah, blah, blah, blah, blah, blah, blah, blah, blah, blah, blah, blah, blah, blah, blah, blah, blah, blah, blah, blah, blah, blah, blah, blah, blah, blah, blah, blah, blah, blah, blah, blah, blah, blah, blah, blah, blah, blah, blah, blah, blah, blah, blah, blah, blah, blah, blah, blah, blah, blah, blah, blah, blah, blah, blah, blah, blah, blah, blah, blah, blah, blah, blah, blah, blah, blah, blah, blah, blah, blah, blah, blah, blah, blah, blah, blah, blah, blah, blah, blah, blah, blah, blah, blah, blah, blah, blah, blah, blah, blah, blah, blah, blah, blah, blah, blah, blah, blah, blah, blah, blah, blah, blah, blah, blah, blah, blah, blah, blah, blah, blah, blah, blah, blah, blah, blah, blah, blah, blah, blah, blah, blah, blah, blah, blah, blah, blah, blah, blah, blah, blah, blah, blah, blah, blah, blah, blah, blah, blah, blah, blah.
Don't tell anyone, but I don't want to die.

## *August 28*

The lunar month of Av has always been the worst month for the Jews. Both the first and second temples were destroyed on the ninth of Av (August 7th this year, three weeks ago today). Weddings and court dates are avoided. It is the winter of Hashem's love, the eleventh lunar month. It should come as no surprise then, that I've been stuck out here most of the month of Av, that this is the month plagued with demons and loneliness and grief and boredom. Elul begins tomorrow but I am not confident that the demons will disappear, much as I would welcome any change in my fortunes (don't the Inuit have a September whaling season? Shouldn't there be open water then?).

The demons are outside all of the time now. For the most part I ignore them. They run away when I go out to collect snow, or relieve myself. But I can see their dark red shapes dancing away through the driving snow and thick mists. When I'm in the tent they'll creep right up against the walls. I know they're there because all of a sudden the wind will stop blowing on just one spot, indicating a sheltering presence—not that the demons are sheltering per se—they're growing bolder. And then yesterday (I think it was yesterday) late in the afternoon (as best as I can judge time) they took up a new game. While I'm sitting in my sleeping bag staring out at nothing, the tent filled with the dim yellow light of storm obscured sun through the walls, the light of an overcast shadow glowing through yellow fabric, I heard a voice directly behind my head say my name. Just that, Sarah. I spun around, snapped out of my daze, and stared at the tent wall, heart rate full-on accelerating. And then I hear another voice, similar, also directly behind me say my name. Except the second time, it says, Sara. Suddenly there I am, taunted by demons, one saying my English name, the other my Hebrew name. I thought, maybe

I'm already dead, and these are minions of Gayhenom taunting me as I make my way towards judgment. But almost immediately I became aware of an overwhelming need to urinate. I was sure I was alive. I was less sure that I wanted to venture outside, though. I reached down into my sleeping bag and found my pee bottle. Mostly full, much too full to pee into. I held it for a minute, waiting, willing the urge away. Nothing doing. Finally, I pulled on my down top and my shell over it and my booties and crawled into the vestibule, momentarily sealing myself in after zipping the main tent door shut. I unzipped the outside door and it ripped from my hands in the wind. Grey light and snow and wind and in the distance I could see red and brown shapes dancing away out towards the ice. I squeezed my eyes shut and when I opened them again there was nothing but the storm chilling me quickly and the still unsecured tent door flapping like a wildly waved pennant.

I hurried over to my spot, took care of business and emptied the bottle. While I was out, I figured I'd walk over to the kayak and bring back a couple of packs of noodles and a few energy bars. As I approached it I could immediately see that the boat's silhouette was broken and uneven, the layer of wind-smoothed snow blanketing it disrupted. I got closer and could see tracks leading from the top of my boat both to the sea and to the tundra to the west. Each slightly larger than my hand, they belonged to four-toed webbed claws. Demons! Why the demons chose to dance back and forth on my boat I could not tell, do not know, but it bodes ill. (Or, it bodes as ill as anything can bode when one waits for an unwelcome yet sure death). The front hatch over my food was almost entirely cleared of snow. A new chill crept into my bones; this confirmed a divine sentencing of my demise. If Hashem is willing to let me see his secret world, the spiritual beings that confirm heaven and gayhenom and all that's in between, then surely, I am not meant to rejoin the ranks of the living. I grabbed the supplies I wanted and hurried back to my tent.

Back inside, I prepared dinner, laying down in my sleeping bag with my arms out so that I could work the stove in the vestibule. The sweet smell of cooking gas blended with boiling spaghetti-water's aroma and a wave of normalcy knocked me off keel. Everything seemed fine. I could have been away for a weekend along the Connecticut coastline, or camping in the Catskills. Or even, if one really suspended disbelief, and only took note of cooking a simple meal in a warm place while a storm raged outside, I could have been making a Sunday night dinner back at Columbia, maybe during a March rainstorm, perhaps after waking up late, lagging from Saturday night's revelry, a textbook in one hand, a wooden spoon stirring sauce in the other. And reeling inside of my sudden comfort, easy happiness, the reality of my situation, ever-present, struck me again: I'm going to die. And I felt so sad for myself. I thought, I'm eating pasta now, and everything seems ok, but the truth is, in a few days, or weeks, I'm going to run out of food, and starve to death. Just like that.

I'm annoying myself with my constant bitching about my incumbent demise. Rereading the last several days of this journal is like peeking into a high school girl's dark diary. Morbidity, like the tide, washes in twice daily. Sure, it's a little higher today, a little lower tomorrow, but the tide's pretty much the tide. And blah, blah, blah, blah, blah, yikes!

Happy are all those who fear Hashem, who walk in his path.
They will reach heights when you nourish them, they make you happy and please you.
They will drink from you the way fruit grows on the vines behind their houses,
their houses will be planted like olive trees around your table.

Behold, because they are blessed and strong who fear Hashem.

You will bless Hashem from Zion,
and you will see good in Jerusalem all the days of your life.
And you will see sons born to your sons, peace descend on Israel.

But I will have no sons. And the sons that I don't have, won't bear children either. And my parents will never see grandchildren; I will never give children to them. I will never carry Udi's child; my child Udi will cease as well. It all ends with me. I fear Hashem, and yet no peace descends on Israel. I do not see good in Jerusalem all the days in my life.

Then, this may also be a test of my faith. I should be able to trust that Hashem orders the world and it moves according to his plan. I should believe that if I do not make it, then that is Hashem's will, and salvation awaits me in Shamaim with my parents. And I should believe that if I am to survive, and my role in this life is meant to continue, then my survival is not beyond Hashem's means to facilitate.

Momma, Eema, I wish I had been able to talk with you before you died. I wish I could have once, just once told you how much it meant that you came to see me despite our fighting.

## *August 29*

I think it's tomorrow, but I've been dozing in and out of daydreams which confuses things considerably. But for the sake of argument, let's consider this Friday, August 29, and not just Thursday's late afternoon. (Though I must also confess the possibility of losing or gaining a day somewhere earlier in the trip. Especially during the nightless summer days when I'd stopped looking at my watch, which I've since misplaced altogether). But that's all distraction and digression.

Here's the point. Yesterday, while I lay rustling in my sleeping bag, immobile, I could not help but think about my situation for what must be the umpteenth time. I'm stuck, I'm miserable, I smell, I've got no chance of survival, yadyahdyah, blah, blah, blah. And I just got completely sick of my own company. My whining bored me, irritated me, got under my skin. I was disgusted with myself. For the past several days, every time I go to recite tehillim, I find myself instead turning to the Book of Job, indignant at the lot Hashem's given me. But this onset of self-revulsion, of antipathy for my pathetic sniveling, forced me to think further about Job's plight.

I rehearsed the actual story. First, Job is a rich man and very pious. He prays all the time, offers sacrifices on behalf of his children lest they screw up at their feasts and so on. Then along comes the Satan, to Hashem, and he says listen, the only reason this guy's great is because his life's so easy. So Hashem gives the Satan permission to do as he likes to Job, so long as he does not lay a hand on him. Well, no sooner said than done. The next day, a succession of messengers arrives. Each is the sole survivor of some terrible calamity. Job's livestock has been killed: five thousand camels, thirty thousand sheep, something like five hundred oxen, and so on; Job's fields have fallen to pestilence; and his ten children, assembled at a feast, have been slaughtered. Job takes all of this in stride, "Hashem gives, and Hashem takes away." And that's it, he changes nothing else.

Well, time passes. Hashem assembles his angels once again, amongst them the Satan. And, once again, Hashem asks the Satan if he's seen his good servant, Job, and isn't Job just such a great guy? (I mean, yeah, kill all the man's children and make him a pauper and the best he comes up with is: some days God's good, other days less so. Sure, how could you not be proud of that particular creation). The Satan rejoins that yes, so far Job just continues to bless Hashem; but let something bad happen directly to Job, and then, the Satan swore, then, Job would curse Hashem. So Hashem okay's this next plan of attack. He gives the Satan permission to do what he wants to Job so long as he spares his life.

Again, the Satan promptly gets busy and Job comes down with the rash to end all rashes. I shouldn't make light. He's horribly mutilated with boils, sores. He sits in ashes and scratches himself wishing to die. In fact, he's so miserable that his wife asks him why he doesn't just curse Hashem, be smote and get it all over with. (Sounds familiar, right?) But Job refuses to sin. Job says that he wishes to die, wishes that Hashem would finish what's begun and kill him, but that he, Job, will not sin. No, Job will do nothing wrong, for he is a pious man.

There Job was, ranting and raving against the evil turn done him, but adamantly refusing to redress Hashem for it. Along came three of his friends, wise old men. And in turn they beseeched Job to be a supplicant, pray to Hashem, ask forgiveness for his sins. But Job asked, for what sins shall I ask forgiveness? He declared that he would do nothing at all, that he was strong enough to meet the challenge of continuing to praise Hashem even while he continued to receive such unjust treatment at his hands. Each of his friends appealed to him more fervently, and he rebuked each one in turn. Throughout, this single question continues to burn: If Job is so pious then what sin could he possibly be being punished for? This goes back and forth for quite some time in poetic language. Job's friends insist he must have done something wrong and claim that they are wise enough to know the symptoms, and Job rejoins that he's just as wise as they, and he'll simply bear the test, having done no wrong. And eventually, it becomes clear that for Job, worship has become a sort of endurance sport. Job takes a certain perverse pride even, in suffering while refusing to bend, while refusing to curse Hashem. He's strong enough. He's got the gumption to stick it all out. Pain, loss, grief, misery. He never doubts that God's done all this to him. And he never waivers in his steadfast refusal to repent (for what? Repent for what?). *And these three men ceased to answer Job, because he saw himself as a righteous man. And then rose up alone Eliyahu ben Barachel.*

Eliyahu says, "Because I was younger, I did not speak, believing myself lacking in wisdom... But because no one would speak the truth; I realized that wisdom comes not from years but from Hashem...My belly is now full of wind; my belly is like a fine wine waiting to be opened...Who are you, Job, to consider yourself right against Hashem? Who are you to dispute the judgment of your maker? Who are you to impugn what Hashem metes you? ...Hashem communicates with us all the time, he lets us know when we stray by bringing misfortune and so guides us back to his graces."

But does Job fall down on his knees and pray to Hashem to forgive him? No. He does nothing. Eliyahu, incensed, speaks again, says that all wise men will see the emptiness of Job's words, will realize that Job adds to his sin with his speech, with his failure to speak (what sin?). And then Hashem himself comes down and demands to know who darkens counsel so, who dares to refute the impeachability of his judgment? Yes, Job's obstinate refusal to curse Hashem in the face of trial, is also based on his conviction that this is all trial and not punishment. In fact, Job rebels against Hashem by refusing to repent, refusing to accept that he must be wrong about his righteousness, his innocence. Even after Hashem comes down, and demands to know who he thinks he is, Job refuses to respond. Job says that he's already answered twice, and will not be swayed. He is innocent. Naturally, Hashem doesn't take that answer very well, and tells Job off fiercely. At last, after this tirade, Job repents and Hashem finds favor in him, gives him new children, lets him live to hundred and forty, restores his wealth.

While the wind whips outside and the demons play hide and seek over the top of my kayak, I mull over this strange story about Job and Hashem and the Satan. Between wind gusts and taunting, demonic calls I hear the singsong study voice of Rabbi Shem Tov, analyzing scripture in the linoleum-floored room where we Hillel-house women met Wednesday nights to learn. Because I've found myself as indignant as Job at my poor chances, my misfortune, I worry that I am guilty of Job's transgressions. It's a strange story, part psalm, part parable. At its beginning, the thing reads like Hashem betting a man's life against the Satan; by its end, the Satan plays no role and the man being bet represents a subtle and insidious brand of iniquity. Clearly, the Satan is part and parcel of Hashem; his suggestions are not idle, but in fact what Hashem feels to be Job's due. And the hints of Job's sin can be found right at the beginning of his story. He offers burnt sacrifices on behalf of his children after each of their feasts lest they have sinned while drinking, or thought unpure thoughts, lest they fall from Hashem's grace, lest Job's wealth be threatened. Clearly, Job believes in Hashem—but he believes in him as if grace in the eyes of the Lord could be gamed. He believes in him insomuch as if he does X, then Y must necessarily follow. Job thinks his reason equal to that of Hashem. Therefore, he can never imagine that he might be punished for a sin outside his awareness: *these three men ceased to reply to him because they saw he was convinced of his righteousness.*

Eliyahu indignantly explains that when bad befalls one, invariably some justification, *possibly beyond our conception*, lies behind it. For Hashem controls everything and nothing transpires without his decree. Because who but Hashem can break the dawn, raise the sun, cause rain to fall? Job thinks he can, by doing X and earning Y. He believes that God is a system of accounting. Three burnt offerings equal another year of good fortune. What greater sign could there have been than in a single day, all of Job's livestock, children and servants dying, all in separate events? For fuck's sake, his sheep are destroyed by clouds of fire! He must have known that this only happened by Hashem's will, and if by Hashem's will, clearly he had fallen afoul of Hashem's favor and must seek forgiveness; but he doesn't.

So then, I must ask, logically enough, whether I too am not traversing an increasingly furious sea of signs. I must think whether I have sinned. I don't want to believe I have. After all, I am the first among my family to be ba'al t'shuvah and return to the faith of my forefathers. I am the only orthodox woman in my family (what's left of it). Surely, I must be better not worse. But then, few feared Hashem as did Job, and yet he should've known better than he did. Perhaps, this scourge, these bombings, this rampant murder of our children on buses, in squares, in random places, perhaps it is all a series of alerts, the lighthouse on a shoal growing ever closer. But then, I am no prophet; I need not interpret the fate of my people, only my own. I must concede the possibility that I have sinned and am being punished.

Can such loss be punishment? Can anything I can imagine doing demand such a price? Is this a string of warning buoys? First, I fell from my parents' graces, was cut off from their love. Next, my father was made to witness his fellow office workers dying around him, his friends, his life, his complacency devolving in a burning solvent, a jet-fuel funereal pyre; and as if that wasn't enough, he then found himself frozen alone in grief, unable to catch up with a world reinterpreting itself past that event. After that, I lost my parents. I awoke on a hospital gurney seeing black, my eyes bandaged, screaming, before slipping into opiate-induced sleep. When at last I could see, I couldn't walk. When finally I could walk, I wasn't whole. I look at myself and I see scars. I take off my shirt and find a body that could only be loved by din of a miracle. And I found I was afraid, always, too fearful to live, too fearful to die, denied any peace, any rest. I am scarred. Now this,

this journey, this attempt to make things right with my parents, this which has instead absolutely rived me from the practice of my faith, from the manners of humankind. Are all these brightening beacons of my damnation? Is even this a last chance to repent? Do my cramped legs and itching scalp and nagging boredom and haunting hunger and horrible, horrible fear of certain death all dictate a constant canvassing by the Lord to do t'shuvah?

Then I will repent that I might be saved, yet, from this fate. Tomorrow is Shabbat; rather, tonight is Shabbat. I will spend this Shabbat, this holy day beseeching Hashem to forgive me, to save me. No miracle is beyond his power, no act too great for his strength. He can yet rescue me. I will put my faith in the Lord; I will be his supplicant. I will beg his hand and his help; I will walk in the path of the righteous, for beautiful are his commandments. And Hashem will take me out of this place. I will reach my Udi, my love. The wind will change, the ice blow north. The water will clear, the skies relent, the sun emerge. The snow will melt, a second summer briefly dawn, and I will reach the mouth of the McKenzie in several days hard rowing. And then I will head home to my people, our land, to my Udi, our love. I will. I will. I will.

## August 31

And nothing. I prayed more like it was Yom Kippur than Shabbat. So that I would not be impure before Hashem, I used some of the water I'd made from snow Friday to wash my hands. Then I spent twenty-four hours pleading with Hashem to spare my life. And nothing. I looked outside this morning, and though the storm's fury has somewhat relented, travel is hardly plausible. A pea-soup fog lingers over the two foot deep snow plain stretching from the mountains out over the sea. The ice seems here to stay. My prayers are yet unanswered.

It occurs to me that perhaps, because I'm praying for something, for rescue, for clear water, Hashem deems my supplication unworthy. But I can't not want to survive. I can't pray without wanting Hashem to aid me. It's a terrible catch-22: Hashem will only rescue me if I pray to him without my explicit intent being to solicit rescue—but then even thinking in those terms puts me afoul of the ontological basis of Job's sin. Attempting to discern a way in which I can properly get Hashem to rescue me is still an attempt to force Hashem to act on my behalf rather than submitting to his will and unconditionally repenting my sins. Each permutation feels like another attempt to properly decipher a system. I should simply take these misfortunes as signs of my evildoing and repent without hope for my future because the Lord my God the Lord is One. (Perhaps I will only be saved if I despair of my situation and yet continue to pray? Can I truly despair? And will despairing of the possibility of Hashem's salvation be itself an indication of inadequate faith? Part of me knows that the answer is to accept whatever Hashem offers, because it is all part of his plan. But I can't. I'm not built that way. I can't not want, not grieve, not fear).

Listen, Hashem, I understand that I know nothing. All is within your reason and I do not attempt to know your will. Please, look on your servant, Sara. Find what is good within her. Deliver her from danger that she may continue to serve you and bear children into your service and fulfill your commandments.

Please, God, please take me out of my suffering. I hurt everywhere and have no solace. I am cramped and afraid. The ice has landlocked me. Winter comes. I don't want to die.

I am despairing.

I suppose that I will continue to pray, even in my despair.

Can one despair and maintain faith at the same time?

It's certainly possible to grieve, to mourn, to feel sad while keeping one's faith constant. Those things are not incompatible.

But despair might be. Losing hope would seem to run counter to belief in the divine. Apathy rarely inspires impassioned prayer.

In the end, this isn't that different from the rest of life. I'll continue as best I can and try to survive as long as possible. I'll struggle, trying to be the best Jew possible, trying to keep up with my Yiddishkeit. And I'll be vaguely miserable, miss my parents and hope that at some point things will be different (perhaps in the after-life).

Originally, I was drawn to orthodoxy because I looked around at my surroundings and realized a spiritual wasteland. It didn't take any great genius to see that a life spent chasing social status in the form of designer jeans, husbands, jobs, homes, vacations and children hardly guaranteed happiness and fulfillment. As I grew older, I realized that without purpose, life cannot have meaning, even if it escaped the shallow prescriptions of my wealth-addled peers. None of this is new or unique. I am not the first to seek. Gradually, I discovered Yiddishkeit. I discovered faith. I discovered the worship of Hashem. And it makes sense. I became devout. I moved to Jerusalem. In the busy bustle between work, Hebrew class, Talmud and Torah classes, a social life comprised of Jews, and the exploration of a beautiful new country, I found my life filled with meaning. I was content.

Can I not have that sense of meaning and fulfillment now? I'm finally alone with my God. It's just me and Hashem (discounting the demons, some bears nearing hibernation, and the contents of my kayak). I will fill my last days with meaning. I won't ruminate about the past or imagine a lascivious future filled with Dalias and Udis. I'll just live these days, pray to Hashem, concentrate on my faith. Whatever comes will come.

## *September 1*

September! The weather's finally broken but that doesn't do much good. The ice is where it was, under the snow, over the water. I can't see any leads from here, none. What water I do see seems to be small melt pools formed by underlying pressure. The snow glistens grayish pink in the dim sunlight. You'd think Arctic winter had fully arrived. September 1! Not good. I haven't seen the demons for the past two days, but their footprints are all over and around my kayak, they've really scratched up and gnawed at the wood in spots. My muscles atrophy more each day; I've got half the strength I had when the ice first stopped me two weeks ago. It's been this way two weeks. Holy shit. I've been here at this campsite over a week. Speaking of which, my tent shows a lot of wear. The color has literally faded to half its former brilliance—and I'm not talking about dirt here. It's washed out. I hope that doesn't reflect an equal decline in tensile strength, though soon there'll be enough snow to build a snow cave, which will undoubtedly provide better, warmer shelter anyway. I've also noticed fatigue in the stitching that holds the pole-clips to the tent body, and likewise in the fly's seams where they're stretched over the poles and at guy-out points. I don't want to resign myself to morbid thoughts, but I doubt I need the tent to last much longer. My supply of fuel is finite (though there's always the option to scavenge for driftwood, dig for it beneath the snow, and attempt to make a fire). I suppose I'm gradually resigning myself to trying to make it through the winter (though my supply of food is also finite). I don't know what the policy is for search and rescue. If my pilot has his shit together—unlikely given all the misinformation he fed me—when I fail to call for pick up from Aklivuk, he'll notify the NPS Rangers and the RCMP. They, in turn, may or may not have the resources to mount a search party. That party, then, may or may not actually find me. My father never would have carried an emergency transponder beacon, and I haven't either. No radioing for help, not that there ever was.

Well, I can actually see where I'm going out there today. I guess I should take some initiative and go for a walk, stretch my legs, get some exercise. It'll do me much more good than sitting in this tent. Maybe I'll build a fire as well, conserve fuel for the time being. It can't hurt.

—Later—

Polar bear, I saw a polar bear, not a mirage, not a possibly imagined ghost of a white slip trailing me, not a delayed nightmare, the real thing. I just got back into the tent and wanted to write this right away, but maybe I should take a few seconds to collect myself. Ok. Here's what happened:

I left the tent a few hours ago intending to go for a walk. I wanted to explore the immediate area as well as get some exercise. Like I wrote earlier, the weather's taken a turn for the better, so I dressed in fleece with a Goretex top and bottom, gloves and a hat. I wore two pairs of wool socks inside my waterproof rowing booties, and then my tevas over that, figuring it would be my best option for warm dry feet in the snow. That worked fine as a system.

At first, I walked towards the mountains. Going was slow. With almost every step, I postholed practically up to my knees. Occasionally, I would step into a drift, and sink in to my waist, which required a rather unfun extrication process. Escaping a snow drift is not bad practice for falling through thin ice over water: you lean forward and try to slide out on your stomach, get your knees above the surface of the snow. Invariably, this activity simply serves to sink your arms in deep, leaking snow into your gloves, which quickly melts and refreezes into a nice ice bracelet. Once I managed to free a leg from the drift, the temptation to try and stand would overwhelm me. I couldn't seem to learn from my mistakes; I'd end up doing a wide split and sinking back in, this time with my legs spread apart. The proper procedure for escaping this compromising position, I discovered, calls for pitching forward, which lifts both legs out behind you, but points you ninety degrees away from your intended direction. Then you must slither along until you reach snow shallow enough to walk in again. How do you know when you've reached such snow? You don't. Basically, you crawl until you want to stand. You attempt to stand and either sink or not, usually not.

The pea soup had lifted into a low gray ceiling whose textured underbelly gently swirled as the entire mass moved in the wind. Occasional breaks in the cloud cover would announce themselves in a bursting streak of light across the snow, instantly grabbing my attention. I would look up from my plodding path, blink stupidly in the crazy glare cast by the low sun across the snow, now more blue than red. And if the break was wide enough, deep enough, the mountains to the south would appear like behemoths playing hide-and-seek around a corner, their massive white flanks glinting where snow melt turned to ice, gave way to coal black rock.

I spent what felt like an hour slowly trudging towards the mountains, desperately wishing for snowshoes. The further I went, the more frequently I wallowed into deep drifts. The distinctly uphill approach began to wear on me. I had discovered little of interest, no surprise caches of driftwood, no obvious, open fresh water. My face was cold from the wind but I was sweating under my Goretex. I decided to turn around.

Retracing my steps, walking in an already broken trail, knowing where the deep drifts were, let me move much faster. I made it back to the tent site in I think less than half the time I'd taken marching south. I was back, but I didn't feel like packing it in just yet. I couldn't quite stand the thought of awkwardly stripping off my wet fleece sweater and damp socks inside my cramped vestibule, then putting all of it down in my sleeping bag to dry from my body heat. Nor did I relish zipping myself back into that confining cocoon and spending another cramped day staring at a yellow wall that continued (and continues) to keep its secrets to itself. (Fine, so sometimes it does give up its secrets, and in hallucinatory fits, sagas play out against its screen).

How did it happen that I've been writing for this long and still not gotten to the polar bear? It's going to sound anticlimactic when I finally do. Anyway, I stood outside the tent, rapidly cooling off, panting, a bit out of breath, and thought about where else I could walk. And there it was, plain as day, the flat ice stretching in front of me, my nemesis, my final way out. I thought, why not explore this rare ground, this occasional terra firma, this hallucinatory fit of non-land? I even dared to hope that after heading out a short ways, I might find a system of open leads, a clear path towards Aklivuk, towards the McKenzie, where, if anywhere, there'd be more open water. But walking out onto the ice also struck me as a potentially deadly choice. Thin ice concealed beneath snow, old seal breathing holes, mazes of open water: all potentially awaited me out there.

In truth, there was little reason to hope for a navigable set of leads when I couldn't even glimpse the hint of one from shore. Standing there though, in the stamped out clearing between my kayak and my tent, I daydreamed about finding a narrow system during my reconnaissance mission, open water just barely wide enough for the gunwales to slip inside. I thought, I will pack the kayak, yoke myself to the haul lines and drag it out. Then slowly navigate, regularly hauling the boat over short strips of ice. I foresaw the leads growing progressively wider as I made progress eastwards. The weather cleared somewhat. Muted sunlight glinted where long dirty ice floes touched the water's surface and were washed the brilliant blue of a calving glacier. Yes, it was worth the risk of exploring the ice—so long as I had a probe to determine the solidity of what lay ahead.

I rooted around in my kayak until I found an old trekking pole with the basket removed that I occasionally use to stake the boat down. Plunging it ahead of me, I tenuously made my way out onto the ice. The surface, which just days ago closely resembled a scale model of tectonic upheaval, proved remarkably even. Before each step, I rammed my rod down through the snow, connecting with the solid ice below with a resonant clunk. I grew slightly more intrepid. I hastened my pace. Unlike my earlier walk on land, here, few obstacles slowed me. Checking back occasionally to ensure a beeline away from my tent, I traveled north easily. Alas the prognosis was not good: snow covered ice as far as the eye could see. Once in a very great while, I would encounter pools of water that had welled up over the ice through temporary pressure cracks. These small basins rippled in the wind, teal ice readily visible beneath their surfaces; I easily circumvented them.

Disheartened by my bleak prospects, I thought to turn back. My campsite was now barely visible, a tiny spot on the horizon. The vastness of my surroundings—flat white extending in every direction—gave me a sort of vertigo. Yet, I enjoyed the freedom of movement, the risk of sudden objective hazards rather than the slow doomed wait back at the tent. My limbs and my lungs reveled in exercise. If nothing else, I've become a hardcore athlete this past year; I don't handle immobility well. I wanted to prolong my awkward walk, bent over, jab, step, jab, step, jab. Rather than head further north, the exposure of which unnerved me somewhat, I decided to turn east. As long as I kept my tent in sight, off to my right, I would gradually arc back towards shore. When I'd gone far enough, I could cut back to the tent.

On my new course, the injured tendons along my right leg flared up almost immediately. It took nearly a year's worth of physical therapy to get that leg remotely functional after the surgery. The blast nearly severed it mid-thigh, shattering the bone and tearing the tendons there. When I came back to the States for the remainder of rehab, I could barely get around even with a brace and a cane. PT freed me from those supports, and after a year of serious athletic training in advance of this trip, I was essentially pain free. Two weeks inactivity and I've lost months' of progress. My leg will never be the same; I'll have to keep on top of it for the rest of my life (presumably not very long). I felt disheartened by the pain, by my recovery's lost ground. I tired of stooping at each step to prod the ice. Again, I considered turning around, heading in, nesting in my sleeping bag, wrapped in warm waves of my own scent. But this new feeling, the annoyance with my own whining, emerged. A separate being, a cruel and unforgiving Sarah stepped outside my body and sneered at my pathetic sniveling. Hounded by this fictive, harsher double, I plodded further along. The snow, seen now through my leg's ache, my back's ache, stretched out interminably grey. I cautiously kept glancing back at the dirty yellow spot that was my tent. And I walked, halfheartedly plunging my trekking pole, suddenly less concerned about falling through the ice than about my waning stamina.

Then I arrived at the tracks. I had the same sense of surprised discovery as if I'd stepped out of dense woods onto the shoulder of an eight lane interstate highway. The wide thoroughfare of giant paw prints, each big enough to swallow both my feet, blinded me. I considered my options. I could ignore them and continue on eastward. I could head back to my campsite now. Or, I could follow the tracks back to the landfall from which they led. The advantage of this last option being that I'd be heading away from the bear, and, I wouldn't have to worry about punching through the surface, allowing me to walk at a normal pace. I opted to stand there, stretching my back and shaking my legs. The wind began to strip warmth off the surface of my layers and from my exposed face. September 1 and the weather hasn't climbed above freezing in a week. I looked towards shore. As I'd walked, I'd noticed the irregularity of the land's edge; long spits of uneven, even rocky, ground dashed out to sea. I saw that a cliff band of muddy rock emerged from the water's edge parallel to where I stood. This was one reason not to head back along the prints: they might take me to a spot east of the cliffs, and I'd have to traverse back to my tent over uneven, drift-riddled territory without access to the relative flat of the ice. I felt the unmistakable urge to pee. I didn't like standing in the middle of fresh, big bear tracks. It made me queasy. There was nothing to be shy about. There was no one anywhere near (I wished there were).

And I, Sarah, an ultra-orthodox Jewish woman, dropped her pants in the middle of a vast exposed territory, the only spot of color for miles, squatted, and relieved myself. When I was little, really little, four or five, my father and I were traveling somewhere by train, perhaps we were going to see his office, and he had to take me into the men's bathroom on a Long Island Rail Road car to urinate. On the back of the door, visible over my father's shoulder, someone had crudely inked a disproportionately large vagina onto the black outline of a woman. It looked more like a crab or a spider than anything else, a yawning vertical oval with four or five black lines coming straight out from each of its sides. I don't know what I thought it was at the time, but I stared at it, fixated, while holding up my little jumper and peeing. The image remained with me. Now, somehow, when I find myself particularly exposed, or considering sexuality, I imagine this giant maw, obscenely stretching from mid-belly down, hungrily gaping. It's gross. I peed as quickly as I could, eager to cover myself.

I'd pulled up my pants and was adjusting my underwear when I realized I was not alone. Apparently, the bear also thought his little highway the best path back to land. He stood about fifty yards off, massive. I couldn't imagine how I'd failed to see him until he got so close. I vaguely wondered if perhaps there was open water behind him and he'd swum. I vaguely considered inviting him back to my tent for some tea and dry noodles. It's been so long since I've opened my mouth and made words that I'd greeted him like a neighbor in the elevator before I could process rational thought, "Hello, Mr. Bear. Fine afternoon isn't? Good day for a swim if you can find the water."

He wasn't overly impressed.

"What's the matter, cat got your tongue? You know, if you chew instead of trying to swallow them whole, you can avoid that problem."

Still no response from my big white friend. For the second time in an hour, for the first time in a week, I found myself with high-stakes options, none of them good. I considered carefully. I could, A, turn and run like hell. This choice could well trigger a chase response in the bear, and he'd win that race. B, I could continue to strike up small talk until I annoyed him enough that with a grunt he wandered off. C, well just as I was about to consider C, the bear yawned, twisting his head mildly, which pulled his black lips back from his gums revealing the most impressive set of teeth I'd ever seen, not to mention one of the longest tongues. I completely spaced out on my actual situation and just admired the efficient, elegant and yet overwhelming mass of that animal. After a week of flat snow and synthetic camping material, I reveled in an ocular orgy of richly textured fur, thick firm paws, shining eyes, rounded ears, deep black nose. Those teeth! Here was life, vital, charged. Get a grip, Sarah, I chided myself, perhaps out loud, I don't know. First things first, I needed to break eye contact with the beastie. The last thing I needed was him thinking I was challenging his authority and trail. I demurely turned my head to the side. In turn, he stuck his ass up in the air while bringing his head down low, stretching his front legs out before him. Those paws!

Desperately, I tried to spark my groggy mind into recalling

my bear training. My mind wasn't all that interested, it wanted to consider the faint deep smell of Udi's shirt in the afternoon after a day's work, a combination of his body musk, barracks' coffee, deodorant and lightly applied European cologne. If the bear was a dog, I could have interpreted his odd stance as an invitation to play (also potentially fatal). Since he was a polar bear, I considered it probably prelude to a charge, even as he lifted his front right paw slightly above the ground to get an even better stretch in and yawned again, this time with a slight grunting moan. Come on brain, I thought, work with me.

I remembered the things to do to avoid having a bear visit your campsite in the lower forty-eight and tried to dismiss them quickly, flip through the files to the next section. I remembered that for a grizzly bear, the key was to not surprise it, and then if you encountered one, to talk to it, turn your head to the side, and then slowly back up without running. If a grizzly charges, play dead, shielding yourself with your pack or whatever else you have on hand. But for polar bears? I remembered a man in Fairbanks suggesting that the appropriate order of interaction was to avoid them, ignore them, and if those failed, shoot them.

The bear stood up out of his stretch, arching his back upwards. He was huge, unbelievably big, gorgeous. Subconsciously, unconsciously, bizarrely, I lifted my trekking pole to my shoulder like a long skinny rifle, and adopted the marksman's stance I'd learned during my mandatory military service in Israel. I sighted down the length of my beat-up black pole, highlighted with splashes of green and yellow enamel paint, took careful aim at the divot where the bear's nose met his skull between his eyes and yelled, "Pow!" at the top of my lungs.

He stared at me. "Pow!" He turned his back to me. "Pow! Pow! Pow!" I yelled, raising the tip of the pole with each recoil. He loped away further out on the ice, heading north, his spade-shaped white tail almost immediately beginning to blend in with the landscape. I didn't wait around; I turned and ran.

I ran like I've never run before. Gone were my worries about weak ice and booby-hatched seal holes. I made a break for it, turned everything to maximum go, pole waving wildly out to the side from my pumping right hand. My teva soled booties gave uneven traction in the snow, I felt myself slipping and sliding, considered the danger to my joints, but never broke stride. I ran until I reached my tent, radically out of breath, sweat-soaked, feverish. I planted the pole in the snow behind the kayak, and leaned on it, gripping it with both hands gasping. Once I was certain I wouldn't puke, I crawled over to the vestibule, stripped off my wet clothes, and wormed into my sleeping bag, where it's safe. Then I wrote this. I'll have to go out and build a fire now. There's no way those clothes will dry otherwise.

## September 2

Last night, I dreamt that I fell asleep in Udi's arms, the slight bulge of his stomach nestled in the arch of my back, the tops of his thighs cradling my bottom. I wiggled my body until I could pull my head under his chin and the blanket over my shoulders and felt the rich rustle of fresh, dense sheets against my bare skin. With each inhale, I felt him exhale, the two of us working in easy opposition, like the casual balance of a locomotive gaining steam. I fell asleep in Udi's arms and dreamt that my mother was driving my father and me out to Montauk, where we would put in, and row to the tip of the north fork where she'd pick us up again. "Be careful with my Sarah," she said. "She's the only daughter I've got." My father winked at her, licked the tips of his lips, and offered to help "correct" that situation as soon as he got home. I yelled at them to stop being gross and my father laughed.

I dreamt that I woke Udi by rotating in his embrace until I faced into his neck, and then rubbing my hands up and down in his thick chest fur. Though I couldn't see them, I could feel his eyes gradually opening. I pulled his head down so that he kissed me and I moaned. Deep in the dark, way under the comforters, like exhausted teenage sisters confiding in each other long after they were meant to bed, I told him that I'd dreamt about my parents. He ran the balls of his fingers down the muscles along my spine, easing and arching my back. He whispered that his son's favorite animal was the bear, and that when they flew to New York to visit his son's mother's family, his in-laws would take their grandson to The Bronx Zoo so that he could see them. Udi had planned to send him to Katmai National Park in Alaska on photography safari to take pictures of the grizzlies after he completed his mandatory military service. How many young men, Udi wondered, would choose a few weeks in nature over the sexualized beaches of India after three years in the army? I made curlicues in his chest hair and felt his heart beating through my fingertips. His hands found my sides and traced the scars along my ribs. Blinking in the dark like a sated cat, I murmured first in English, then in Hebrew, I love you, I'm sorry. Ochevti lach, sholach lee. He slipped a hand under my cheek, cradling my broken ear and kissed the top of my head. "I understand, Sara. I understand."

I dreamt that I smelled his musk and twang, sleep stale, pungent. I breathed in until my chest ached and held my breath until I woke up in my sleeping bag in my tent.

The weather continues to clear; the ice shows no signs of doing so. This is the moment in which a larger party would begin silently wagering which man might die first and what he'd taste like.

Still, my encounter with the polar bear has given me a modicum of courage and a certain measure of hope. I can't imagine that he got that close to me unobserved unless he was in a hidden lead. There must be more clear water to the east. Perhaps not all is lost. My thought is this. I'll eat a fighting-sized breakfast today, spike my oatmeal with butter, pack in as many calories as I can. Then I'll harness myself to the kayak and start pulling, following the path I made when I ran back from the bear encounter. As long as I stay on that track, I won't have to worry about the quality of the ice underfoot. I can make it back there in less than a day. I'll stop there. After making camp, I'll go on a second reconnaissance mission, with the trekking pole, to find either water leads or more safe ice. Tomorrow, I'll either follow my newly broken trail, or, I'll tow the boat to the open water I've discovered. I don't know what I'll find, but it has to be better than sitting here waiting for a miracle (not that I would rule a miracle out of Hashem's ability to perform, nor from my wish list. A strong wind blowing the ice northwards remains the best hope).

Well enough writing. I've got a plan to execute!

—Later—

Defeat, absolute defeat. And it's so disheartening to look at this diary and see my hopeful exclamation followed immediately by word of my plan's failure. I began as I said I would. I ate an extra hearty breakfast, broke down my campsite, and packed everything into the kayak (which I was pleased to be moving after seeing just how bad the damage around the hatches has become. These demons are really something). Using two-inch webbing, I rigged a crude waist-belt and chest-harness. I ran more webbing from these back to the kayak's tow ropes. In all, it took perhaps as much as two hours before I was ready to set off. After a brief last look around the small spot of Arctic shore I'd called my own for more than a week, I clipped in and prepared to haul off, eager to make up time lost breaking down the campsite.

And that's where my problems began. At first, I couldn't budge the kayak from its grave in the snow, period. I tugged and pulled, but the bow was beneath the snow line, and so rather than rise up, it submarined beneath the surface, the hull grating against the gravel ground. I stopped and thought about what I could do. Unwilling to despair, I reassured myself that once I had my little ship above the surface of the snow, she'd coast easily. I remembered my mother putting small branches behind the wheels of our car for traction when we'd gotten stuck one winter. We'd driven my father to Glen Cove in the middle of a snow storm so that he could row back to Northport in simulated arctic conditions (little did he know). My mother thought we might as well have lunch while we were there—a meal notable for her profound and vocal mix of anger and anxiety. I kept quiet; I'd wanted to go with him. The storm picked up, and by the time my mother finished her third cup of coffee, insisting that there was no rush for us to get to the pick up point, I couldn't see three feet out the window. Then the waitress came over and said there was a call for my mother. Apparently she'd given him the restaurant's number, knowing all along that he wouldn't make it. He'd capsized after encountering very rough seas once he was out into the sound, and just barely managed to land on some massive estate's lawn. My mother became instant action, bundling me up and out, throwing random, excessive money onto the table and rushing for the car. Of course, it was snowed in, the wheels spun and spun on the ice they were making. Then, my mother did her little trick with the sticks to get us traction that inspired me today. To make a long story short and get back to today's events, though her driving probably endangered my life as much as going along with my father would have, I loved her for flying along snowy roads like a rally-car driver; I loved her for risking us for him—despite the anger and anxieties his follies caused. In no time flat, we pulled into the drive of a gaudy mansion only to find my father sitting in front of roaring fireplace, a wool blanket wrapped around his still dripping wet suit, sipping a hot toddy and charming his hosts with tales of his sea-borne adventures. He was in no rush to leave.

"Come in, have a seat, meet the Englanders, Jerry and Gayle," he motioned to us without getting up from the easy-chair. "I was just telling them about the time Sarah and I were practically lifted out of the water by a surfacing nuclear sub near Mystic."

I thought my mother was going to kill him. But he simply smiled and smiled at her glare. Meanwhile, Jerry and Gayle, a tidy, elderly couple, she with her bleached-orange hair done up and jewelry donned despite wearing a sweats-suit and slippers, rushed to bring us chairs and drinks, cocoa for me, rum spiked tea for my mother. So we sat down, and were told, once again, how wonderful it must be to have such a bold and heroic patriarch at the head of our household.

But I digress and digress and digress. This has been happening lately, I sit down to one thing, full of focus, eager, energetic, and then twenty minutes go by and all I've done is daydream. It took me two hours to break down my campsite. Usually, I could have gotten that done in less than twenty minutes. But every few minutes I'd find myself standing there, holding something, wondering what it was for, or what I'd meant to do with it. I've never been this absent-minded. I feel totally disconcerted by the whole thing. And I still haven't gotten to the point.

Ok. Thinking back to my mother's example, I decided to try and build a ramp, with traction, of sorts. I stamped out the snow in front of the boat to make a gully about fifteen feet long. Packed down, the snow's surface came to just below the boat's deck. Then, using a paddle, I shoveled some of the snow immediately in front of the bow out of the way. Next, I unscrewed my paddle and placed both blades down along the snow ramp under the bow. This, I thought, ought to work. Harnessed up again, I resumed pulling. Nothing doing, the sides of the kayak had compressed the snow around them into ice during my first attempt, and were thoroughly lodged. Still unwilling to give up, I tried to lever the boat upwards using a paddle. At first, the paddle's arm simply sank into the snow. I tried bracing one paddle half over the other's horizontally-aligned shaft. This worked to rock the boat free, though I worried constantly that I would irreparably damage one of the paddle blades and be absolutely fucked if and when I ever reached some open water.

With the boat's hull loose, I replaced the two paddle halves in the gully, got behind the boat and shoved. Now it slid up and out and onto my gully, where it sunk in somewhat, but not too bad. At last, I thought, progress, and resigned myself to not making the day's distance goals.

With the paddle stowed beneath the deck's elastic cording, I hurried around to the front of the boat and harnessed myself in for the third time. Forward ho, I thought, and began to pull. Yes, I could make forward progress, but at tremendous effort, very slowly. Each step forward required a lunge. The boat simply sunk too low in the snow. Moving forward meant displacing a snow path two-feet wide and one foot deep. It's no sled, my kayak. I determined to continue. Perhaps I'd have an easier time out on the ice. Sweating profusely, I reached the slope of the beach. Everything hurt (hurts). My right thigh throbbed and throbbed. I pulled forward and the front of the bow hung over the drop-off onto the beach, poised, ready. I pulled again and it tilted downward and started to slide on its own, quickly gaining a bit of speed, but not so much that I couldn't keep in front of it. This is great I thought, this is what I was hoping for. Then it plowed into the bottom of the slope where the beach meets the sea. Its nose dove deep into the snow, the back swung around, and it rolled upside down, twisting my harness straps and pulling me over. I hadn't thought to use the outriggers while hauling (not that they would have helped, not really).

I picked myself up and promptly tripped on the tangled webbing. After unclipping from the tow-leads, I stood up again. A bit more exertion and the boat was upright once more. Favoring my right leg, I hobbled around, clipped back in, and renewed hauling. Progress came at tremendous cost. An hour later, I had covered at most a hundred feet and was dizzy from hyper-exhaustion. A kayak is not a sled. The left side of my upper lip twitched uncontrollably. My body drooped into the leads, and slowly succumbed to gravity. The snow burnt against my face and bare arms. Gradually, I pulled myself into a limp sit, crying. I must have made a bizarre and pathetic sight: a sobbing woman, stripped down to a tank-top and shell pants, crumpled in the snow five feet in front of a kayak, its snow-wake stretching back a hundred feet straight out from the shore; and me and my boat were the only break in that orange-lit white-clad landscape for miles and miles. Disheartened, I realized that my only options were to build a new camp where I was on the ice, or haul my way back to shore. Thinking that the haul back along broken trail would prove much easier than the haul out, I elected to turn around. The way I see it, if the ice does break up, I don't want to be out there when it happens. If I really believe it won't, then I've stopped hoping even for a miracle.

Pulling back in, the already broken trail was much easier, though I had a lot less to give to the effort, having exhausted myself on the way out. When I reached the beach's slope, I feebly attempted to haul the boat back up. It was too hard; I couldn't muster the effort; I didn't care enough. I left the boat at the shoreline staked to the trekking pole. Wearily, I pulled out the tent and pitched it on its former footprint, then the sleeping bag and pad. All the while, my body began rapidly cooling, so I kept adding clothes, shivering, drawn.

Now the day's nearly over, and I'm back in bed, so to speak, in the same spot, scrawling in this diary once again. Hopeless. Broken. Emaciated.

## September 3

I'm wrecked. Walking to my pseudo lavatory—a pit of frozen waste carved in the snow a hundred feet from the tent—muscle and ligament pain made me scream twice on the way out and three times on the way back. That's not counting my groans when I heard the joints on my right side popping as I squatted. So much for taking advantage of the good weather today.

Time passes anyway you look at it. They told me it would heal me, this inevitable pulling away from trauma's port. In fact, each day just takes me further along. Progress is a fallacy contrived to keep people striving.

This is what I know:

1. The kayak that my father built with his own hands out of carefully selected teak and pine is not a sled.
2. With each passing day, the likelihood of the ice breaking up diminishes.
3. My choices are to attempt to winter here, hoping against hope for rescue, or to give up.
4. Fear-of-death *plus* disgust-with-life = motivation-to-try-and-survive-winter *minus* apathy.

I'm not sure what I should even be doing to try and survive. Basically, an attempt at a winter in the Artic (crazy! hello!) should translate into a whirlwind of activity right now, especially while the weather holds up. I need to identify any potential food supplies, gather fuel, choose an ideal location, possibly attempt to kill something that could be eaten. These aren't optional items, a list from which I can choose any two of the above. Fuel, food and a campsite are crucial. This tent will not survive the winter. My best bet would be to find a decent snow drift and begin digging a snow cave. The tent can then line the floor of the sleeping ledge to keep my sleeping bag dry.

I need to lay in a supply of driftwood. Now, while the snow's only a few feet deep, I can still locate large protruding logs along the shoreline. Once surveyed, these can be chopped into manageable pieces with my hatchet. The wood must be stored next to the chosen campsite, ideally on top of a nylon surface so it can begin to dry. I can probably scrounge something from the kayak, maybe cut up an old dry bag. A separate cooking pit should be carved out of the snow next to the snow cave. All that alone is at minimum a week's worth of work. The wood gathering might actually take longer. I should switch to wood as fuel for all cooking and snow melting for which I'm not confined to a tent, conserving my supply of white gas for storms when I'm tent-bound.

Then there's the issue of food. If I ration, I probably could stretch my supply out to two months. That's running a serious calorie deficit and assuming an absolute minimum of exertion. Basically, it would mimic concentration camp conditions. (Is that it? Are my people simply, always, destined to suffer: my grandfather in the camps, my mother killed by terrorists, myself at the mercy of arctic winter? And how much worse can I get? I'm already weathered skin over bone, scrawny, practically genderless. No one will rescue me for my beauty). Obviously, I need to get some more food. The question is how. There are three possibilities: killing an animal, finding edible plants, fish. Of all the choices, plants would be the best if A, they weren't all under several feet of snow, and B, I had a guide to edible greens. As it is, even if I could get down to the grasses and tubers of the tundra, my chances of giving myself the shits are just as good as those of filling my tummy.

Without a gun, killing an animal seems endlessly complicated. It requires finding an animal, figuring out some way of trapping it, and then slaughtering it. I haven't seen any wildlife in days. They're out there still, I'm sure, but I wouldn't have the slightest idea how to go about trapping let alone killing them—and that ignores the kashruth issue entirely. Theoretically, if I want to kill an animal, I need to capture a kosher one, which rules out bears, foxes, rabbits and squirrels—the latter two being the easiest to capture. Then I need to somehow kosherly slaughter it, an act for which I'm neither trained nor qualified (not to mention that in the case of quadrupeds such as musk-ox and caribou, it requires the use of a specialized knife and inflation of the lungs. Oh, and I'd have to discard the hindquarter). Then the meat needs to be soaked in a saltwater solution to remove any blood. The ocean would come in handy for this if I could get down to it. (If I could, I'd row all the way to Aklivuk). In hindsight's clarity, a molting goose would have been ideal, but they've long since taken from the ground. In a life and death situation, there's dispensation for eating non-kosher animals. But does that come into play only after I've exhausted my entire food supply? Or could I begin trying to set up traps now? Not that it matters. The closest I've come to an education in trapping was a field trip to the Museum of Natural History, which had a display of bird snares used by early, indigenous people.

Which leads our rousing debate of Sarah's survival options to fishing. I have an emergency fishing kit: hooks, nylon line, a few split-shot lead weights, a very small red-and-white bobber. Bait can be improvised. Alas, there remains the question of habitat. To fish, I need to find a stream. Now this should not be impossible. There's almost certainly a stream within four miles (four hours on this terrain). A fast moving, relatively voluminous stream fed by snow runoff might, just might, still be ice-free. It's just a matter of finding it, finding it and catching enough fish to last eight months—they'll keep; frozen in the snow they'll keep.

Maybe I shouldn't even bother.

How much fish would that even be? In Israel there was always fish as a first course with Friday night dinner. One medium sized fish (two pounds?) served four people who expected to eat more. I can stay hungry a bit, so that's two meals out of a medium-sized fish, or, about a fish and a half a day. I'm definitely going to loose my teeth to scurvy. Ok. A fish and a half a day times eight months is how many? I can never keep straight which months have thirty-one days and which have thirty (February has twenty-eight). I wish Udi was here! No, I wouldn't want Udi to have to go through this. I wish Udi would rescue me. Let's call a month thirty days, which gives us 240 days. Oh, who are you kidding, Sarah? What kind of perfectly two-pound fish do you expect to catch? Catch as many as you can, as soon as you can, before the ice closes up the stream, which will happen soon. 360 fish. I need to catch 360 two-pound fish, freeze them, and keep them away from predators.

I'm totally fucked.

Don't give up yet.

You still have to find a stream.

Streams can be found.

You still have to get up out of bed.

I'll feel better tomorrow.

This would have been so much easier if I'd simply gone back to Israel after finishing rehab. I could have skipped this whole dying in the Arctic episode, and instead jumped right to the new apartment. Right about now, I'd be meeting Udi on the bus while on the way to the Lavanah Superstore to buy linens. If, if, if. If I'd never become orthodox and moved to Jerusalem, if terrorists had never flown planes into my father's office building, if my parents had never come to visit me, if that young woman hadn't decided to kill herself by exploding in the middle of a crowded café, if I hadn't survived the attack, if I hadn't decided to finish my father's boat and complete his retirement dream, if I'd found a more knowledgeable outfitter, if I'd started two weeks earlier or packed an emergency transponder, if I stopped whining so much, and instead began searching for that stream. If I didn't keep worrying that like Job, I was being punished rather than tested. If only Hahsem forgave me and renewed my fields and gave me twice as many children (or parents, for that matter).

How long could it possibly take to walk to Shingle Point from here? I must be close, but how close? Walking close? Well, Sarah, you could answer that question if you knew where you were, if you hadn't forgotten the bag with the maps, right? (Sometimes, lying here, I can't help but wonder if I didn't simply misinterpret the outfitter's directions to go to Gordon instead of Kakiovic, and whether that map would have directed me to stop in the right place instead of rowing on through the fog. How did I manage to miss a whole town? Fuck). But how far can I possibly be from the endpoint of this trip? I mean, wouldn't it just be hysterical if I was like, say, a day's hike away from civilization while I attempted to catch a fish for every day in the year. A kayak is not a sled. And you can't leave home without your stuff—not you anyway.

Here's the deal. Tomorrow, you'll survey the region, you will. Finding a stream's got to be the first priority. To do that, walk along the shoreline going west; you saw nothing to the east two days ago (two days already! Time fucking flies; I'm cursing too much). Ok. You find the stream as quickly as you can tomorrow. By the stream, you look for a campsite, some slightly wind-sheltered dell in whose slope you can dig a cave. In both directions, you look for driftwood. It's most likely along the shore. The day after tomorrow, assuming you've found the dell and the stream and so forth, you pack up and move. This may mean hauling the kayak again. But this time, don't haul it full. Make trips with stuff until it's empty, then haul it. After that, the days' work should fall into a logical progression. Half your time you fish, the other half you chop/search for wood. Ok. Now you can go ahead and spend the day daydreaming about Udi while your muscles slowly recover.

I wonder if I will tell Udi the full extent of my arctic portage when we meet. At first, I'm sure that I'll just tell him that I'd finished kayaking a section of the Northwest Passage the prior summer. Then over time, Udi will gradually realize the missing year in my chronology. One day, he and Sara will be walking through the old city, perhaps at the beginning of spring when the peach trees and honeysuckle blossom. They'll stroll along enjoying the distinct end of winter, marveling at the beautiful ancient buildings inside the walled city. Some moment in the conversation will arise and Udi will turn to Sara and point out mildly that she left for her trip in 2003, and then returned to Jerusalem to rebuild her life in the fall of 2004; and what happened during that year in between?

Sara will look up at him and smile mischievously and say, "Well, I ate a lot of fish."

"Did you now? Were you sampling many kinds or just sticking to one favorite?"

"Mostly just one."

"Did you at least cook it as many ways as there were days you ate it?"

"I pretty much always fried it in a pan over an open fire—when I cooked it."

"When you cooked it?"

"If I cooked it."

"One day you'll tell me where you were and what you were doing."

"One day."

And they'll keep walking, possibly deciding to stop at the shook, inspired to pick up fish for dinner. There Udi will point to each kind of fish in turn, all ugly creations dredged from the Mediterranean, and ask, was this the kind of fish you ate? Sara will shake her head no at each one, Udi finally tossing his hands up in mock exasperation. Then he'll turn all business, pressing their sides with his thumb to judge the firmness and freshness, also checking their eyes for glaze, and at last selecting a particularly choice specimen, a knobby black fish with spines along its back.

Or perhaps it will be completely different. Udi may come over to Sara's apartment with a promise to cook for her bearing bundles of groceries. She'll stand at the doorway of her kitchen, prodding him to tell her what concoction or confection he has planned for them. He'll be secretive, elusive, alternately telling her to put any fears from her head and simply giving his name, rank and serial number. But when he unwraps blood-wetted butcher paper to reveal thick tuna filets, she will wistfully ask if she'd ever told him about the winter she ate nothing but fish for 240 days.

"Never," he'll say, continuing to chop cilantro.

"It's better than Atkins."

"Maybe I should try it."

"Not so good for the teeth though."

"You just have to remember to eat them with lime."

"That must have been my mistake. What are you planning to do with that fennel?"

"Udi Haverstein, Colonel, Army, number 98112745."

"We have ways of making you talk young man. For example, we can tickle the backs of your knees, or abandon you in a remote snow cave."

"Might as well kill me now because I'll never talk."

"So, you may have noticed there's a year missing from my life. I spent it in the Arctic."

Udi will look up from his chopping, knife still poised, and acknowledge that he'd noticed the unaccounted for year, alternately allocating it to her rehab process, an extended stay back in Northport, or to some unspeakable calamity.

"Yes, calamity. I don't know how I survived."

"Apparently on fish."

"But you have to realize that I was out there for the entire winter."

Udi won't reply, but as he scoops up the cilantro he's finished chopping, will nod to her to continue, the sense of play drained from his face and replaced by a sad seriousness. Sara will step into the kitchen and pull out a stool from under the breakfast bar.

"I never told you this, but I got stuck at the end of the summer of 2003. Ice hemmed me in. I couldn't finish the traverse."

Now seated, Sara will watch Udi crush garlic cloves beneath the flat side of the knife's blade, pressing against it with the palm of his extended arm, and then finely mince the broken cloves. She'll continue in a quiet, low voice, confident of Udi's attentiveness.

"My father had often warned that this was the one great danger of the trip: early winter. He said he couldn't emphasize the need to get an early start strongly enough. In years where the ice broke up late in the summer, he felt it wasn't worth making an attempt at all. The guaranteed ice-free timeline would simply be too short. I don't know what exactly went wrong during my summer. Maybe it was the early winter, maybe I didn't make the time I should have, maybe my start was later in the season than it should have been."

"But you didn't make it."

"I didn't make it. The ice closed in around me and it became impossible to row—there was nothing to row in! The ocean might as well have been an ice-skating rink, except that snow buried its surface."

"But what about the whole story you told me about the ice temporarily blocking you in, but then a day coming where the weather changed, the ice blew out to sea, and you made good time and you got to Aklivuk after all."

"That day came the following spring."

Udi will silently resume his cooking duties, splashing olive oil into a pan over the stove, scooping the chopped garlic between his fingertips and the knife's blade and unceremoniously tossing it into the pan. His rough manners with the food, his back to her, his silence, all will make her anxious. But she won't speak first. Finally, he'll ask her why she hasn't trusted him enough to tell him these basic things.

"But surely you must have noticed that there was a year unaccounted for, Udi."

"Sara, I'm just not sure I buy this whole story."

"I couldn't make it out before the ice packed me in. I had to spend the winter."

"I don't see how you could have survived. On fish alone? How could you have caught a winter's worth of fish in a few days—or even a month? Something doesn't add up."

"The garlic smells good, Udi."

"Sara, you explicitly, explicitly told me that you were so afraid because the ice blocked you in earlier than it should have, but just as you were about to despair, the weather changed and—if you remember, you had me tell that story back to you that first night that we…"

"Just because you're angry I haven't told you doesn't mean it didn't happen."

"Maybe if you told me you were rescued, or that the weather changed after all, or that you hiked out or something—then maybe I could believe you. But this story you're telling me. I don't believe you could've survived."

"I'm still praying to Hashem for that day when the weather changes."

"What's that?"

"Udi, the story about the ice clearing—it was true, it cleared for a day. I rowed a bit. But then it came back stronger than ever. Dibuks, you know demons, came out of the north and danced on the edges of crashing ice floes, whispered to me through the walls of my tent. I was doomed. But when I realized the hopelessness of being there, I settled in for the winter. I found a stream,

I fished, I created an Inuit style cache of my frozen catch, dug a deep snow cave, and hibernated, eating fish, rationing driftwood to make small fires and melt snow."

"I don't buy it, Sara."

"I practically lost my mind. But then, just as my fish supply ran out, the night broke, days grew longer, the sun emerged and returned to its half-mast highpoint on the southern horizon. Warm winds washed snow out to sea and the weight of fresh water broke the ice into smaller and smaller pieces—"

"I don't believe you could have survived the winter."

"I dragged myself out of my eroding snow cave, looking for all the world like a musselman liberated from a concentration camp, skin and bones, dirty long-haired, ragged. But there was my kayak, and there was water, and I knew, I just knew that I would persevere."

"Sara," and Udi will turn from the counter where he'd finished mixing his rub and begun applying it to the tuna. "Sara, no way, okay? There's just no way. I'm a colonel. I know about survival—you didn't make it through an arctic winter with just summer supplies and the fish you caught in a few weeks before the streams froze up. Maybe if you told me that you'd killed a bear or a musk-ox or something—no. That you are here clearly means you made it out of the arctic. So don't feed me these stories."

But I will survive. I will, I have to.

## September 4

There are no demons and I can't survive the winter. Demons don't break into kayaks and tear apart dry bags in feeding frenzies. I'm not sure what kind of creatures left their clawed footprints and burgled my food supplies—fox, wolverine, seal, other. But when I went out to the kayak this morning, bright and early, still aching but functional, the weather clear—both bulkheads looked like exploded flowers blossoming out onto the snow. I thought that I broke into a run, but in fact I simply plodded along through the snow, down the steep bank to the beach and the sea where my father's final triumphant handiwork spewed shredded synthetics in outdoor fashion's violent neon colors. Blues, reds, greens, oranges, pinks and yellows littered the endless white. Small bits were scattered far out on the ice, and in every direction except towards my tent. More fluttered away in gusts of frigid breeze blowing south from the pole.

I wanted to sit, not go any further. In fact, after returning to the tent, I did nap before waking to write this. My exhaustion now borders on complete immobility. However, just as I continued to walk when I thought I ran, I continued to walk despite wanting to sit. Near the bottom of the slope, I slipped, tumbled and slid, coming to a stop when my feet rammed the side of my savaged craft. With difficulty, I hoisted myself back upright, leaning on the kayak's side, desperately struggling to overcome defeat. What could I possibly have done for Hashem to curse me so completely?

The hatches had been chewed open. I was so foolish to believe the scratches and gnaw marks the work of supernatural demons. Ordinary animals, as eager to survive the winter as me, smelled their way to my boat, and over a period of days and nights, chewed their way in. I almost can't believe the totality of the damage. Every dry bag was torn open. While I kept some supplies inside bear canisters, which were the only intact items, 99% of my food was in simple dry bags; all of that is gone. The canisters were really just meant for trash and what I might have out overnight. My extra clothing was chewed up, the sweatier the better. Fortunately most of what I would wear is in the tent, and thus preserved, but I doubt if what I have left can get me through a winter whose warmest days rarely crack the negative forty Fahrenheit mark. The damage doesn't stop there. The sail, carefully stowed, was ripped apart in an apparent effort to get to the bags below it. They must've really had a party last night! Yesterday while I ached too hard to get out of bed, they must've been blowing the final locks and celebrating their success. My stove gas, stored in square plastic containers, was chewed through too—though not consumed—and leaked out everywhere. I now have the fuel in my stove's metal canister, about eight ounces, and a twenty-two ounce square container that was miraculously spared; all in all, I have fuel for seven days.

Despairing (despair now so familiar as to nearly lack impact), I opened the bear canisters and took inventory. Though I knew the red one only contained trash, I hoped to find scavengable items. Instead, a stinking mess of tampon waste and fermenting discarded couscous met me. The other canister held what I will now depend on to survive: eight packets of instant oatmeal, two couscous dinners, a bag of dehydrated turkey, a package of beef jerky, a ten-ounce stick of vacuum-sealed cheese, and a pound of gorp. In addition, I have here in the tent—well all of it's here in the tent now, but I had additionally—a pasta dinner, two bars of butter, and a vacuum sealed steak. Of course, I'd thought to only bring vacuum-sealed items rather than cans because it saves so much weight; stupid, stupid, stupid! But how could I have known that every time I attempted to live, Hashem would strike me down?

What have I done to deserve this?

I didn't black out right away after the blast in Jerusalem. There was a moment after the deafening noise when I realized I was on the ground and covered in mangled metal—from what, I don't know—and I screamed out, Momma. I tried to move, but I couldn't. There was heat everywhere; I saw flames. Light still reached me from the front of the pastry shop and I could see movement amidst the debris. I couldn't hear anything though I knew rescuers must already be attempting to enter the café. And then my eyes cleared further. And then I saw my mother's arm, by itself, laying on top of what might have once been a chair, her hand curled, her palm turned up to heaven, a broken rugelach just out of reach. I knew it was her hand because she still wore the sea-charm bracelet my father had given her for their twenty-fifth anniversary. And then something fell, or blew, or collapsed, or maybe my mind cracked, and next I woke up several days later in the medical center, bandaged everywhere, surrounded by bright, sterile lights.

Well there's no point anymore. I have no fuel, no food, no backup gear, and no will left. I'm going to take a nap now. And when I wake up, I'm going to take another nap. I only pray that I don't dream about the blast, about the wretched pain of surgery after surgery to remove the shrapnel from my body, bits of glass, and screws and nuts and nails and wire, the litter of some Jericho lot, the remnants of the last bomber's razed home. What was the point of all that surgery? Why try so hard to live to only die?

And then after all my naps in two weeks or so, after the last of the water and the last of the fuel, I will meet my maker. I will ask Hashem why. Even Hagar, after Abraham cast her out of his house and into the desert at my namesake's behest, even she had her prayers answered, was rescued by an angel. Why not me? Why must his chosen people suffer so?

But now I go to sleep.

—Later—

I didn't sleep well, and I didn't dream about terror, but I did dream. First my father waved goodbye and walked out onto the ice. Then my mother did the same thing. Next, Dalia waved to me, blew me a kiss, and disappeared. Last, Udi waved and turned to go. When he was nearly out of sight, heading due north it seemed, he turned on his heel, and still walking backwards, he yelled out, "A kayak is not a sled." Then they were all gone.

The dream woke me. I tried to get back to sleep—waking meant cooking some food, eating, all of which seemed way too difficult and tiresome. I must have fallen back asleep because I dreamed the same dream again. Again it woke me, and I shouted out, "No, a kayak is not a fucking sled." My voice startled me. I don't usually speak here. The only sounds I hear are small ones: the stove's roar, wind, pen on paper.

I fell asleep a third time, and for a third time, I dreamt the same dream. Except this time I woke myself screaming, "I do want to live. I do. I want to live." And for the first time, I believe myself. Yes, now that my doom seems assured, I've finally realized that I want to live. Three is a magical number, three is a biblical number, three is the number of proofs one uses to confirm something, three is unimpeachable. Yes, I believe myself. I want to live. I don't know why, but I do.

For my whole life, I've been trying to decide why one lives. I've struggled to find meaning. That quest brought me to religion, found me Hashem, allowed me to reject the petty shallowness striven for in my home port. But even with the blessing of Judaism to give me purpose and direction, life refused to come easily, and still I wondered why it was worth it. I don't need to reiterate the contents of this diary, the itinerary and log of this trip, the arch of my existence. But now I suspect that at the base of everything is the simple desire, the simple joy, of breathing another day.

I want to live.

I just don't know how quite yet.

## September 5

After writing in this diary yesterday, I took another nap. When I woke, it was the beginning of the long twilight—night is still only a couple of hours. Hungry, I dragged myself up onto my elbows and sorted the now grimy cookware and stove. An impulse to break free of this musty tent washed over me, and I dressed myself, decided to cook my couscous outside. I walked to the edge of the bluff overlooking my kayak. Some movement below deck inside the bulkhead contorted the mountain of synthetic confetti, probably field mice and other small rodents scrounging for the last crumbs. Food is dealt with efficiently here. With the paddle blade I've pressed into service as a shovel, I carved a small seat for myself overlooking the expansive, ice-covered ocean. A place from which I would scan for leads if I had my binoculars. I think about my forgotten necessities, how they languish somewhere, do not really exist without me, cannot reach any potential. Leaning over to prime the stove, I saw just how weathered my fingers have become. Black grease plasters deep cracks that notch my dry skin as regularly as a prison calendar scratched in a wall. My fingernails are long and ragged, regularly catching on the pilled edges of worn fleece. Warmed somewhat by the stove, its heat reflected by the snow surrounding my recessed seat and stove platform, I mechanically performed the necessary steps to cook, filling the pot with a bit of water and a lot of snow, adjusting the flame, adding more snow as the snow in the pot melted, pumping more pressure into the fuel canister, finally turning everything off and pouring my boiled water into a Ziploc bag full of couscous.

With the stove off, I put my gloves back on. Though the skies have cleared and the winds died down, it's cold, certainly below thirty degrees, even in the sun. I let the bag of flavorless pasta slowly swell in my lap, and stared out at the boat Abba built, brightly front-lit by a strong sun low behind me. My own shadow stretched practically out to the frozen sea. He'd dreamt of this boat and this trip for as long as I could remember. All of our trips were tainted or fueled, depending upon your perspective, by his idea that they were really training sessions for the big one. The trip existed before the dream of the boat. But later, it took on an equal importance, though its form morphed over time. Initially, he thought to traverse the arctic in the same craft as its original navigators, the Inuit. He researched a kayak built around a bone and driftwood frame covered in taut sealskin, marveled at the great distances these original boats traveled, the many years they lasted.

For two years, he punctuated nearly every family dinner with facts and statistics about Inuit seamanship. We heard about the lost paddler who turned up on a Scottish river before white people discovered Canada, about boats who'd kept their original skins for as much as a century and frames that had been reskinned over so many generations that only carbon-dating could determine their provenance. Of course, he also bemoaned the rapid pace at which traditional kayak construction's art was being lost. Perhaps he imagined himself apprenticing to some Inuit wise man, gradually learning the intricate handcraft by which the boats were constructed without metal (just as Solomon's temple was built without metal, without the material of war). Obviously, whalebone and sealskin were not available, let alone legal, in Northport. By the time I became his regular paddling partner, he'd settled on a wooden boat. The advantages of fiberglass: weight, durability, hydrophobia, never outweighed the appeal of rowing in a boat he'd made himself.

After years of research, when I left for Columbia, he began construction. Progress was slow. Selecting and seasoning wood drew from a pool of time and energy already largely devoted to paddling, work and my mother. By the time I left for Israel, he'd cut most of the spars for the frame, but not yet begun assembling them. The skin was wholly unfinished. Then came September 11. It changed everything for him, his attitude towards this project and this trip included. On one of the mornings we'd prearranged for me to come into the office early so we could talk, he called nearly delirious with exhaustion. He'd just returned from a shift volunteering at the Red Cross tent down at ground zero after spending the entire night working on the boat after spending the day before that working at the tent. This was the first period in his life since college that he'd pulled an all-nighter; but he was pulling them nearly weekly.

I asked him how the kayak was coming. Instead of answering the question, he launched into a dry-mouthed monologue on redemption. Redemption, he explained, was the end result of the process of reuniting with oneself. In the past—or for those still religious, in the present—necessarily it meant a return to God's grace. But in the absence of grace, in the absence of the concept of grace, humans continued to discover themselves complicit in a world beyond their morality, survivors without any right to survive, distanced from the earth and from being. For neither the first nor the last time, I saw how deeply my father longed for Hashem, yearned to appeal to Him for understanding and peace. (But then, what understanding or peace has Hashem yielded you, Sarah?). I pleaded with my father to just try going to synagogue, try da'avening, try mourning within structure. "I cannot be among the living, Sarah. I can't act like myself. I'm afraid that I'll jump out of line at the airport and flee, or that I'll yell out to everyone on the LIRR to duck down quick, or that worst of all I'll tackle some innocent man because I'm certain he's a terrorist about to explode. But all of that's just half the battle. I also want to scream at people and demand that they understand me, that I am a ghost, a mistaken survivor. I belong in the rubble. It's better down amongst the workers, in the smoke. I suspect they may feel similarly.

"I just can't keep on this way—and I don't want it to stop. I don't want the pain to stop. I don't want to forget about Samba the security guard. I don't want to forget about Mary, my assistant's sister who was last seen helping her pregnant boss down the stairs. I don't want to stop crying when I see all the faces photocopied onto handwritten descriptions with loved one's contact numbers. I cry when I see how the weather has warped the thin paper flyers, rain-spots, mud, wind, tape yellowed over time. And yet somehow these thin sheets endure. Some are replaced with fresh copies weekly. Hope against all hope that by some strange chance, their loved one was hit by a brick, stunned not killed, wandered outside the normal circle of hospitals, and now lies in a bed suffering from amnesia, hardly whole but still alive. And then there are the pictures so old that the ink has begun to run, the faces eroding in streaks and spots, maybe they got the call that there was something to bury, a finger with a ring on it, a piece of leg, a bone shard, confirmation. Most confusing are those signs to which people, family, have attached flowers, at once holding out hope and mourning an obvious fate.

"I keep looking for my face on a sheet of paper with your mother's phone number. I keep imagining how it might read. I'm certain that my number amongst the living is a clerical error that will inevitably be corrected. And so, Sarah, I come home and I work on this boat. I build out of the day's memories, spars hewn from silences as all work stops and a flag lies flat over a small appendage, a flesh-smeared piece of steel, DNA, proof. I plane the sides of the skin to cut through a sea of the drowned, to bear me over them, to carry me to the far shore intact. I must redeem myself. I've done away with power tools, I want to be invested in every atom of this creation, imbue it, and then ride it to safety. I have to go to the artic as quickly as I can, as quickly as I can cut scuppers and mold bulkheads. Redemption only comes with risk. I can be saved only if I can be lost. I must be saved; I am lost,

Sarah. I'm so lost."

I thought about my father's plea and the intricate, delicate workmanship with which he had made a fast, agile craft out of a heavy design. And I knew, I just knew, that no matter how many neshamot were memorialized in each of my father's strokes, in the effluence of scarred memory from him to wood to craft, I simply knew that a kayak is not a sled. And I need a sled.

I need a sled because there are no demons; there have been no miracles to save me; food will run out very soon; and if I don't start moving I will die here. I need a sled because I want to live.

I cannot hope against hope that the water will open. I cannot rely upon prayer to save me while my food supplies dwindle into nothing. I cannot rely upon canonical edicts to determine who I can love when. Not if I am to love myself, not if I am to be loved by a man I could love, not if I am to live.

If I am Job, then this is my curse. If this is the best Hashem can give me, then tomorrow I will walk without Hashem. I will destroy my father's kayak with the hatchet, and fashion a rough sled onto which I can tie down the rest of my food, fuel, clothes and gear. I'll harness myself in, and walk along the frozen water as long and as far as is necessary.

I watched the sun change colors in a rippled kaleidoscope projected across the snow, a deepening shift from gold to orange to red to purple, a color wheel spinning with chances, with opportunities to survive. I no longer will; I must.

## September 6

It was not without sadness that I took my hatchet to my father's kayak yesterday, and chopped free our linked neshamot from its frame. But it's done. It wasn't hard to build. All I really need is a flat piece of wood to function like a toboggan, something that will float on the snow instead of sinking into it, something light.

I split one side off the boat along the seam, and removed most of the skeletal spars, leaving only two runners lengthwise along the edges that extend from the rear to about two feet shy of the front. I also retained the few cross-spars that joined the two runners. Overall, it's roughly six feet long, and took about an hour to fashion.

It's not without fear that I set off on this new venture today. It's Shabbat, after all. Yet here I am, writing in my diary, preparing as I would for any other day of adventure, cooking half of my steak (I'll make the rest tonight), and suiting up. For the second time since coming to this campsite, my tent's broken down and all my gear stowed. Everything's strapped down to the sled with the forward deck bungees, the remains of the sail cover the cargo load and are held down by the rear decks bungees. In fact, I'm ready to go. I'm perched on the sled's load, which is the perfect height for a seat, writing this entry as a kind of break between loading everything up and the certain exertion of forward motion. All that's left to do is strap on some chopped up pieces of the old kayak that I'm taking along as firewood, take off my heavy coat and stow it along with this journal, and start pulling. The weather's clear; winds are low; a golden expanse of snow stretches out from here due east; there's no reason to delay. I'm off.

—Later—

I can feel myself changing again. My body isn't used to this version of exertion. Hopefully, Aklivuk isn't too far, because I'm hardly making the time I would rowing. As best as I can tell, I'm pacing at about a mile an hour, and can pull for about six hours before needing a real break to melt water and eat. But it's progress. I'm camped for the night now. And I can feel my body transforming already, long dormant leg muscles awakening, a set of chest muscles I never knew I had straining against the webbing harness. The sled works, its jagged back end leaves strange tailings in the snow, but it floats along the surface, and the surface is flat enough that I do not need it to track, and so its flat bottom suffices. Snowshoes would help my effort. I sink about a foot in with each step. My feet get cold, my calves wet. I expend far more energy than I'd like just breaking trail. But I'm moving forward. Too tired to think, I watch this majestic landscape, jagged mountains on my right, a great flat plain to my left, all blanketed in glittering white. It seems too large to pass, and then disappears behind me. Ok, I'm lying. Everything hurts and I don't know if I can go on. But does that sound any better? Does it capture the spirit of what's happening for me? I've decided to live, and am making progress, that's all, that's everything.

## September 7

Each step seems like it must be the last. Tenuously I move my foot forward, terrified of the inevitable pain pressing it down through crunching snow will bring. I force it down, compressing the endless glittering crystals into a slippery ice surface beneath my now ragged Teva's sole, launching an invasion of stray and seeping snow up my pants' legs, down around the tops of my socks. Over the hours, the melt-freeze cycle of body heat and more snow and more snow forms an ice cuff around my ankles, a painful shackle that makes me silently gasp at each step, makes me ask, do you really want this, Sarah? Really? Yes, I want it, yes. I want to go on.

It occurs to me, reaching down into my sleeping bag and rubbing the useless, swollen appendages I once called feet that I have shown a remarkable aptitude for providing myself with just barely enough to proceed. Boots! What I would give for a pair of boots. This level of imposed objective hazard, not quite enough to stop me outright, but everything but, seems contrived, ludicrous, unfair. True luxury would be a pair of the lined plastic deals outdoor stores carry for would-be mountaineers and the occasional, hyper-geared winter-weekender. Now I could use those. The constant abrasion from sinking through with each step is taking a clear toll on my booties, the seams seem sanded and smooth. Snow balls around stray threads until my feet resemble a shaman's bell-ringed moccasins. Who knew that snow abraded so? I worry that despite everything I might overcome, my feet will stop me. I imagine painfully shuffling a foot out of a posthole, the toe scraping along the hole's front, only to see a clear tear along the bootie. The next step would bring the sudden feeling of wet, and then of freeze. I'd stop. I cannot do this barefoot. The pain of freeze. I lose feeling in my feet fairly quickly into the day. But then, for no apparent reason, as I trudge on through this endless wilderness of nothing, of white, of crystal, a foot will suddenly warm, shooting crippling pain through it. I want to puke the first time in the day that it happens. By the third, I hardly even pause.

And I ask myself, are you sure it's worth it to survive?

And when I whisper, yes, out loud, I'm thrilled.

But it would be so much easier to stop. There's still time to stay in my sleeping bag and give up, nestle down into its depths and fade away as dark sets in. There's still time for that with all my body parts intact. But each time I think I can't take another step, each time the landscape seems too endless, the landmarks stationary, impassable, (they are mountains), each time, I surprise myself with one more step and then another.

A light snow began falling just a few hours into my walk today. I plodded on through dim gray light, the snow blocking the wind. Pulling the sled takes so much more exertion than rowing that I hardly dress warmer than I did while paddling during the summer. On top, I only wear a sports bra beneath a light polypro long-sleeved shirt. Three loops of webbing run from the sled to my body. Two form an X across my chest and the third runs around my waist. I long to free myself from this makeshift harness, from the weight of the sled. Sure, it works, it floats on the snow; I can pull it. But then it doesn't track either, the broken line of its tail carving a wobbling trail as it shifts first left, then right, as I turn and pull, lunge to drag it forward. I'm stripped down to keep from sweating—sweat is death; as soon as I stop, wet clothing rips the heat from my body like a central park mugger stripping an old lady's purse from her arm—but without clothing there's little between my skin and the constant chaffing of inch-wide webbing. I've wrapped bits of my animal-shredded clothing around the straps, but even these twist and abrade. My chest is raw with rubbing.

I remember Scott's men, who dragged a sled full of rocks, geological samplings, back from the pole. Even at the end, even when they knew they were short on time to live, making poor progress, they never abandoned their some hundred pounds of stone. They had a sail on their sled, but the wind didn't blow (until it really blew, confining them to tents). I regret not fashioning some fixture to mount my kayak's mast on the sled and hoisting what's left of my sail. There are enough days with wind that such an arrangement would unquestionably ease my burden. I might even be able to ride. But the mast is two days back, lying by the rest of the remnants of my original trip. I try to take inspiration from Scott, who couldn't bear to have gone to the pole for nothing more than ego gratification, and thus died still trying to advance science with his precious specimens. I wonder if I'm here for anything more than ego gratification, and suspect that I am pulling my own weight—trying anyway.

But there's also something peaceful in crossing this desert—and this is a desert once the snow covers the land, as inhospitable, continuous, barren and awesome as the Sahara. Finally, after all this time, I'm really alone. It's just me and the snow, nothing else.

Now the real work can begin. The flagellant purge of sweat work, of pain, primitive electro-shock therapy.

I don't have to worry about bad dreams or insomnia or haunting evenings. Sure, I fall asleep to my own crying, both for my breaking body—the red welts across my chest, a lure for the eye away from my scars, and my feet, which even if I survive, may well be lost—and for my Abba viEema who are dead, dead, dead. But once asleep (and quickly so), I sleep the slumber of the righteous. My body passes into a zone borne by exhaustion past the treacherous shores of all mismatched memory and terror-induced nightmare fantasy. I sleep the way I imagine coalminers sleep, and child laborers, those condemned to the salt mines.

And really after an hour or two of this screamingly slow pace, things begin loosening up. I fall into a rhythm just as I did while paddling. Despite the pain, my trembling feet, and a tenuous store of supplies, I'm not afraid. Though, at best, two long days hauling cover the distance of an average day rowing, I'm satisfied with my progress. I've given myself up for dead so many times that I've accepted death's inevitability and so any progress is better than none at all. The barrenness of the landscape, the absolute absence of animals—though they must be here, obviously, they raided my food cache—the tremendous feeling of aloneness, indescribably comforts me. I feel washed clean. Sure, in all likelihood, this will prove to be a pyrrhic exercise, a great burst of exhausting energy that wears down my food supply, and my muscles and my stamina. I could be spending my last days lying in my tent writing in this journal. But even Scott pushed on long past when he had any business hoping (if I get back, when I get back, I want to find out if his rocks were ever used by anyone, retrieved from his found sled the following spring). Why shouldn't I do the same? He died enamorate of his men, committed to his mission, honorable. So let me fall in my traces, collapse days after the end of my food, succumb trying.

One foot at a time, Sarah, then the next. That is the meaning of life. You step down with the numb block of your frozen, teva-shod foot, breaking through the snow, leg twisting and quivering. Then you twist, bringing the sled forward with your waist and your chest, push the other foot into the snow, leaning forward, pulling the sled further still. And so on and so forth, mile after mile. I am a trained athlete. I can endure.

But my feet, oy, my feet. That's the weak link. If I only had the booties, or only Tevas, I wouldn't try this altogether. With good boots I'd be fine, but this is pure torture. They haven't turned white, or worse yet, blue or black; but it can only be a matter of time. Yet it turns out that I'll do anything to live, anything. It's so true, and yet somehow I've always failed to see it.

## September 8

Maybe we live to try and live? Perhaps it's the simple satisfaction of working towards our own sustainment that satisfies our insatiable need for relevance in life. It's worth it because I work for it.

There's not much to say about today. I'm exhausted. I made worse time but walked longer. My feet continue to hold me up, and without such an excellent apprenticeship in pain, I could never bear the chafing on my chest. Of course I tried taking the chest harness off and only pulling with my waist. Nothing doing. The angle between my waist and the tip of the sled is not great enough to lift the leading edge out of the snow. It digs in and the sled takes on snow, doesn't slide. The weather was better today, gray, but clear. I could see the mountains, their shine blunted by overcast. From the ice, the land's contours radically shift like a lapping tongue, grabbing fingers. Bluffs turn to beaches turn to inlets turn to bays turn to cliffs. Staying far enough north allows me to walk in a straight line, unimpaired by land's irregularities.

The weight of these last weeks, these last two years, sloughs off me. Whole days elapse without any care but my feet, my chest and the landscape. Delirious with walking, with pulling, with staying at the precipice of my breaking point, time circles, nipping at my heels; I forget when I left, or how long I've walked, where I set out from and to where I'm headed. Only when I realize that the day must end, food come, rest, do I slowly remember when I set out, why I'm walking, where I must go. But writing, in an eddy off the day's exertion, depleted, language plays tricks on me. Sentences collapse together and expand. Random Hebrew words intersperse the English I write in, but I cannot access enough Hebrew to write in that language right now. The act of towing a homemade sled, sledge, sled across snow, in makeshift shoes, sinking in at every agonizing step deserves its own word. I try to compose one and my mind conjures a list of anglicized Yiddish: putz, shmutz, shmatah, shmuck. My pain is parabolic, easing as I set into the work of pulling a sled, and then slowly reemerging as I approach the day's terminus, peaking in a deafening crescendo as I make camp stumbling on my knees. But as the pain ebbs into effort each morning and I see the vastness of my surrounding, everything is beautiful. The sun breaks through at an oblique angle and underlights the clouds, coloring them like a midday sunset. Snow expands in this great plain so far that it can be dizzying to see. I think I can see the curvature of the earth.

I grew hot pulling today, and stripped down further. On top, I wore only my sports bra and the bone, tied to a length of string around my neck, the scars along my sides and chest showing for all the word to see (though there is no world to see anything). Udi fades from me, as does Dalia, and my mother and father, and even Marie, who I do hope to see soon, who I would survive for. All of it slowly disappears in my hard won, postholed foot-prints, themselves paved over, caved in, covered by the sled. All the bears, the one that might have chased me, the one on the ice and the one at my campsite, slowly recede from their primacy in my personal hierarchy of fear. Capsizing, hypothermia, exploding buses, modesty and shame, all seem safely contained behind fogged glass. I don't know why, but I'm not questioning it.

Yes, I have continued to cry myself to sleep, wishing my father were with me, wishing my mother were with me. But what daughter doesn't mourn her parents' death? I walk and I feel the bone swinging against the bare skin between my breasts and it drives me forward like the drummer on the back of a Greek warship beating out an unstoppable, unalterable pace. When I break to catch my breath, to drink some water, eat some gorp, I find myself tracing the forbidden network of my scars, touching my body. This is me. It happened to me, and I am choosing to pull, to haul forward.

## September 9

This is a push to push as far as I can push. I've stopped rationing food. There's no need. I need everything to walk, and when it all runs out I'll drop. With luck, that will come after I've reached civilization, rescue, people, Shingle Point, Aklivuk, some other settlement, whatever, whichever. I don't feel my feet anymore and I don't look at them. They've almost certainly begun to die; there's not much I can do about it though. The booties wore through, as I suspected they would, and I wrapped the sock, bootie, teva combination in sections of sail cloth and then smeared the whole thing over with tent sealant from my repair kit. This solution means that I cannot take the combination off easily, but it also keeps my feet dry. Nothing I can do about it.

The trip goes on and on and on. It seems endless, the paddling followed by the waiting, then the attempts to dig in and stick out the winter, now this walking. But during this stage, I'm least tormented by myself. My mind checks out as I succumb to the effort of pulling. Miles go by and all I see is my surroundings, I marvel at the constancy of its beauty like a child in wonderland, even as it changes. The temperature dropped radically by this morning, and with it came clear skies and a brisk wind. I put on more clothing. Cream puff clouds whipped through purple blue sky that seemed to meld into outer space. The low bright sun cast long shadows from the mountains that stretched endlessly out, shifting with the day like the pointers of giant sundials.

Most beautiful of all are the dry snow crystals that float in the air and twinkle, daytime stars, magic. Then the sun sinks further, the shadows lengthen still, and a warm glow permeates the endlessly rolling snow cover. I wish I could access those famed forty native words for snow, because to name it "snow," over and over, feels tedious and false. For long periods of time, I leave my body and watch myself plod forward, so slowly I seem to be standing still, and yet making progress, always progress. And there I am, hunched over, the sled ten feet behind me, a ribbon of compressed snow, dimpled by paved over foot prints, stretching back to my point of change. And then this dizzyingly unending expanse of golden, glowing white beneath a purpling sky. From above my body I dance and sing and cry. I feel free. There's nothing to do but walk in a straight line. That's all. So long as I keep on, I live, I am allowed everything.

*September 10*

My luck has changed. I'm very excited. About ten hours into my day, I passed the point of a long spit of land. Something compelled me to look back at it, and on its eastern side, sheltered behind a rocky rise, was a small cabin. I could almost immediately tell that there were no tracks nearby; snow drifts rose several feet up the door. Still, I dared to hope I might find someone, might find rescue. I turned and started dragging my load towards it. In fact, the cabin was empty, though my presence negates that now. It's more of a shack than anything else, a dirty shack. Old, and I mean old, cigarette butts mix with grime and decayed fish scales on the wood floor.

A rough table built from two by fours topped with a broken-off piece of composite-board sports a nasty, quasi-translucent patina, a mélange of fish detritus, old hooks, blood, fat, grease, ashes, and who knows what else. When I lit the oil lamp, also on the table, it warmed the frozen, congealed slime, making it tacky. But still, it's a table. I haven't seen a table in nearly two months. There's also a bed of sorts, which I'd be afraid to lie in. It smells, even in the cold, even after what seems to have been ages since this place's last occupants, it smells bad. But tonight I'll roll my sleeping pad out over the top of it, and then my bag on top of that, and I'll make do. I'll sleep under a roof.

Best of all are the cans of food. Cartons of canned pineapple sections, condensed milk, spam, spaghetti-Os. Someone's laid in a store of supplies that could last a family a summer. Perhaps that's what it's for: a family fishing camp, accessed by boat when the water's open. But for now, it's my salvation. I only wish they'd left a map, or some other indicator of the distance onward from here to Aklivuk. There are pots and pans. Dinner's cooked and now I've put a kettle of snow on the stove. I'm so grateful for this place that part of me really wants to spend a day scrubbing it down and cleaning it up, surprise it's owners when they return in spring, repay them. Any cleaning I gave it would probably be the first it ever received. But I know I won't actually do it. I must keep focused on the end goal.

I'm feasting on spam and spaghetti-Os, the first non-kosher food I've eaten in over five years, and sipping condensed milk straight from the can. The milk is so good! Fuck! Still, it's as if at any moment the lightning bolt will streak down from heaven, and then I remember that I'm allowed to eat this food because it's to save my life; but even that rings false, because I broke with Hashem to make this last leg of my journey, because I already felt as if I'd been struck by lightning. They say that sinners are rewarded in this world and punished in the next, the devout pay for their sins now and see their rewards in heaven; what if I'm using up my good deeds, squandering my share of the world-to-come, on a miserable survival bid to live in a hostile and unforgiving world? It doesn't matter. I want to live.

My pot of snow has melted into lukewarm water, and it's time to begin the inevitable, painful task of dealing with my feet. I'm afraid to leave them frozen. So, I'll have to cut away the sail cloth, remove everything, and soak my feet. I want to pray but I won't.

## September 11

I'm loathe to leave the luxury of this shack. The small fire in the gas stove has not only warmed the space but unleashed a torrent of rotten fish smell. Nonetheless, this is four-star luxury. A bed, a table, a roof, warmth. My belly's the most full it's been in weeks. I carefully defrosted my blackening feet last night, and can actually wiggle my toes this morning. Who can blame me for not wanting to re-swaddle them like a homeless person, dip them in the can of marine sealant stowed in the cabin, and resume my indeterminate march through the snow? There's possibly enough food here to last through the winter, if I rationed (granted, that would be one hell of a rationing). But I can't stay, I must move on. I'm committed (and even if I waited till the water opened next spring, I no longer have a boat).

And even if I wasn't committed, even if I did have a boat, today is two years to the day since my father left the relative comfort of his office and walked to save himself, into a world made unknown. I think that if he were here with me now, he would scream at me to shake off the false safety of this shack and get moving. So I will.

—Later—

I wonder if I wouldn't be better off amputating my feet. Every step brings tears to my eyes. The marine sealant made the sailcloth brittle and strips have begun to chip off. Worse still, my feet quickly went from rewarmed to refrozen, but without the generalized numbness they had the first time. This round, I can clearly feel the frostbite's ice crystals rubbing against and piercing the still living flesh deep under the skin. I should never have rewarmed them; I can't believe how bad it is. And pulling the sled, God, pulling the sled. Really today was an anguished blur. When I felt that I could bear no more, I rested and made lunch, but then I continued again. I lost all sense of time – but the long autumn twilight indicates that I've made it till at least early evening—I'm amazed I continued as long as I did. When I finally stopped, I lay on my butt with my legs up, pedaling them in the air, trying to shake out the buzzing shooting pains, tears building behind my eyes and an itching, frustrated scream putting pressure in the center of my head. Make it stop.

It occurred to me, not for the first time, that perhaps there are two of me: the me that wants to live and the me that quietly sabotages my chances of doing so; me the victim and me the terrorist. The terrorist double of myself does not wander buses waiting to explode but instead roams my mind triggering irrational fears, horrible breaks from normalcy. She suppresses the part of my mind that knew not to defrost my feet until after I escaped. She convinces me of demons, and of my desire for my own demise—all the while distracting me from the very real animals attacking my food stores. She sends me on dangerous trips, grievously unprepared, grieving too greatly to perform well. She tells me that I cannot be loved. She wants me dead. And I do not know where this other half of myself comes from. Maybe I earn her, deserve her. She flits into the shadows once her damage is done, lingers beyond the range of my questioning. And then when I least expect it, sabotages me yet again, though any success on her part would be suicidal. I wonder if this second of myself is the fear my mother said terrorists are so overwhelmed by that they must share it. Perhaps at the very last moment, while connecting the loose wires in her coat, the woman in the Heavenly Delights Pastry shop realized that she'd sabotaged herself and at the moment of her immolation, after it was already too late to not kill my parents and herself, realized she was the victim of herself. Or maybe Hashem, who can't seem to help but curse his chosen people, is the terrorist—no, I don't believe that. God didn't make me come here. We, his chosen people, are the terrorist, choosing to believe that the horrors that befall us are somehow part of some master plan. I will never believe that my parents deserved to die.

Eventually, I caught my breath, and began prying open some cans I ransacked from the shed. Tonight's dinner consisted of boiled Spaghetti-Os spiced with spam, mmmm, good. As tantalizing as the food was though, calories upon desperately needed calories, I could hardly force it down. A combination of nauseating pain and conditioned revulsion to unkosher food nearly overcame my force of will as I lifted each trembling spoonful to my mouth. Waves of vomit still rise up through my esophagus intermittently, burning the back of my throat when I swallow. And equally often, my legs do the marionette twin-kick of a hanged man inside my sleeping bag. Before going to bed, I break my moratorium on prayer, only to ask that the week's worth of cans I dumped in the snow when I realized I could not bear their weight do not constitute the difference between someone else's life and death.

## *September 12*

My feet are horrifying. I wonder if I shouldn't have stayed in the shack until I'd gotten well, and then proceeded to pull further. I don't know how much longer I can continue—and this time it's not me crying wolf, or making yet another assessment of my own doom. The straps from the sled have left raw red marks criss-crossing my chest, describing the original contours of my breasts, which have largely disappeared through exercise and a long-running calorie deficit. I'm worried that the increasingly exposed flesh will eventually become infected. I have no way to treat it if it does. I tried pulling the sled today using only the waist belt, but he nose wasn't lifted high enough, and began to shovel snow, ending progress. But it's my feet that will stop me. Why did I let some foolish nostalgia for September 11 convince me to leave the shack behind? I should have rested for a few days. I don't have enough food to justify a halt here where I am now. I can't afford to dig in. I'll have to keep going.

—Later—

This will be my last journal entry. I'm going to take a great risk. Judging my current condition, there's no other choice. Everything will be left behind, this, my confidant, included. I can't justify the weight, any weight. If I'm able, I'll come back for it before flying home. There's a roundness to beginning this book here and leaving it here as well, a holistic completeness. And the end is in sight, literally.

My feet kept turning pins and needles, phantom pains shot from my toes to my ankles. My sleeping bag confined my legs like a woolen cast. Instead of sleeping, I dozed between sessions of seething pain, of sucking in my breath through clenched teeth, my chest arched, my legs stiff. Finally, irrationally, I decided to leave the tent, shake out my legs, pee. Teva's back over my tattered foot-wrappings, I unzipped the vestibule, and stepped out into a moonless black shattered by infinite pinpricks of multi-hued starlight. For a moment, I forgot my feet.

A cold wind roughing my face reminded me that I did have a purpose in being out here. Intending to walk over to my pee spot ten feet from the tent, I turned north. Red lightning danced through the sky. My father once emailed me a link to a picture of this on northernlightphotography.com along with a long explanation of why the red borealis was rarer than the green. Urination long forgotten, I stared up at shamaim, light arcing overhead, and wondered if my father's neshamah wasn't watching out for me after all, hadn't beseeched Hashem to give me this small gift of beauty. Because as time faded into flashes of light, my pain temporarily disappeared as well, and it seemed that despite everything, two months struggling to survive could culminate in a simple phenomenon more exquisite than a wrecked body's demands. I too could transcend. Flawed, still I might live. And then as if in confirmation of my father's presence, my eyes tracked a series of bursts to the east, and where the horizon touched down, saw light. Not stars, not atmospheric abnormalia, but the haloed twinkle of a town's incandescence. I turned my body towards them and focused. I closed my eyes until the static faded and my eyelids showed black, and then looked again. What I saw was unmistakably a concentration of manmade light, a town, Shingle Point, or even Aklivuk, it has to be. Three or four shaky strides later, I stopped running, and considered just how far away those lights were: almost certainly at least ten miles, probably not much more than twenty.

Even that short burst of energy had brought pain flooding back into my feet. I looked down at them and thought about how I might cover these last twenty miles before me. At best, I've been making seven or eight miles a day. That pace will continue to slow as my foot situation worsens. At that rate, the best I can hope for is to arrive at the lights in three days. During that time the weather could easily change and a storm could pin me —and if a storm stops me? Well I doubt I have fuel left for much more than a week. There's also the real chance that my feet will give out before then. Certainly, after three more days of this, I'll lose them when I reach medical care. They'll chop them right off (perhaps a foregone outcome anyway). And the pain of three days more walking—

The alternative is to eat as much as I can and then leave now, carrying only a single nalgene of water, the stove, and pockets full of gorp. Without the sled, I should be able to reach anything I can see by true night tomorrow. I want to leave quickly, before first light, while I can still take a good compass reading of the exact direction I need to go in. After nightfall tomorrow, I can correct any navigational inaccuracies by redirecting towards the lights. But this whole plan depends on carrying nothing extra. My inventory should be:

| | |
|---|---|
| Gorp | 1 lb |
| Down Parka | 3 lbs |
| Stove and fuel | 3 lbs |
| Nalgene w/water | 2 lbs |
| Sailcloth sack   (to be fashioned) | 1 lb |
| Knife/matches/compass/whistle | 1 lb |
| Total weight: | 11 lbs |

That's already too much weight, and nothing I can easily leave behind. Without the stove, I can't make any water; I'll need to refill the nalgene at least twice, which is two liters of water for each stop—one drunk there and the other carried—a gallon and a half of water for twenty to twenty-four hours, barely enough, not enough really, not if I had to be able to perform the following day.

Of course, each snow melting session will use more fuel, lightening the load. I'd like to add a can of spam to that list, which I could eat an hour in for energy. In fact, I think I will do that. An extra pound for the first hour is worth it for the additional food. As a compromise, after the second water refill, I'll ditch the stove, which will drop me to a comfortable eight pounds of carry-weight. I wish I had Gatorade powder or something to dump in the water and give me a little extra energy. Well this is the last push; I can afford to suffer.

What are you waiting for, Sarah? What if those lights turn off?

I'm not quite ready to leave.

Ready for what? You're scribbling in a journal you're about to wrap in a piece of sailcloth and secrete in a tent that will inevitably rot out here through the winter only to fall though the ice in the spring. You're wasting travel time to scribble on litter.

I know, and yet there's nothing for it.

Well, let me light the stove, and while I cook my thick meal, I'll keep writing. Once that's done, I'm off.

But why are you hesitant? The sooner you zip the vestibule shut behind you (it's tacky, but you'll do it), the sooner you'll arrive at civilization (such as the civilization at Aklivuk is). An early winter, who ever thought there'd be an early winter?

What am I even going back to? Suddenly, with the hope of salvation clear before me, realistic for the first time in three weeks, return terrifies me. The will to live came upon my abnegation of faith. How can I live without Hashem? What else will I be but an orthodox woman?

I can see it. I arrive at Aklivuk, and sink back into the hands of medical professionals. As soon as I'm stabilized—and after my final march, I'll be much worse than I am now—they'll fly me to the closest hospital. There, surgeons will decide whether I ever walk on my own feet again. Other doctors will treat me for dehydration and malnutrition. I'll sleep for days on end.

Meanwhile, I'll end up in the news: Woman walks out of arctic carrying only a rucksack, wearing homemade shoes, etcetera, etcetera. But they'll only be concerned with the high-impact portions of my story, its physical aspects, how I intended to row, was caught on the ice, eventually made the hard choice to walk, finally saw lights and made a last break for it, abandoning everything at my final camp. Though they may note that I embarked in the stead of my father, they'll care little for my own spiritual struggles, my attempt to purge myself of anxiety, the loss of my life's meaning—faith in Hashem—and simultaneous embrace of my own desire to live (perhaps I'm just more afraid of dying now? Afraid of facing Hashem in the heavenly court and being judged poorly?)

Maybe I'm leaving this journal behind so that no one can analyze it, deconstruct it, reorganize my secret confessions into pet theories and psychological profiles. My story will leave me and become something separate from myself. And like it or not, I will become an object people judge. The uber-outdoorsy will dissect the minutia of my account and point out my all too evident errors; they would do much better. At the opposite end of the spectrum will be those who deride my trip as foolish, self-destructive artifice, an egomaniacal, contrived adventure. I suppose many people simply won't care, too busy aspiring and consuming to notice.

The best I can hope for is that the great middle, where, in all honesty, I belong, that group happy to believe, desperate to believe, in whatever, God, country, their neighbors, right and wrong, will read a corny, inspirational story about the indomitable human will to live, of a terror-survivor who refused to hide. Maybe they'll imagine that they too could make it, if mysteriously ripped out of their comfortable lives and put in the very path of adversity (which is, after all, terror's threat). And in that imagining, some suppressed nexus of fear may see a crack of light, the hope, the dream, that they might overcome terror's paralysis, might actually win against this scourge. If my making it means nothing more than that for two minutes, while watching the morning news, or reading their daily paper, that group with which I feel greatest kinship realizes some moment of relief from their lives, then it will be worth it, for the summed two minutes of the hundred million Americans who occupy that country's middle, far outstretches the duration of my suffering, past, present, future.

Or, perhaps, none of that will happen. The lights will be further than I expected, or will belong to roving snow-mobiles that continue further east and elude me. A storm might blow in over these next twenty-four hours. In the ensuing white-out, I'll wander in circles, or walk past Aklivuk, missing it by mere miles. Yes, I may make this attempt only to end up out of food, out of fuel, unable to return to my tent. There is still plenty of opportunity for me to fall face down in the snow, and gradually stiffen with cold. Any eventual magazine article may be little more than a footnote saying that Sarah Frankel, who attempted to traverse from near Prudhoe to Aklivuk, was found dead, apparently on foot, miles from her tent and equipment. More damning still, would be to arrive at the myriad deltas of the McKenzie, and find open, uncrossable, channels of water. The worst possible scenario would be to find myself stopped within sight of Aklivuk, just a mile or two away, and unable to contact the people: to sit down, as if behind a wall of glass—or more fittingly, ice—and slowly starve to death while looking at paradise.

There really is no choice. It's this push, or head back to the cabin. My feet won't make it for three more days pulling a sled. (So start walking, Sarah).

Yes I could die.

Yes, I may go back to a world in which there is no spot for me (again).

I'm afraid that I will die (or, worse, wish that I had).

But, Udi and I will take our son, Yechil, to the Jerusalem zoo. It will be late autumn, November. The sun's warmth will contrast strongly with crisply cool air that threatens full winter. Yechil will insist on walking between us, only letting our hands go to point at the animals (and sometimes, embarrassingly, at the other patrons). A certain melancholia will ebb into me with the autumn cold. Transmitted through our son's hands, it will reach Udi. He'll look over at me

No. So where does that leave me? Another false orthodox pretending behind a shatel in a marriage I don't want to a man repulsed by my deformation; I'd rather not. But I cannot imagine a world for me outside orthodoxy. I don't believe I can simply go join some non-religious community where no one could understand me. The possibility that I'll get back to civilization and return to normalcy and easily go back to my own life without doubt or crisis has also crossed my mind; and I rejected it. If these decisions bear no lasting impact, then everything I've written in this log of my soul will be rendered meaningless, will have amounted to naught. I cannot accept that.

It is written that there is repentance for all sins except those done with the expectation of repenting – but if I repent right now, will the lights of Aklivuk magically disappear and in their place the demons return? And if I don't repent now, aren't I working under the assumption that I'm going to sin for a while and then potentially repent after I arrive home, which is specifically disallowed? I wish I were smart enough to puzzle all that out, but I'm not. I'm no theologian. My stomach's stuffed and I'm wasting time I should spend walking east. Maybe I'm only imaging the lights; they're a mirage conjured by my need. I could be eaten by a polar bear. Sure, I may die, but so what.

I'm sad to leave this behind, this, my only confidant these past two months. It's been a devoted listener, an unerring recorder, an unflattering mirror of the lies I've told it. Ultimately, it shamed me into truth, proved instrumental in the excavation of my will-to-life from under the rubble of those two explosions. And it continues to do so, even after I've told it that it will not survive, that only one of us will walk out of here and that one is me. I wish I could bring it. But any extra weight I carry had best be food or fuel. I cannot afford two pounds of paper, or nostalgia. Perhaps it's better I don't remember these confessions anyway. But I'm afraid of being so very alone once I return to the world of people, especially without this friend, a tangible record of why everything.

This last walk, this last ditch burning of my every reserve, may also trigger some final vision in which I will find the answer by which to live. In the absence of this diary, its truth may be burned into my flesh, inscribed in my very being. Yes, it doesn't hurt to hope that somewhere in the falling crying pain of stumbling for twelve, or twenty, or thirty hours on stumps of frozen feet might bring some spirit quest dream, a final purge and replacement, an imbuement of self. I can't know.

The night fades, and if I am to see the star I track, I must leave.

Goodbye, I will set sail now into my uncertain future.

One step, and then another, and yet another still.

I will live.

## Acknowledgements

I couldn't have written this book without the thoughtful comments and patient rereads of Alexandra Enders and Heather Laszlo, as well as those of my aunt, Barbara Keiler. I am deeply grateful to Jon Waterman, whose account in *Outside Magazine* first suggested that one could row the arctic, and who kindly answered my ignorant questions about the Beaufort Sea; to Jill Fredston's *Rowing to Latitude* and Victoria Jason's *Kabloona in the Yellow Kayak*, which immeasurably enhanced my understanding of the arctic; to Francois Camoin, Ellen Lesser, Douglas Glover and Christopher Noel, my writing teachers; to *Hunger Mountain*, which first published a section of *Sarah/Sara*; to my mother, who showed me what it meant to sit in front of a computer and wish for words; to my father, who assured me that I was right to risk to write; and to all of my friends who believed in this book when my own faith waned, especially Susan McCarty, Mary Domenico, Cheyenne Rothman, Peter Chaskes, Dylan Keefe, Rachel Paul, Michal Woynarowski, Rene Ravenel and Emily Riehle.

I am especially thankful to Elizabeth Clementson and Robert Lasner for making this happen.